Black Rose

Works by K.L. Bone

Rise of the Temple Gods Series
Rise of the Temple Gods: Heir to Kale
Rise of the Temple Gods: Heir to Koloso
Rise of the Temple Gods: Heir to the Defendants (coming soon)

The Black Rose Series
Black Rose
Heart of the Rose
Blood Rose (coming soon)
Shadow of the Rose (coming soon)

Other Works
The Indoctrination

See www.klbone.com for more.

K.L. BONE

First Edition October 2014
Second Edition: August 2015

DEDICATION

This novel is dedicated to my mother, Tracy, and my mum, Teresa,
for supporting me through every twist and turn
of this story and its path to publication.

To my writing partner and friend, Jonny R. –
thank you for all your encouragement, support, humor,
and everything in between.

And to my teacher, friend and lifelong mentor, Mike S.

CHAPTER I

FOR THE FIRST TIME IN *over six hundred years, Mara dreamed of the sea.*

As she walked beside the ancient wall, her feet sank softly into the sand. Mara was reluctant to face the water that foamed in soft waves behind her with an elegance held only by the sea. The sky was painted in pinks, oranges and reds. The sun slowly rose from the water, as though emerging from the ocean's deep blue waves. As Mara finally turned, the scene, so clear in her mind, was even more beautiful to behold. Taking a deep breath, Mara could taste the salt on the tip of her tongue. She closed her eyes and took several steps forward, allowing the sand and salt to saturate her pale skin as it absorbed the first rays of the rising sun.

As she reached the edge of the water, she lowered her hand, allowing the foam to wash over the tips of her fingers. She knelt upon the beach as the wind bit at the edge of her full-length royal blue gown. A shadow fell over her face. She did not need to look up to know who it was. "Philip."

"Hello, my lady." His voice was deep and gentle, the way it had sounded all those centuries ago.

"Is it my time, my lord? Have you come to take me away?"

His bronze hand came into Mara's view, raising her chin to meet his crystal blue gaze. "Do you truly wish it?"

"Every day." Her usually strong voice came out soft and unsure. "I have much to atone for."

He stared at her for several moments, and a look of sorrow came into those blue eyes. "You know that you cannot stay here."

"Why? It should have ended, all those years ago." The wind blew her hair softly behind her. "I should have followed you into the sea."

"Do not say such things, my lady. You must go back. He needs you now."

"Needs me?" she whispered, confused. "He has not needed me in centuries."

"If you do not find him, he will surely die."

With those words, the dream changed. The purple hues of the sky began to spread, swallowing the lighter pinks and reds that lay throughout the clouds. It spread from the water to fill the sky, all the while changing from purple to gray. The water grew darker and rose in ever- increasing waves before rising up in a high wall which reached to blend with the darkening sky. The water and sky turned black as the ground beneath Mara's feet transformed from soft sand to hard stone. The sun dimmed to a small flame, becoming the only light visible in the darkness and Mara once again found herself standing inside those dark, horrifying chambers.

She closed her eyes, but was unable to block out the sound of the young woman's voice, begging for the release of the man Mara knew would be lying on the blood-soaked sheets. Her eyes opened against her will and she saw him there, lying nude across the bed. A beautiful woman lay naked beside him, terrible in her wild beauty, a bloody, silver knife clutched in her left hand.

"No!" Mara screamed as she was pulled from the dream in a violent jerk. "Edward." She called out the one name she had not spoken since the night Phillip had died. "Where are you?"

She hugged her knees to her chest, her body shaking from the impact of the dream. She fought to draw several deep breaths before turning to glance at the small clock. It would be just after midnight at the Ciar Court—crazy to call this late.

Yet no sooner than this thought entered her mind, she disregarded it. Rising from the bed, she grabbed her phone from a small desk in the left corner of the room. She dialed a number she knew by heart, despite rarely ever calling it. Moments later she was greeted by the secretary of the Ciar Court Guard.

"I need to speak with Edward," she told the young woman on the other end of the line.

"I'm sorry," the woman replied. "The captain is away on assignment."

"Then patch me through to whoever is in charge of the guard while he is away."

"Do you mean Sub-Captain Jake?"

"Yes! Jake, Garreth, whoever Edward left in charge."

"Umm, I'm sorry." The woman did not sound nearly apologetic enough for Mara's taste. "Sub-Captain Jake gave orders not to be disturbed."

"Tell Sub-Captain Jake that it's a pretty woman on the other end of the phone."

"I think he's with a pretty woman," the secretary replied. "Which is the reason he is not to be disturbed. I'm sorry, ma'am. I can either take a message or you are free to call back tomorrow."

Mara sighed. She would have to do this the hard way.

"Tell the sub-captain that Mara Sethian of the Black Rose needs to speak with him. He can either come to the phone, or I will get on a flight and knock down his door!"

"Did you say, Black Rose?"

"Yes. The Captain of the Black Rose, to be more precise."

"Oh," the woman said, suddenly sounding much younger than she had over the past few minutes. "Right away, Captain. I will get him right away."

The other end of the line went quiet as the call was transferred. Approximately thirty seconds later, a rather tired-sounding male voice came on the line. "This had better be important."

"Jake," Mara said, "when exactly did Edward get the crazy idea to make you his second?"

A moment of silence followed before Jake answered. "He ran out of all other candidates for the job."

She laughed. "Yes, I figured that is what it would take."

"How are you, Mara?"

"That depends, Jake."

"On what?"

"Where's Edward?"

"All these years and the only thing you want to know is the location of another, more powerful and better looking man? I'm hurt."

"You're right, Jake. Where are my manners? How are you? And do you happen to know where your better looking half is?"

It was Jake's turn to laugh. "I am doing rather well. Edward was sent to deliver some messages to the Arum Court." He paused. "Come to think of it, I would have thought he would be back by now. Did you ask for him when you called?"

"Yes."

Jake's voice took on a far more serious tone. "Wait. You actually called for Edward? What happened? You never call for Edward."

"Sometimes I do."

"No. You never call for Edward. Not once in six hundred years. You ask about Edward, but you never actually speak to Edward. What the hell is going on?"

Mara paused before answering, "Just a bad dream."

"A dream?"

"If you hear from him, I want you to call the Rose."

Jake gave a slight gasp. "You are giving me a direct line to the Captain of the Black Rose? Must have been a terrible dream."

"Let's just say," she replied slowly, "it was as deep as the sea."

Chapter II

Lady Sandra walked down the long hallways of the Arum Court. The walls of the palace were generally painted in deep reds or royal blues, but as Sandra began to descend, the colors began to fade. The walls of the lower levels ran deep underground, built in blocks of black stone and enchanted to withstand the ravages of time. A light chill filled the air, causing Sandra to shiver in her thin blue shirt.

The man walking by her side was Regald, Captain of the Arum Court Guard, who had served as her bodyguard for the past several years. He was tall with pale skin, short golden hair and green eyes. He wore a long-sleeved shirt of crimson with a small black rose upon the single pocket on the left side.

"So," Sandra asked the captain as they descended the darkened hallway. "Do you know why King Mathew has ordered us into these," she searched for the word, "charming chambers today?"

Regald hesitated before answering. "No, my lady. I am afraid I have no idea."

She looked at him in surprise. "Does that worry you?"

Regald gave the slightest of nods. "I am not normally excluded from the king's plans." They were ushered through a tall wooden door and into a circular room featuring torches burning sporadically along the dark walls.

"Line the walls, please," a younger guard called to the arriving crowd. "Please everyone, backs against the wall." Sandra took several paces further into the musty room and stepped to her left. The wall behind her back was slightly damp, causing her to step forward to keep her blouse from touching it.

"Do you see Darek?" she asked, inquiring as to the whereabouts of her fiancé.

Regald glanced around the room as he moved to stand beside her. "I do not see him, my lady."

"Hmm. I wonder if he will be here later."

Her gaze traveled the room. It was barren, save for a single silver table standing at its center. Thick, silver chains lay upon the top. As her gaze traveled downwards, she realized they were bolted to the floor. Sandra's eyes shifted back to Regald's warily. "What is this room used for?"

He looked apprehensively at the table. "Once long ago, this room was used to..." He searched for the word. "...punish prisoners. But it has not been used for such in more than a century. I have no idea why the king would want us down here."

An uneasy feeling began to settle over Sandra as she glanced through the silent faces of the small crowd. She again searched for Darek, but the Crown Prince was nowhere to be found.

A soft click was heard and all eyes were drawn to the left. A tall, pale-skinned man was led into the circular room, moving forward slowly. His legs were shackled together and his arms were bound behind him in thick chains. His shirt had been removed and his hair hung loose around his shoulders in long, dark strands. As his face came into view, a light murmuring rose through the crowd and Regald whispered, "By the Gods."

"What is it?" Sandra kept her voice quieter than the soft hum surrounding them.

The man was led toward the table by four figures covered completely in dark blue, hooded robes. When the table was reached, they guided the unresisting man to its sleek surface, expertly transferring him from his bonds and into the thick, silver chains. Once secured, his body lay taut across the table, the metal cutting into his wrists.

The guards stepped back as twelve more hooded figured entered the room, each wearing dark red robes. Their movements seemed to flow as one as they stepped forward to form a circle around the bound man. The four members in blue stepped back toward the wall. As one of them walked past Regald, he asked, "What is going on here, Kala?"

"King's orders," the woman replied.

"What... Do you have any idea who that man is?"

"Do not insult me, Regald. He is the Captain of the Ciar Guard."

"Then what, in the name of all that is sacred, is he doing on that table?"

"I do not question the king's orders, Captain. I merely carry them out."

He looked back at the man chained to the table. "You do understand that they will come for him, don't you?"

"I am not afraid of our sister court," came her curt reply. "And if you interfere, you will be chained right beside him."

"It might be worth it."

Kala met his gaze with blazing golden eyes, then resumed walking forward, eventually stopping on the opposite side of the room.

Sandra looked closely at the captain and could almost see the color draining from his face. "What is going on?"

Regald shook his head. "He is Edward, the Captain of the Ciar Royal Guard."

"Then why would the king order him harmed? Will that not anger the Ciar Court? "

"Yes, it will. However, I fear that it will not be the Ciar guards who will come for that man."

"I don't understand. Who will come for him, if not his own guard?"

Regald either did not hear, or chose not to answer as his attention was drawn back to the twelve hooded figures. Moving in unison, they had closed around the silver table in a tight circle and then, as one, tossed back their hoods, revealing twelve women with matching black hair pulled back with silver bands. Their reflective, catlike eyes were a green so pale it was almost yellow, with black, vertical slits where a pupil should have been. The prisoner remained silent.

Sandra watched as the women raised their arms, each revealing the black handle of the long whips that they had carried with them. Each of the whips had three leather straps attached to the main handle with a sharp, triangular piece of silver metal on each end. The jagged edges of each metal piece would tear skin from bone when dragged across the prisoner's vulnerable flesh.

Sandra's gaze traveled back to Regald, who motioned for her to remain silent. She turned forward. Her eyes scanned those whispering around her before turning back toward the circle. She caught the gaze of the man lying on the table. His eyes were jet black, the darkest she had ever seen.

The room began to spin. Sandra closed her eyes to steady her vision and found herself standing in a rose garden. Red and violet roses surrounded her, climbing the garden walls to blossom in a beautiful cluster of royal colors. The full moon was high above her, reflected in the calm waters of the pool before her. She wore a thin gown of royal blue. Her long black hair was curled in luxurious waves framing her face and flowing gently down her back. A gold chain with a white, rose-shaped diamond nestled at the hollow of her neck, visible in her gown's plunging neckline. A smile graced her dark red lips, extending to her rouge-tinged cheekbones.

A man stood behind her. His white shirt was closed at the upper chest with silver buttons that blended with the moonlight. The top of the shirt should have been laced together, like something out of the Renaissance, but instead the silver strings hung loose on either side, allowing his pale throat to lay bare to the cool night air. He stepped closer to Sandra and placed his arms around her gently. Her smile widened as a mild gust of wind sent ripples through the previously still water, distorting their reflection.

The ripples slowly spread through the water. The reflection of the moon vanished and the pool changed from dark blue to black. Then she was falling, her thin frame tumbling towards the dark night water. She closed her eyes, but instead of water, she hit stone.

"Sandra?" Regald's deep voice pulled her from the vision. "You don't have to watch this." But it was too late. The whips rose high in the air before crashing simultaneously onto the man tied to the table. When they pulled back, blood ran in long streaks down his skin. The prisoner was silent, but Sandra knew that he would not remain so for long.

She searched the scattered pieces of her broken memories for anything about the man chained to the silver table, but it was to no avail.

She closed her eyes again and this time found herself lying on the stone floor. The stone was smooth beneath her fingers, but also cold. She tried to rise. Something crashed into her, knocking the wind from her lungs, keeping her pressed firmly to the floor. She lay still for several moments before again attempting to see her surroundings, this time raising only her head.

A man and women lay upon a bed near the center of the room. The woman was topless, her pale skin glowing in the darkness. Her long black hair hung around her in wild curls. Her laugh was like sweet music carried upon a summer breeze; like the ringing of bells that only angels should be pure enough to hear. She tossed her curls to the side, revealing the man lying beneath her.

His chest was streaked with lines of blood. A thin, silver blade was clutched in the hand of the beautiful creature who lay upon him. Sandra's gaze followed the bloody lines from the man's open chest to his face and found herself staring into his dark gaze.

The whips whistled through the air, pulling Sandra again from the strange vision. The room had fallen to silence as the man chained on the table gave a deep moan. Sweat poured from his skin, mixing with the ever-increasing amount of blood now streaming from the table.

She searched her memory, but no answer came. The whips struck again, and this time, he was unable to suppress his screams. Sandra's heart cried out at the sound, yet she did not know why. Another scream shattered the room and she had to resist the urge to scream with him. She closed her eyes, but it was only to see the same man, being slowly cut by the blade of a woman Sandra had never seen before.

The whips again rose in the air. Without thought or understanding, she took several steps forward before breaking into a run. Before the guards realized it, Sandra reached the table and threw herself across the injured man. The whips crashed against her body, cutting through her blouse and sinking into the thin flesh of her back. Her high-pitched scream rang through the room, echoing down the halls before finally reverberating back towards her with an almost living force.

Blood slid across her back, running down to mingle with that of the man tied beneath her. Her back felt like it had been lit on fire. As a second stroke came down upon her from half of the whips, the guards had moved into the next stroke before realizing what had happened. The second stroke slid past the ragged tatters of her shirt, pulling more flesh from her body. Her vision swam. The pain was nauseating.

Regald bolted to her side. "Sandra," he whispered in horror.

She heard his voice as though from a distance. "No more," she said as the world began to dim. "No more."

CHAPTER III

SANDRA AWOKE IN AGONY. THE lines of ruined skin burned with fire from the antiseptic which had been slathered over the open wounds before her back had been bound in thick, white bandages. She started to rise from the bed where she lay facedown, but then thought better of it as she experienced a searing pain with the contraction of each muscle. She took several deep breaths before trying again, this time moving more cautiously.

Slowly moving to a seated position, Sandra found herself facing the deep green of her fiancé's eyes. At just over six feet, Prince Darek was a handsome man. His skin held a healthy bronze tan which matched his sandy brown hair, just a shade darker than blond. He wore a pair of black slacks with a long-sleeved royal blue shirt kept closed with buttons of silver which matched the simple silver chain worn loosely around his neck.

"Sandra," Darek began. "What? Why?" He shook his head, but seemed unable to continue.

"I don't know," she answered. "Darek, I really don't know. I just... Is he still alive?"

"Yes. He was returned to his cell after you fainted." A hint of anger entered her fiancé's voice. "You threw yourself over him and you don't know why?" He shook his head. "I know you can't remember much of your past, but this..."

"Look, Darek. I don't know!" Her voice sounded strained. "I don't know what I saw. I don't know who he is. I don't know why I threw myself over him." She jerked upright, then regretted it, hissing in pain.

"Look, stop," the prince said. "Lie back down and rest. I'll send someone in to give you something to help with the pain." He stood swiftly from his seated position and walked towards the door.

Sandra sat quietly on the bed. When she managed to find a position that was bearable, she attempted to close her eyes, but did not find the quiet dreams she longed for.

Instead she found herself back in the garden, the roses so vivid in her mind that she could smell their sweet aroma. A light breeze slid across her skin, moving her hair slightly in its gentle breath. She opened her eyes and stared across her fiancé's room.

She could still smell the roses.

CHAPTER IV

THE PAST WAS A forbidden subject, even in the privacy of Mara's mind. Yet she could not prevent her thoughts from wandering into that forbidden realm. It had been nearly eight hundred years since Mara had first taken her vows, foreswearing her life to the service of the courts. The day she had achieved the rank of sub-captain within the Lorcan Guard had been the proudest of her life. But it was a rank that she would hold for only a short time before tragedy would force her to leave the court and swear the remainder of her life to the Order of the Black Rose.

Garreth, Phillip, Mathew, Brendan and Regald had once formed the core leadership of the Black Rose. They had followed Mara without thought or question into what some would come to call the greatest victory that any immortal court would ever hold over another. Philip had been her second in command. Philip, who would forever walk along the sparkling ocean sands in the deepest recess of Mara's memories.

As the limousine pulled up in front of the tall black gates of the Arum Court, Mara ignored the driver's rush to reach her side and opened the door to the long, dark car. She had made this trip unaccompanied, which was unusual for one of her rank and title. Yet, in this instance, Mara felt she should attempt to keep a low profile. It would not do to voice her fears if they proved unfounded.

Mara entered the grounds of the Arum Court quietly, offering the two men guarding the door a smile as she approached. "Hello," she said to the two men in black jeans and loosely fitted, long-sleeved red shirts. "My name is Mara Sethian. I am here to speak with Captain Regald."

The guard closest to Mara removed a phone from his pocket and called who Mara assumed to be someone in the palace. A few moments later, he motioned for her to follow him through the iron gates and into the doors beyond. They walked in silence down the long, wide corridors, painted in deep reds and royal blues and lined with famous paintings along the walls. Walking briskly, Mara passed through corridor after corridor before finally coming to the darker, stone hallways of the Arum Court Dungeons.

Dressed in a crimson shirt tucked neatly into slacks with his silver sword hidden in a black leather sheath, Captain Regald stood against the stone wall with a troubled expression. His blond hair was cropped short. "So, it really is you," Regald said to the captain he had once served. "I had half hoped it was an imposter, so that I could have cut their tongue for lying."

"Now what could possibly have you in a cutting mood? Has someone done something they were not supposed to?"

"Now, Mara," Regald said in a light tone that did not match his hardened expression. "Surely, whatever happened did not rise to the level of warranting your personal attention."

Mara looked into his green eyes. "So, he is here."

Regald sighed. "I expected they would send someone. But I did not know it would be you."

Mara considered him for a moment and then said, "Liar."

Regald nodded. "Yes. But it is the expected answer."

"Where is he?"

"I had to follow orders, Captain Mara."

"Oh no." She shook her head, keeping her tone as calm as possible, motioning to the small black rose etched into his crimson shirt. "You know better. You would never have carried out these orders."

He cleared his throat. "Orders were given..."

"Then perhaps it is time to start following the orders of someone who knows what is good for you."

"What are you doing here, Mara? You came for Edward? You can't even be in the same room with him! He's not..."

Mara's sword was at Regald's throat before he knew she had moved. "You will not speak a word against Edward. Not in my presence." Her voice was far too calm. "Do you understand me, Captain?"

"Yes," he replied, working hard to remain perfectly still under Mara's silver blade.

"Where is he?"

"In a cell, my lady."

"Take me to him." She lowered her sword and sheathed it as silently as it had been drawn. "Take me to him, *now*."

"As you wish, Captain Mara." The Arum captain turned, motioning for a pair of nearby guardsmen to open the tall stone doors which marked the entrance to the dungeon cells beyond. The man on the left side of the doors, also in a dark red shirt, stepped forward.

"I would be honored to escort Captain Mara, my lord. I was about to take new bandages down anyway."

Mara's heart skipped a beat at the word *bandages*. "I would be grateful if you would, Nolan," Mara said to the man who had spoken. She had met the younger man almost ten years earlier. He was one of Mara's favorites among the Arum Guard. He was a tall man of pale skin, green eyes and dirty blond hair.

Nolan moved to the desk on the far side of the room and grabbed several stacks of bandages before walking back and entering the doors to the dungeons. Mara followed closely behind him, her wide black heels echoing across the stone corridor. A chill filled the damp air surrounding them, causing Mara's black shirt to cling to her pale skin. As they rounded the corner, Mara paused.

"Nolan," she said, her voice crawling along the silent walls surrounding them. "How bad?"

"It was bad," came his reply. He then turned to glance at her. "Really bad. He..." Nolan's eyes gazed directly into Mara's. "I've seen worse, but it just...wasn't good." He turned forward again and Mara followed him down several more turns of the dank labyrinth. They finally came to a stone door which Nolan opened with a jingle of silver keys.

They entered the room quietly. Edward's still form lay on the cold slab of gray stone, covered by a thin blanket. Nolan walked around the table and knelt to address the injured man. "Captain Edward."

"Nolan," Edward said, acknowledging him. The single word was enough to make Mara's breath catch in her throat. Her gaze slid over Edward: the long ebony hair, the pale skin and the toned muscles. Then Nolan slid back the blanket, revealing the long strips of pink bandages that covered the entirety of Edward's back.

"Just going to change these," Nolan told Edward who did not move from his still position. Carefully, Nolan pulled back the blood-soaked layers, revealing the ravaged skin beneath. Edward's back was covered with long, precise bloody streaks. The flesh open like a raw steak split by a butcher.

Mara remained still, her heart thundering in her chest at the sight of Edward's injuries. Edward hissed as the thick, white salve was both removed and reapplied to the long, open cuts. Fresh blood seeped to the surface of several wounds as Nolan began to re-cover the injuries, dyeing the thick strips a faint pink.

When he finished, Nolan pulled the blanket back over Edward's body. "Forgive me, Captain. You have someone who would like to see you."

Edward started to rise when Mara said, "No." She drew a deep breath. "Please, Captain. Do not rise on my account."

Edward froze. The muscles in his back visibly tightened. Several moments of dead silence filled the room. Then Edward said, "Mara."

She walked forward slowly, her heels shattering the silence surrounding them. When she aligned herself with his vision, she lowered her gaze to meet Edward's for the first time in six hundred years.

"Mara?" His voice held a tone of disbelief.

She stared into the darkest eyes she had ever known. Her voice was a strangled whisper. "Edward."

"What are you... You're here. You came."

"Of course I came." Hot tears rose to the surface of her eyes. She closed them and was haunted by the image of the woman who had stood by Edward's side all those years ago: the long dark hair, the violet eyes. She fought back the unwanted emotions and shook her head to clear the vision. "I am taking you out of here, Edward." She turned towards Nolan and commanded, "Assist the captain to his feet."

Nolan did not question her order, but instead moved to Edward's side and helped him rise, allowing Edward to lean against him.

"Mara," Edward cautioned. "You can't just walk out..."

"Watch me."

They walked unhurriedly down the dungeon corridors. Halfway down the tunnels, Edward began to stumble. Mara caught him, moving to his left side, opposite Nolan. The doors opened before them and they walked out of the cold hallway and into the room beyond.

"What are you doing here?" a guard Mara did not recognize asked them. "Why is he out of his cell?"

"Because he is coming with me." Mara searched the room for Regald, but he was nowhere to be found. She leaned Edward against the stone wall before turning to address the unfamiliar guard. Mara pulled a small, rose-shaped badge from the silver chain she wore under her shirt and flashed it at the guard. "Black Rose."

The man took half a step back in surprise. Then he bent to one knee, lowering his gaze toward the floor. "Forgive me, Captain. I did not realize."

"Help us out of here and consider it forgiven," Mara told the kneeling man. He rose instantly and assisted Nolan in supporting Edward. The foursome walked slowly down the colorful halls beyond the dungeon before finally emerging into the sunlight. The limousine in which Mara had arrived was awaiting her return. Nolan helped Edward into the car before sliding in after him. Mara gave a brief word of thanks to the other guard before entering the limousine herself. When they reached the palace gates, they were waved through—no questions asked.

Edward's breath was shallow as he leaned back in considerable pain. "Mara, I..."

"It's all right." She soothed him. "Try to sleep. It will be less painful if you do." Mara gave Edward the full weight of her gaze. "I've got you." Edward closed his eyes at her words, allowing Mara to shift her attention to the younger man.

"Captain Regald left on purpose," he informed her. "He's too smart to put himself between you and the king."

"If that was true," Mara replied, "he never would have touched the captain of another guard. Especially not this one."

"Come on, Mara. Should he really have known that you would come for him?"

Mara fought to draw a tight breath. She let it out slowly, her gaze shifting involuntarily to the man beside her. Her eyes closed of their own accord.

Edward stood in a crisp white shirt with silver buttons and ruffled sleeves. A beautiful young woman dressed in a pale blue gown stood gracefully on his arm, her long dark hair blowing softly in the wind. Her gentle laughter, the essence of joy.

Mara opened her violet eyes. "I will always come for him."

CHAPTER V

MARA KNOCKED ON THE STONE door. A few moments later, it was opened by a man with sandy brown hair and matching eyes. Dressed in a silver shirt of the Ciar Royal Guard which bore a small black rose denoting his former service and black slacks, the man offered a quizzical look that lasted for several long moments before recognition settled in his eyes. He stepped back, motioning for Mara to enter the room.

"Hello, Jake," Mara said to the Sub-Captain of the Ciar Guard.

"See, I knew you would rather see me than Edward." He flashed Mara his best smile.

"Actually, I came with Edward."

Jake's smile disappeared as though in slow motion. "Sorry...would you say that again?"

"I came with Edward."

Jake gave a hard swallow and took a step back from the slightly taller woman. "Mara, what the hell is going on?"

"Edward was a captive of the Arum Court. I got him out. It's a bit of a long story as to why. Nolan of the Arum Guard is here and he can fill you in on the details." She drew a deep breath. "But the question that I want to know is this. What the hell happened to cause the Arum Court to think that they could take the Captain of the Ciar Guard hostage and not pay a price for doing so? Doesn't matter what they believed Edward's crime to be, this crossed a fucking line!"

"Wait." Jake put up his hands in the shape of a 'T.' "Where is Edward?"

"In the next room. He slept through most of the flight. They..." Her breath caught in her throat and she struggled to finish the statement. "They tortured him, Jake." Mara twisted her head toward the bedroom door. "Let's go see him?"

Jake nodded. The two walked out of the room and down the hall until they reached the captain's private chambers. Two men stood outside the door, both dressed in identical clothing to their sub-captain, minus the black rose upon their silver shirts. The guards nodded as they approached, motioning them through a set of tall, stone doors.

Built deep into the mountains, the captain's chambers featured walls of pale gray stone. A bed sat in the center of the room where Edward lay, covered with thick blankets which were used to fight off cold nights experienced within the mountain tunnels. Over the years, many members of the guard had moved out of these ancient sanctuaries for a more modern form of living. However, the Royal Guard steadfastly remained.

The room was lit by a roaring fire which provided both warmth and light to the vast room. Jake moved forward quietly while Mara remained in the back. When Jake reached the bed, he eased back the blankets which covered Edward's ravaged back. Jake took in his captain's injuries for several moments before replacing the blanket.

"You know, Captain, our men have not had a decent excuse to openly engage the Arum Court in a few centuries. I don't suppose you feel like telling me who, exactly, is responsible for these injuries?"

"We are not going to war over this, Jake. Do you hear me?"

Silence followed as Edward and Jake stared each other down. Then Jake asked, "Do you want to tell her instead?"

Mara stood on the opposite side of the room in tight black jeans and a scoop neck shirt. Her long hair was pulled back and held in place with a thin, silver band. A silver rose mark was embroidered onto her black shirt and a thick, silver necklace encircled her slender throat, supporting a diamond cut in the shape of a white rose. Even her violet eyes had a touch of silver near their center, a mere glint in the darkness. She stood perfectly still, her right hand on the hilt of her silver blade, hidden in a black leather sheath tied to her left hip.

"Mara?" Edward asked in a voice hoarse from screaming.

She walked across the room, her steps the only sound in the silent chamber. Edward started to rise. Mara shook her head and knelt down, placing herself at his level.

"You came. I thought it was a dream."

"Thought," she asked softly. "Or hoped?"

He leaned forward, closing the distance between them. "Mara." His gaze searched her violet eyes as a look of pain crossed his features. Mara shifted her gaze to the floor, ripping her eyes from his view.

The sound of laughter slid into the room. It was the most haunting sound Mara had ever known. She shook her head and reached for Edward's arm, gently pulling it towards her. She placed her cheek against the back side of his hand and dug her thumb into his wrist, letting the strong beat of his heart drown out the echoing laughter. Edward reached forward with his other hand, placing it upon the side of Mara's neck, his own fingers finding her heartbeat.

The laughter rose in volume. Edward pulled Mara towards him, placing her head against his chest. She crawled onto the bed, driving the memories back with the steady rhythm of his breathing and the strong beat of his heart.

Edward kept one hand firmly on the side of her neck while gently stroking her hair with the other. "Edward," Mara whispered under her breath.

"I'm here," he answered.

Jake remained silent as the two captains lay upon the bed, drowning out the laughter with the synchronized beat of their hearts.

Yet even as the sound faded, a vision of the young girl appeared. Dressed in a gown of blue satin, she stood upon the stone steps, Edward's hands holding hers. Soft music filled the room as the two bodies swayed slowly across the stone floor. Edward twirled the girl around the room to the beat of his heart.

Mara lifted her head and glanced down at Edward. His chest was covered with blood. She jumped, violently jerking her body away from his. She wiped her eyes, struggling to clear the vision.

"Mara?"

She glanced down in a daze. She tried to smile, but could not bring herself to form the lie upon her lips.

"Mara."

"I'm glad you are safe, Edward."

"Mara," he said again as he looked towards her, but his gaze faltered when it grazed her violet eyes.

"Still..." The single, bitter word spoke volumes.

He did not look up.

"Forgive me, my lord. I must go." She walked towards the door.

"Mara!" he again called.

She stopped walking, but did not turn to face him. "I will always come for you, *mi amor*. But I just...can't." She waited several moments. When no reply came, she continued forward and walked out the tall doors.

Jake, who had been standing against the wall throughout the exchange, ran forward, exiting right behind her. "Captain!" His voice rebounded against the gray stone. "Mara!" He switched to her first name. "It was centuries ago. It was..."

"Did you hear her laughter?" She turned to face the sub-captain, who gave her solemn eyes. "Edward did."

CHAPTER VI

"AND YOU JUST LET HIM go?" King Mathew asked from his silver throne in the center of the brightly lit chambers, the large windows filtering sunlight from every direction. He was less physically imposing than many of the men who stood by his side. Though tall, he was rather slender. His eyes were pale gray and matched his long-sleeved shirt which was closed with silver buttons and cufflinks. His hair was a blond more silver than gold.

Captain Regald knelt on one knee before him. "I am sorry, my king. He was taken while I was away."

"And the guards just let him leave? I want every man who stood between the gate and the dungeon punished."

"For what, Your Majesty? It was the Captain of the Black Rose Guard. No one questions her."

"Mara?"

"Yes, my king."

"Mara came herself?"

Regald nodded.

"The Black Rose hasn't played a hand in centuries."

"Well, I would say that they did so today." He paused for breath. "Forgive my bluntness, Your Majesty. What did you think was going to happen? You had to know Mara would come for him."

"Did I?"

Regald eyed the king carefully. "You and I both know that this had nothing to do with the Black Rose. Harming Edward? You knew that she would come."

"After six hundred years?"

Regald considered remarking further, then wisely decided to keep his thoughts to himself. Instead, he simply stated, "It doesn't matter why she came, Your Majesty. Only that she did and that it would be unjust to punish those who observed her authority, considering it is exactly what we teach them to do."

"I suppose you are correct. However, I want to see the guard responsible for actually allowing them to leave."

"Forgive me, but Nolan left with Captain Mara. I imagine he intends to take the Oath of the Rose."

A stiffness entered the king's features. A scowl crossed his lips. Several moments of silence passed before he finally said, "I suppose there is little that I could devise which would result in a punishment as cruel as that." The king shook his head. "Attend to your duties, Captain."

Regald stood from his kneeling position on the white marble floor and walked quickly from the room. As he passed down the various halls, another guard called his name.

"Captain Regald, Lady Sandra is asking for you."

"I will go to her chambers," he replied. He turned to his left and headed down a different corridor. The walls were painted bright blue, lined with the golden-framed portraits of elegant men and ladies of past eras. When he came to Sandra's wooden door, he knocked gently. Moments later the door opened and he entered the chambers beyond.

The room was immense with walls painted in the same royal blue that filled the hallways. Lady Sandra sat before a huge fire on the far side of the room in a gown of deep green velvet. A leather-bound book sat in Sandra's lap, which she closed at his entrance. "My lady," the captain said to the future princess. "You asked to see me?"

"Yes. I want to know more about the man who was being punished. Who is he?"

"He is the Captain of the Ciar Royal Guard."

"Yes, but...I want to know more."

Regald moved toward a sofa which stood across from her and took a seat upon the cream colored cushions. "Edward has served as Captain to the Ciar Queen, Clarissa, for roughly twelve hundred years. He has trained more members of both the Arum and Ciar Guard than anyone. He also trained several members of the Black Rose."

"Including Mara?"

Captain Regald tilted his head and leaned slightly forward. "You know Mara?"

Sandra tensed and moved to cradle her head in the palm of her left hand. The vision of a tall woman with long black hair and violet eyes flashed before her. Then just as quickly, it vanished. "She is the Captain of the Black Rose Guard, is she not?"

"Yes, my lady."

"I..." She wracked her brain, but the image refused to return. "No. I suppose I do not."

"Well, her identity and position is far from a secret."

"Sometimes I know things and I am not sure why."

"It is to be expected. We know that your memories are scattered at best. Remember, my lady, I am the guard who found you."

Sandra remembered little before waking up in the wings of the Arum Court healers. She had been found severely injured, wandering through the forest. She had almost no memories of her past.

"I saw him," Sandra confessed to the man who had spent the past two hundred years watching her from afar, as though finding her had somehow made him responsible for her safety. She had been grateful for the watchful eye, and upon becoming engaged to the Crown Prince, had shyly asked the king if he could oversee her protection detail. The king had consented and Regald had spent the past few months splitting his time between and the king and future princess.

So it was to Regald, and not her fiancé, that she offered her confession. "I saw him. Edward, I mean. I saw him, or at least...I think I did."

"Saw him?" Regald questioned. "Do you mean...you remembered him?"

"Yes. No. I'm not sure. It was like a dream. Only it was more like a nightmare. What she did to him was...it was so awful."

"She?"

Sandra turned her gaze back towards the bright yellow flames. "There was a woman in a rose garden." She shook her head. "No, there was a rose garden, and then there was a woman in a room of stone the color of obsidian. She was hurting him."

"A rose garden?"

"Yes, full of red and violet roses."

"Red and violet? Are you sure?"

She nodded.

"The Court roses have not bloomed in those colors for centuries."

Sandra closed her eyes and searched her memories. She found only darkness.

"I need to see him."

"My lady." Regald cleared his throat. "Captain Edward is no longer here. He has been returned to his court."

"The Black Rose came for him, didn't she?"

Regald's eyes widened. "How did you know that?"

Sandra shook her head and turned her deep blue eyes on the captain's. "I don't know."

CHAPTER VII

NOLAN KNOCKED ON THE DOOR to Mara's borrowed room, down a few hallways from the captain's chambers. "Come in," Mara called from behind the silver stone. The door opened with a soft click and Nolan entered quickly. Mara was seated in front of a mahogany desk, reading over a small stack of papers scattered in front of her. An unmarked bottle of a clear spirits sat on the edge of the desk, half empty.

She read to the end of her page, before raising her head and glancing at her visitor. "What can I do for you, Nolan?"

"Captain Mara," he began. "I have watched you over the years, and tales of your guard are legendary." He knelt in front of her. "I humbly ask to join the ranks of your service, my lady. I would like to join the Black Rose."

Mara stared at him from her seated position by the desk. "Tell me, Nolan. How old are you?"

"Forty-seven, my lady."

Mara nodded in thought. "That makes you, what, eight hundred years younger than I have been Captain of the Rose?"

"Yes, but you were younger than I when you were named a sub-captain."

"Tell me, have you ever been in love? I am not talking about a one night stand or a generic girlfriend, but rather, a real, true once in a lifetime love?"

"I thought I was once or twice. But it wasn't with the right girl."

Mara eyed him critically. "If you join the Black Rose, you will never find her." She turned to her drink and took a deep sip.

"I don't need to fall in love, Captain. I would rather serve the realm."

"Serve the realm?" Mara said sarcastically. "What do you know of service? You, who have lived in the realm of peace bought by the blood of Roses?" Her speech slurred as she stared into the eyes of the younger man.

"I am brave. And I very much want to join your ranks."

Mara glanced down at the silver rose embroidered on her black shirt. "I suppose," she said slowly, "that we seem majestic to you? The feared Order of the mighty Black Rose. The slayer of daemons, procurers of kings? Is that how you see us, young lord? Are we glamorous, mystical, majestic as the knights of old?"

He drew a deep breath before answering. "I see you as the protectors of the realm, my lady."

Mara gave a harsh laugh. "The Black Rose does not defend, Sub-Captain Nolan. We are not saviors—we are killers. We do not protect; we destroy. We are glorified assassins and the best at what we do. Look at you with your pretty, idealistic eyes. Almost thirty years of living and still as optimistic as a child."

She poured more of the clear liquid into a narrow glass and drained it dry. "The Black Rose destroys the soul of all it touches. It betrays every moral, standard, value, and person you have ever held dear. I have done things, Nolan. Things you can't even imagine. And for that, my soul burns in the fires of eternal torment, while my body still breathes."

Mara refilled her glass and took a long, slow draught before turning her violet gaze back upon the younger man. "You want to serve the realm? Then marry a kind woman and teach your children to dream of a world where the Black Rose is no longer needed. A world where I am condemned for my crimes, not honored for them. A better world, Nolan. One where someone like me will never again see the light of day."

Without knowing how to respond, Nolan rose from the floor and walked towards the silver door. As he stepped out into the hallway, Mara's voice cut through the space between them. "Nolan."

He turned back towards her.

"Tell Captain Edward you want to serve under him. I will use my authority to sever your vows to Regald. Serve him well. Then we will see if you still desire to become a member of the famous Black Rose."

Chapter VIII

1400 AD

MARA WALKED ALONG THE CRYSTAL sand of the beach, the waves crashing softly in the gentle ocean breeze. The water was the deepest blue Mara had ever seen. The sky was clear with not a single cloud. She inhaled deeply, tasting the salt on the tip of her tongue. Her white cotton gown swirled around her body, and her long hair blew behind her from the soft ocean wind. Mara knelt, running her hand through the warm, golden sand and then looked up, gazing to the blue sea where water broke in white waves.

"Hello," whispered a small voice. She turned her head to face the young boy who had walked up beside her. His bronze skin was kissed lightly by the sun, and his short blond hair blew in the wind. He wore a pair of leather pants and a white shirt closed with small, sapphire buttons. Her gaze traveled up to view the boy's young face, and she found herself staring into a pair of blue eyes; eyes the color of the sea, with a touch of white running through them as though the waves of the ocean moved gently within his azure gaze.

"How old are you, child?"

The boy held up four bronzed fingers.

"What are you doing out here on the beach?"

"Mommy told me to come here," the boy told her.

Mara forced a soft smile upon her full lips. "And who is your mommy?" she asked, knowing the answer.

"Sophia. Please, can you help me? Mommy is really scared. She sent me here." There were tears running down the child's rosy cheeks.

Mara held out her arms to the young boy, who trustingly came into her embrace. "What is your name?"

"Dorian," the child answered quietly.

"Well, Prince Dorian, there is nothing to be scared of anymore. I will take you to your mother."

"You can?"

She pulled back slightly. "Yes, child. In fact, I have a secret to tell you. Do you think you can keep a secret?"

The child stopped crying and nodded.

"This, my prince, is just a bad dream, that's all." She fought to maintain her smile. "Just a bad dream, and dreams are nothing to be afraid of."

He looked at her quizzically for a moment before returning her smile. "Can I wake up now?"

Mara's heart lurched as she stared into his trusting blue eyes. "Yes, child. I am going to make the bad dream end. All you have to do is close your eyes. Do you think you can do that for me, little prince?"

The young boy nodded happily as Mara placed a hand upon the hilt of her long, silver blade. Then the child closed, what Mara knew, would be the last eyes to ever hold the sea.

Chapter IX

Present Day

Mara awoke to find Garreth sitting beside her. A former sub-captain of the Black Rose, Garreth had spent a lifetime attempting to avoid any position of command within the courts he had devoted his life to. He sat beside Mara dressed in a dark pair of blue jeans and a white t-shirt. His blond hair was shaggy with bangs that were just beginning to obstruct the view to his pale green eyes. "You need a haircut," Mara said groggily, a persistent pounding against her left temple.

"Hello, Mara," he said to his former captain. "I would say that I was surprised to see you here. However, after seeing Edward, I would honestly expect to find you nowhere else."

"Go away," Mara told him. "Or at least kill the lights."

Garreth glanced toward the desk at the empty bottle, and then back at her. "Are you drunk?"

Mara gave a deep groan. "Not anymore."

"Mara? You don't drink alcohol."

"No," she replied. "The Captain of the Black Rose does not drink alcohol. I, on the other hand, drink just fine."

He sat in silence for several moments and then said, "Mara, are you okay?"

"Aren't I always?"

Garreth shook his head. "I spoke with Nolan when I arrived. Glorified assassins?"

Mara closed her eyes as the previous night slowly returned. "Please go away."

"Destroyers, not protectors?"

"Well, aren't we? You should know, you were one of us."

Garreth drew a slow breath before answering. "I haven't seen you like this since the night Phillip died."

"A lot of people died that night."

"But you only cared about one. I came as soon as I heard. It must have been hard for you to see—"

"Him that way," she finished for him.

"Mara, are you okay?"

Her head continued to pound insistently and anger slipped into her usually calm tone. "Stop asking me questions to which you already know the answer! Do you think standing over me like this helps anything? Do you think I want to see you any more than him?"

"Mara!" he cut in. "Stop it! It was six hundred years ago. It was—"

"She was wearing a blue gown of silk. She was dancing in his arms where she belonged. He spun her around once, twice, thrice."

"Mara." This time his voice was gentle. "That was a long time ago. She died a long time ago."

"I know." Her voice decreased in volume. "I know she died...except when I look in his eyes, watch him breathe, listen to the beat of his heart. Then she lives. I can see her dancing in his eyes."

"You have to stop punishing yourself for what happened. It was—"

"If you say it was not my fault," Mara interrupted, "then I swear to the Gods I will slit your throat where you stand."

Silence followed her threat. Garreth's eyes shifted around the room as he considered his words. "Have you ever considered that perhaps your forgiveness lies in his arms?"

She shook her head slowly, the anger vanishing from her now hushed tone. "In his arms," she echoed his words. "In his arms, listening to the sound of his heart, is the only place I have ever known peace. And the one place...the only place that I can never be—is with him." She searched Garreth's pale eyes. "I am not worthy of his forgiveness, Garreth. I will never be worthy."

CHAPTER X

EDWARD AWOKE IN CONSIDERABLY LESS pain than when he had first arrived back in his chambers. The expert healers had gone to work on his injuries. Between their careful ministrations and powerful salves, he was beginning to feel more like himself. He opened his eyes to find Garreth sitting in a chair that had been pulled beside the bed.

"Hello, Captain."

"Garreth," Edward said to his longtime friend. "You need a haircut."

Garreth gave a soft chuckle. "Mara said the same thing."

"So, she is why you are here."

"I am here because someone tried to kill you, Captain."

Edward met Garreth's light green eyes. "Is she okay?"

Garreth shook his head and sighed. "Why the hell do you two fight each other? You should go into that room, throw her down on the bed and let go of the past once and for all."

"Garreth! Be serious."

"I am being serious! Do you think this is what *she* wanted? She would kick both your asses if she could see this."

Edward shook his head. "You don't understand."

"Of course I understand," Garreth replied, frustration filtering through his voice. "She was my sister, Edward. And she would not have wanted the two of you, who she loved most, to suffer in this way."

"I should have been there. I should have stopped it."

"There is only one person to blame for the fact that both you and Mara were not there that night. It wasn't you and it wasn't Mara. If you still must insist on blame, after all of these years, then at least place it where it rightfully belongs."

"If I had done my job, instead of letting everything else get in the way."

"You mean instead of following your heart? Please, for the love of all the Gods, Edward, my friend. Please, let this go. Forgive yourself and forgive her, too. She is self-destructing and from where I am seated, you don't seem far behind her."

"Mara does not self-destruct. Haven't you heard? She is the cold-hearted, fearless, merciless Black Rose."

"Edward!" he said sharply.

Silence followed as the captain stared down at the blankets in sudden shame. "I'm sorry, Garreth. It's just, seeing her again, it's just not..."

"I know," Garreth replied sadly. "I know what the two of you do to each other. I know all too well." He ran his fingers through his shaggy blond hair. "But you need to understand, she feels the same way."

"She should have left me there. She should have..."

"She wouldn't be able to live with herself if she had."

Edward raised his gaze. "I know."

CHAPTER XI

MARA LEFT THE COURT WITHOUT saying goodbye to the captain whose life she had saved. Instead, she had turned to Jake, instructing simply, "If you need me, do not hesitate to call." She had offered the sub-captain a slight bow and then turned and walked quickly from the room, exiting the long, gray hallways of stone. Two hours later, she was seated on a private jet on her way back to the house of the Black Rose.

The Black Rose Guard lived in an ancient castle nestled in the Lethia Mountains. It was an isolated, dreary place known for spectacular thunderstorms and a fog that put even the Scottish moors to shame. The drive to this desolate and remote castle was a slow one in which vehicles needed to carefully tread the gray, steep roads on the mountains. Once, long ago, this hidden land had been the heart of all the immortal realm, and the ancient keep a glorious, hidden castle. But as the years passed, the courts had moved on to warmer, less remote locations until all that remained were the members of the revered Black Rose.

Mara had been picked up by a driver at the Lethia airport and began the four hour journey into the heart of the Black Rose. She attempted to sleep throughout the ride, but found herself unable to quiet her mind long enough for sleep to come. She shifted again, fighting her rising memories.

Liza. She closed her eyes against her will and saw the young girl sitting beside her. With pale cheeks, ruby lips, luxurious black hair, high cheek bones and violet eyes, Liza had been a beauty among beauties with a heart of profound innocence. It was no surprise that Edward had lost his heart to her. Liza had stolen all of their hearts in one way or another, even Mara's.

"We have arrived, my lady," the driver said, pulling her mind back to the present.

"Thank you," Mara replied, and then waited while he came around and opened the door. She stepped out into the damp air. The sky was a cloudless gray over the ancient stone towers which constituted the keep of the Black Rose. She walked across a narrow, wooden bridge that stretched over a stream of gray water and walked toward the tall stone doors. They opened far before she reached them, and she stepped slowly over the bridge.

Two men stood on either side of the door, both in black from head to toe, a silver rose embroidered into their black shirts. They had matching, shoulder-length brown hair and golden eyes. "Captain Mara," they both said and bowed their heads slightly as they opened the door for their captain.

"Hello, Brian. Aiden."

"Sub-Captain Brendan is awaiting you, Captain."

"Yes, thank you."

She walked past the guardsmen and into the old castle. The vaulted ceiling rose nearly twenty feet high and was made of gray stone. Large rugs had been placed upon the stone, in deep, crimson reds that were beginning to fade. Narrow spiral staircases stood on either side of the walls leading to the levels above. Mara took the stairs on the left and began the slow, careful walk towards the upper levels of the ancient castle. When she reached the top level, she continued past her chambers toward those of her second in command, Brendan.

She knocked on the tall stone door and entered without waiting for an invitation. Brendan sat at his desk, leaning over several sets of papers. His dark brown hair was cut short against his skull, his skin pale from the lack of sunlight associated with the area. He looked up, turning his ice blue gaze upon Mara. He stood from the chair and offered a low bow to his captain, bending at the waist and remaining perfectly still for several seconds.

"Rise," Mara instructed him.

"I am glad to see your safe return, Captain."

"Thank you," Mara replied. "The guards downstairs said you wished to see me."

"Yes, my lady. I just wanted to report that all has been quiet while you were away."

"Has Sean returned from his protection detail?"

"He returned two days ago, after seeing the Prime Minster safely through his South Ciar tour."

Mara nodded. "Is that all?"

Brendan stared at her for several moments in silence, unspoken questions burning in his eyes.

"Captain Edward is alive and back in the Ciar Court," she said in a dry tone, answering his unspoken question.

"Thank the Gods for that, my lady."

"It was a necessity," Mara replied. "If Edward had died, that would leave Jake in charge of the Ciar Court Guard."

Brendan cringed slightly. "No one wants that."

"No," Mara said in a voice that withheld even the slightest ounce of humor. "No one wants that."

Other questions burned brightly through Brendan's eyes, but Mara was his captain, so instead he offered a low bow and said, "Is there anything else, Captain?"

"No. That will be all for now." She gave Brendan a curt nod, then turned and walked back towards her own chambers.

Mara's chambers were made of the same granite that formed the rest of the castle. The floor was covered by a thin black rug. A bed stood by the left wall and a writing desk sat in the right corner of the room near one of two small windows. A fireplace was situated along the wall closet to the door, but no fire was currently lit.

Mara walked across the room and pulled back the black curtains covering a window and pushed open the glass panels. A cool breeze flowed into the room, allowing the fresh wind to saturate the stuffy air surrounding her. Mara slowly peeled off her clothes and walked towards the private bathroom attached to the room. With black marble tiles, a shower and a Jacuzzi tub that was far too large for its single inhabitant, the bathroom was one of the only rooms within the ancient castle to have been fully refurbished within the last century.

Mara turned on the water and waited several minutes for the temperature to rise before stepping into the steaming hot water. She closed her eyes, allowing the feel of the water beating against her skin to soothe her taut form. She lost track of time standing in the hot water, drowning out the world. By the time she stepped out, her normally pale skin had been beaten red by the heat of the water.

She wrapped herself in a black towel and bound her long black hair in another. She dried her body thoroughly and then walked back towards the bedroom. The cool breeze filtering in from the window was soothing against her flushed skin. She lay down on the bed with the towel wrapped tightly around her. As her head touched the familiar black pillows, a sense of calm began to descend upon her. Here, among these desolate chambers, Mara was able to drown out the dreams, the memories chased back by the cold mountain winds and the familiar gray stones that she had called home for the majority of her life.

Mara threw off the towel and slipped under the black covers that cascaded over her bed. Moments later, she slipped into a deep, dreamless sleep.

CHAPTER XII

SANDRA ENTERED THE ANCIENT GARDEN. Black roses ran wild, climbing the ancient stone walls, thorns piercing the crumbling gray rocks. A pond was in the garden's center, the water covered in a layer of thick, green moss making the water appear almost sickly in the fading light. Sandra approached the water's edge and closed her eyes, allowing her mind to change the bleak scene.

As though stepping into a dream, the moss vanished from the water, transforming it to a clear pool that reflected the stars above. Her thin, black gown melted away to royal blue, the skirt becoming fuller as she gazed into the sparkling crystal water. The reflected image was of a woman Sandra had never seen. The same pale skin, long black hair and rouged lips, but the eyes...the eyes were violet. Violet with a glint of silver at their core. Sandra stared mesmerized into the reflective pool. She had never seen such eyes.

A man approached her slowly, his image gradually appearing in the reflective surface of the water. His pale skin seemed translucent in the encroaching darkness. She studied his reflection. Shoulder-length black hair blended into his long black coat. A crimson shirt of silk was tucked neatly into long black pants. He stepped behind her, his arms slipping securely around her thin frame. The woman in Sandra's reflection smiled with a sparkle in her eye that matched the brilliance of any star.

Sandra turned around to face the man who held her and realized with a start that his shirt was not crimson—it was white. White silk soaked with thick, wet blood. Sandra lifted her hands, her fingers suddenly dripping with immortal blood. She screamed, jerking her body away from him. The man reached forward and grabbed her, saving her from toppling into the mossy water behind her.

"Sandra!" Regald's voice broke the trance. His black eyes faded to green and she found herself held tightly by his strong arms. "My lady, what did you see?"

"The other captain."

"You mean Edward?"

She nodded.

"Edward once stood as a guard within these walls. These are the old castle grounds of the Lorcan Court."

"The Lorcan Court?"

"Yes, the court that existed before they split into the Ciar and the Arum. But no one has lived here in at least five hundred years."

"The royal chambers," Sandra said in an uncertain tone. "I need to see them."

Regald nodded. "Those chambers are underground." He reached back to the black bag lying on the ground behind him. After a few moments of fiddling with locks and opening zippers, Regald produced two flashlights. "Not nearly as fancy as the firelight that once lined these walls, but much more practical for our immediate purposes."

Regald led Sandra to the edge of the garden, but paused when Sandra stopped at the entrance. The violet-eyed woman once again stood at the water's edge. Edward stood beside her, his shirt crisp, white and clean. "*I love you, Edward.*" Her words danced upon the wind.

"My lady," Edward replied to the violet-eyed woman, her royal blue gown billowing around her in a soft breeze Sandra could neither hear nor feel. "I am not worthy of your love."

"Edward..." Her voice was the definition of tenderness. "How can you think such a thing?"

"My princess." Edward turned slightly to better see her eyes.

She reached out her pale hand, brushing her fingertips against the side of his face. "I've loved you all my life. Are you saying that you do not love me?"

"You know I do." Edward's voice was soft and deep. A sad smile graced his handsome features. "But, my princess," Edward drew back, facing away from her, "this can never be. It is forbidden."

The woman with violet eyes reached her hand forward, silencing his words with a caress from her pale hand. She studied him for several long moments, her hand sliding down the side of his face as her finger traced their way lightly over his lips. "I love you," she spoke softly. "I cannot imagine life without you."

His eyes searched the irresistible depth of hers and slowly, ever so slowly, he leaned forward and pressed his lips against hers. The kiss was deep and passionate, his arms grasping hers in a firm grip as she opened to him as a flower to the morning sun. The kiss lingered for a long time, his hand rising to the back of her neck, drawing her more tightly against him. Then he finally pulled back as though in a daze.

"My lady," he said. "I am so sorry."

"For what?"

"I love you. But, this..." He shook his head. "This can never be."

A gust of wind blew through the scattered roses, taking with it Sandra's vision. The cold wind caressed her skin, blowing the tears from her deep blue eyes.

Chapter XIII

"Yes, Nolan," Garreth said to the younger man.

"Forgive me for disturbing you."

"Not at all. What can I do for you?"

"I was hoping you could explain a few things."

"About Mara?"

Nolan nodded hesitantly, as though unsure if he was crossing a line. "I know that something happened between her and Captain Edward, but I am not sure if I understand."

"You don't." Garreth motioned to the wooden chair beside him. Nolan took several steps forward and took the offered seat.

"Tell me, Nolan, have you ever had a great love? One that burned you through and through? Stole your heart in a way that you knew you could live a thousand years and it would never be the same? A love you would give your life for and know that the one single moment of happiness received in return would be worth all the years of living without?"

Nolan shook his head. "I can't say that I have."

"Nor have I."

Seconds of silence passed between them before Nolan said, "But I would like to know why both you and Mara have asked me the same question."

"I've never had a love like that, Nolan," Garreth said to the younger man. "But I have seen it."

"With Edward? Mara loved him?"

"Oh yes. Mara loved Edward."

"Then why?"

A glassy look came over Garreth's expression. "Mara loved Edward and Edward loved Mara. But not as much as they both loved another. I have seen things, Nolan. Things that dazzle, things to dread, but never in my life have I ever seen anything that haunts me as much as the power of one, true love. It was magnificent, terrifying and something that I have spent my life both dreaming of finding and dreading the day that I do."

"Wait, I don't understand," Nolan interrupted. "They loved another? Who?"

Garreth did not move his gaze from the wall. "Her name was..." His words trailed off. "She was..." He could not bring himself to say it. Then Garreth visibly shook himself. "It was a long time ago. It doesn't matter anymore. Mara is gone now. It is for the better, I think. Yes, for the better of all."

"I don't understand. Why did Mara act so strangely? Why did she leave without telling anyone?"

Garreth's eyes finally moved to meet Nolan's. "I'm afraid I cannot tell you that. I shouldn't have mentioned it. It is forbidden, you see, to speak of it."

"To speak of what?"

"Forbidden love," he offered with a bitter smile, the slightest curve of the lips.

"Forbidden love?"

Garreth nodded. "It is forbidden, you see. What happened that night was the greatest tragedy this court has ever seen. And I am forbidden to even tell you her name. All you need to know, is that the girl in the room that night wasn't Mara. You must forgive her for losing her temper. Edward and Mara are never together, and for good reason. Live a few hundred years and you will see. It is for the best."

Silence followed as Nolan rose to leave the room. When he reached the door, he stopped and turned back toward Garreth. "May I ask just one question, my lord?"

Garreth nodded slowly in consent.

"Does he still love her?"

"Edward?"

"Yes. Does he still love her?"

Garreth raised his head to stare up at Nolan from his seated position. "He will love her until he draws his last breath."

Nolan nodded and then left the room. As the door closed with a soft click behind him, Garreth whispered under his breath, "Liza...with his last breath."

Chapter XIV

THEY PLUNGED INTO DARKNESS, SINKING ever deeper into the ancient tunnels of black stone. The twin flashlights held by Regald and Sandra provided the only visible light. "I would have waited for daylight," Regald explained, "but it would not have mattered. We are too far down for sunlight to filter through."

"Why did they build underground?"

"For protection, mostly. The tunnels are too narrow to send an entire army inside. Geographically, the area is very stable as well."

Sandra stared ahead, but not even her imagination could form pictures in this darkness. "What happened here? Will you tell me?"

"I cannot. It is forbidden to speak of such things. If you truly know what happened here that night, I will take you to the one who can tell you. But if you do not remember," he allowed several moments of silence to fill the encroaching darkness, "it is forbidden, my lady."

"By whom?"

"The Captain of the Black Rose."

"Black Rose," she repeated. "The woman who came for Captain Edward?"

"Yes." Shadows danced across his face from the dim light of Sandra's flashlight.

"You are not part of her guard though."

"No, my lady."

"Then how can she forbid?"

"I served the Black Rose for many years. Centuries, in fact. When I was released from her service, it was under the condition that certain vows would be kept intact. This, what you ask, is most assuredly one of them." He drew a deep breath. "King Mathew also once served at Mara's pleasure."

"The king was a member of the Black Rose?"

"Yes. A sub-captain."

"Is it true what they say, about Mara?"

"What do they say?"

"That she is cold, ruthless and kills all those who would dare to challenge her?"

Several moments of silence filled the air between them before Regald stated, "As a killer, the Captain of the Rose is most proficient."

"Tell me about her."

Regald shivered. "I will, my lady, but not within the confines of these dark walls. This place..." He shifted his gaze down the hallway as though seeing figures beyond Sandra's sight. "They were children here. Edward, Mara, Garreth, Mathew...they were happy once. But after that night, they would never know happiness again." He shifted his gaze back to Sandra's. "Ask me some night, far from these walls. Here lie the ghosts of still-beating hearts." He turned and walked forward toward the tunnels. Sandra followed in a confused silence.

He led her down corridor after corridor, knowing the way even after all the centuries of abandonment. They finally found themselves standing before a tall stone door covered in black roses on thick, green vines. Regald moved to push the door open, and cut his hand on the thorn of a wild rose bush. Sandra shined the flashlight up and down the door. The roses ran up and down the stones. He moved more carefully and managed to maneuver the door open enough to enter the room.

The same roses ran across the walls of the expansive chambers and then trailed along the floor to reach the center of the room. A little more manipulation of the flashlights and Sandra managed to take several steps forward. In the center of the room was a slab of black polished stone upon which lay not the black roses that had been upon the door, but roses the color of freshly spilt blood.

A light appeared in the far corner of the room; a single flame in the darkness. She stepped towards it, being careful not to trip over the vines. As she watched, the flame split into two and then split again, slowly transforming into a roaring fire.

She reached the flames and stared in awe, watching the fire dance across the cold air. Then, she heard a soft whisper, "No." She turned around, facing away from the light. "No."

The stone was covered with piles of soft cushions and thick, dark blankets. Another fire burned on the opposite side of the room, flames pushing back the darkness. Edward stood beside the bed bared to the chest, his arms held fast by two men standing on either side of him. Standing beside him was the most beautiful woman Sandra had ever seen. She wore a gown of dark fabric and her long black hair hung across her back in ringlets, every curl in its proper place. Her lips were a ruby red.

Sandra started to walk forward, but was stopped by pressure on her right arm. She turned to find a tall man standing beside her with short brown hair dressed in black. The man shook his head and held Sandra's arm firmly. He leaned forward, placing his face by the side of hers. "I'm sorry, my lady. It will be worse if you fight."

"What is going on?" She heard a sharp gasp and turned her head back towards the bed. The woman held a silver knife in her left hand. Blood was running from a shallow gash along Edward's left side. "What are you doing?" Sandra tried to move forward, but was again restrained by the man behind her.

The woman raised her silver blade. Sandra watched in horror as she slid the side of the knife over Edward's upper chest, cutting into the top layer of his skin. Blood swelled to the surface and began to run in thin rivulets down his chest. Sandra's heart began to beat frantically. "Why are you doing this? What is going on?" Then something hard crashed into the back of her skull.

"Liza!" She heard Edward's voice in the background as she fell. Tears sprang to her eyes from the pain as her vision blurred from the force of the blow. Then the same guard leaned down and picked her up, planting her firmly back on her feet.

"Please, Princess," the guard whispered again. "I don't want to be forced to harm you."

"I don't understand," Sandra said, her vision slowly clearing.

"Liza!" Edward fought the hands that held him, but it was to no avail. "Please," he said to the dark-headed woman holding the knife. "Just let her go."

"I don't think so," the woman replied, her voice singing through the room. "She will watch, and she will do so silently." She took the knife, now painted red with Edward's blood, and slipped the metal expertly between the layers of skin on his side, removing the flesh from his well-toned frame. He cried out, a sickening sound between a sharp hiss and a suppressed scream.

"No!" Sandra screamed for him. The sadistic angel gave a nod. The guard hit her with brutal force, this time across her upper back. She fought to stand against the stinging pain, but was hit a second, then third time. She fell to the floor with a harsh thud, her body crashing against the cold stone floor.

"I did this!" She heard Edward's voice again, though it seemed distant to her ringing ears. "Punish me, my lady. Not her. It was my doing."

"I wish I could believe that," came the soft, feminine reply. "But it would simply not be true."

Sandra was pulled to her feet once again, but could not stand on her own. The guard placed his arms around her, holding her upright. She fought not to vomit as she turned back to Edward. Unshed tears glistened in his eyes. "Liza." He again called her by the unfamiliar name.

"Edward," another's words poured from her lips. "Please, stop this. Let him go!" The words poured from her lips uncontrollably. "He is the most loyal of all your knights! The captain of your guard. Please, do not do this."

The woman stepped across the floor and walked toward where Sandra was being held upright by the guard behind her. When she finally reached them, the dark woman leaned forward and whispered in her ear. "The most loyal of knights you say. Well then, we must reward him for his loyalty, mustn't we?"

She nodded toward the guards and as Sandra watched, they began to remove the rest of Edward's clothing. "What do you say to...an experience he will never forget?" Her voice put a chill in Sandra's heart.

The two men began to move Edward toward the bed. He struggled in their grasp. The woman moved the silver blade to Sandra's throat. "You will cooperate," she instructed him, "or else."

"I don't understand. Why are you doing this?" Sandra looked uncomprehendingly into Edward's dark eyes. They were so full of fear she could almost taste it.

The woman stepped away from Sandra and walked toward the bed. "Remember," she whispered, "fight me, and I will personally slice her to bits."

The woman leaned down towards the bed and slid her blade down the center of Edward's chest.

"No!" Sandra screamed as she opened her eyes.

She was lying on the ground, her head cradled in Regald's arms. "Sandra!" he said breathlessly.

Sandra screamed, scrambling to her feet and away from Regald. Tears plastered her cheeks and her hands shook uncontrollably. "Edward!" she called out as she struggled to remain upright. Where moments ago Edward's body had lain, there now stood only a cluster of blood red roses.

"You fell," Regald informed her. "You tripped over the rose vines."

She looked down at her arms and found them covered with scratches. They didn't hurt, but Sandra assumed that they would later on. She took several slow breaths, her eyes readjusting to the darkness.

"Whose chambers are these?"

"The queen's, my lady."

"The queen's?"

He nodded.

"She tortured him." Sandra maneuvered around the vines until she reached the red roses. "She tortured him, sliced into him with a silver blade. His own queen. And she forced the woman he loved to watch her do it."

Regald's voice took on as serious a tone as Sandra had ever heard. "And do you know the name of that woman?"

Sandra nodded slowly then turned to meet Regald's gaze. "Liza."

Regald's expression went slack and they stared at each other, his eyes revealing nothing. Then he turned away from her, back toward the stone door to the chamber, and realized that the roses lining it were no longer black—they were violet. "By the Gods," he whispered turning back to stare at the young woman by his side. "I will take you to Edward."

CHAPTER XV

THE FIRST TIME MARA HAD met Edward, she was five years old. He had come to visit her father, a high-ranking lord among the Lorcan Court. Mara's mother, Princess Mellissa, had been alive then, a tall pale-skinned woman with long dark hair and violet eyes. Mara remembered her as a soft spoken woman with a kind, gentle touch. However, there was little else she could recall of her mother. Both of her parents had died when she was still a child, even by mortal standards.

It was at this young age when Mara declared bravely to the already famous sub-captain that someday, she too would be one of his knights. Her father had responded to hush her, calling for her mother to escort her from the room. Yet when her mother approached, Edward had knelt beside the young girl.

"Tell me your name, child," the knight had said to her.

"Mara," she had replied shyly.

"Well, Princess Mara. Do you know the first rule of being a knight?"

She shook her head, and Edward offered her the full weight of his dark eyes. "A knight must honor the realm and above all else, always keep their word. Do you think you could do that, my lady?"

Mara stared up into his eyes and gave a slow nod. "Well then," the knight said and smiled, "I would say that you may one day make a great knight indeed. I shall look for you, when you come of age. If knighthood is still the path you desire, I will teach you more."

Now, a cold gust of wind filtered into the room of the tower Mara had called home for centuries, pulling her from the recesses of her memories. She slowly slipped the sheets from her thin frame and grabbed a black satin robe that hung on the back of the closet door. Donning the robe, she moved to the dresser on the far side of the room. A tall silver mirror sat atop the dresser. Mara sat in the chair in front of the mirror and picked up a small white brush and began to run it through the stands of her long hair.

It took several minutes for her to completely comb through her tangled locks, still slightly damp from the night before. When her hair reached a point of manageability, Mara pulled the locks behind her and fastened them with a thick black band. Then she proceeded to walk towards the closet, lined with a dozen pair of identical dark jeans, slacks, and long-sleeved shirts in varying degrees of thickness, each marked with the silver symbol of the rose. She selected a thin, long-sleeved shirt and a comfortable pair of dark slacks.

Once dressed, Mara moved from her private quarters to an office used by most members of the Black Rose. Two of her fellow guardsmen were seated inside the office, staring at computers on the left side of the room. Both stood at their captain's entrance. Mara waved them back down. She walked toward the opposite side of the room and entered a second door to her private office, closing the door behind her. Several stacks of folders containing the daily reports lined the dark desk.

Mara ignored the folders and took a seat. She picked up the phone by her desk and dialed the number for the Arum Court. She asked for Captain Regald. "I'm sorry," came the response, "Captain Regald is out of town for the next few days."

"Okay," she replied. "Then would you please transfer me to the king's office?"

A series of beeps come over the phone and a few minutes later, a feminine voice answered. "King Mathew's office. How may I help you?"

"This is Captain Mara Sethian of the Black Rose Guard. I would like to speak to the king."

"Hold, please."

Mara again heard a series of beeps and then proceeded to wait for several minutes. This time, it was a masculine voice that came over the line. "Hello, Mara," the Arum King said. "It has been a long time."

"Greetings, Your Majesty. Yes it has."

"To what do I owe the sound of your voice, Captain?"

"Edward."

"Ah, still sending you to make his threats, is he? Good to see some things never change."

Mara's voice grew constricted. "With all due respect, Your Majesty, you cannot and shall not harm the captain of another court's guard. You know that better than anyone."

"Don't you want to know why I did it, Mara? Or are you ready to jump to his defense no matter what."

"I don't give a shit what you think he did or did not do. You will not harm him again. Do you understand?"

A moment of silence filled the line before the king replied. "Still in love with him after all these years, Mara?" She did not answer. "You know he cannot love you, right? He is incapable of doing so. Or is it Liza for whom you are doing this? Do you think if you protect Edward, you can finally be forgiven for what happened? It doesn't work that way, Mara. You know it doesn't."

"Your Majesty," her words were slow, tight in her throat, "I will make this very clear. If you or anyone on your guard raises so much as a finger against Edward again, it will be the last mistake they ever make."

"Are you truly threatening a king, Captain?"

"Why not? I'm the only one who can."

"Mara." The king's voice softened unexpectedly. "Have you ever thought about putting down the sword, moving into the modern world? You could do it you know, come have a place at court. Pass the mantle on to someone else for a while. Come, Mara, we were friends once."

"Thank you for the concern, Your Majesty. Did you really think I would not come for him?"

Mara heard the king draw a deep breath on the other end of the line. "I guess in a way, I wanted to know."

"Well, now you do. Don't touch him again, Your Majesty. You'll regret it."

"Fearless as ever." He paused. "Mara, if you threaten me, then you are challenging the entire Arum Court. Do you really want to do that?"

"Ask the Muir Court," she replied coldly.

The line went quiet. Mara listened for several heartbeats, then the king said, "Thank you for the call, Captain of the Black Rose."

"Goodbye, Your Majesty."

The line went dead.

CHAPTER XVI

MATHEW WALKED TOWARDS THE DOOR of his private office. He entered the corridor beyond and walked slowly down the hallway, ignoring the occasional guard who stood before various doorways along the hall. He had not spoken to Mara in centuries, instead opting to deal with the Black Rose through intermediaries—usually through Captain Regald. In fact, the last time he had spoken to Mara directly, she had refused his proposal of marriage. It had been just over five hundred years ago. The Ciar Court had split in half and the Arum Court was formed. His uncle had lead the rebellion which had threatened civil war within the Ciar Court. An agreement was reached at the last moment, neither side eager to engage in the loss of more immortal life.

However, his uncle's antics had been less than popular among powerful members of his newly formed court and even less so with the court he had rebelled against. Facing mistrust on all sides, he had turned to his nephew. A sub-captain in the Black Rose Guard, Mathew was hailed a hero by both courts and an ideal candidate to take over his uncle's troubled throne.

It had been then that Mathew had turned to the woman who, even nearly a century later, was still hailed as the hero of both courts, and asked her to be his queen.

"Come with me, Mara," he had said. "Stand by my side and help me to build a better court, to be a better ruler than the ones we once served."

It had taken several moments before Mara answered. "Mathew, you don't know what you're saying."

"Yes, I do. Just think, Mara. We have a chance to build a court better than the ones we once served. We can protect our men and their families." He offered a smile. "It will be everything we ever dreamed of. We can—"

"Mathew, wait."

"Think about it. We could create a court that honors the old traditions. Where the men and women you have vowed to protect would finally be safe."

Mara turned to face him. "And tell me, my lord, in what role would you have me cast within this court which you describe?"

"Why, by my side, of course." He took a step closer. "I would see you made a queen."

"Queen," Mara clarified, "to your kingship?"

"Yes."

"I'm sorry, Mathew. I cannot do that." She matched his gaze fiercely.

"Mara," he responded, "I would offer you my heart, along with my kingdom." He lowered himself to one knee before her. "Please, my lady...be my queen. I will give you control of the kingdom. My rule will be in name only, to your leadership."

"It's not about that, Mathew. Don't you see?"

"Is it about love? Rest assured, Mara, I love you."

"But I don't love you," came her quiet response.

"What?"

"Mathew," Mara started again, "I am sorry if I have mislead you in any way. But I..." She forced herself to meet his gaze. "I cannot do as you ask."

He stared at her dumbfounded for several moments. A glimmer of realization dawned and he looked at her incredulously. "Could it be?" He shook his head in disbelief. "You are still in love with Edward."

She did not deny it, only stood silently, the pain showing solely through her violet and silver eyes.

"Even after what he did to you? After all he put you through. After he..." Mathew took a step closer to her. "He cannot love you, Mara. You know that he cannot love you. He is incapable of it."

"Still," she answered. "I cannot give you what I do not have. I cannot love you when my heart resides with another. I'm sorry, Mathew. I cannot be your queen.

"Cannot?"

This time she spoke more in anger than pain. "Don't you think I want to say yes?" She drew a sharp breath. "What a pretty picture you paint. A court where we are free to rule as we see fit. A way to protect the men without the isolation, the pain that comes with being a member of this guard? To be happy? Believe me, Mathew, if I could give you what you ask, I would. But...you ask for what I cannot give.

"You by my side? Helping me to protect the people from the wrath of a queen you despise?"

"But that is not what you are asking for."

"Yes, it is."

"No. You are asking for my heart, Mathew. You will be satisfied with nothing less; nor should you be. And I have no heart to give." She drew another deep. "If it is any consolation, I would love you, if I could."

"Mara, please."

She offered a thin smile. "Goodbye, Your Majesty." She offered a slight bow. "May you lead your people with the grace of the Gods and the same honor with which you have served this guard for so long."

That had been the last time he had stood alone in a room with Mara. He had left the Black Rose only days later with Regald by his side, ready to take his place as the Captain of the Arum Court Guard after the coronation. Now, five hundred years later, Mathew again stood at odds with the Black Rose captain over the same issue that had ruined his plans all those years ago. With Mara, it always came back to Edward. The love that consumed her—which she could neither embrace nor escape, accept nor deny. He had watched it consume her for centuries, a flame burning through her with agonizing ferocity. Yet, after what happened the night the Muir Court fell and the six hundred years of self-inflicted separation, Mathew had hoped that Mara might, at long last, have banished the Ciar captain from her heart.

Mathew gave a deep sigh as he reached the door of Jayden, one of the sub-captains of the Arum Guard. He knocked only once before entering to find Jayden sitting before a large desk. His bronzed skin was far darker than the king's. His short hair was cropped close to his skull.

As Mathew entered, Jayden gazed up from his paperwork and immediately stood to bow before his sovereign. "Arise," the king instructed, motioning for Jayden to return to his seat before moving closer to the desk. "It's time," the king stated.

Jayden looked up uneasily at the king. "Forgive me, my king, but I would be remiss in my duty if I did not ask...are you absolutely certain that this is the best course of action?"

Mathew studied the sub-captain and considered reprimanding him for the question, but instead decided to offer a decisive answer. "I am absolutely certain," he stated, meeting Jayden's brown eyes. "There is no other way."

Jayden did not question the king further, but instead gave a single nod. "As you command, Your Majesty."

Mathew nodded. "Let it begin."

CHAPTER XVII

NO SOONER HAD CAPTAIN REGALD entered the gates of the Ciar Court Guard, when he found the silver tip of a broadsword at his throat. "Well, look what we have here," Jake said to the Arum captain.

"Jake," Regald said, standing as still as he could with Jake's sword pressing lightly against his flesh.

"You think you can torture the captain of this guard, and then waltz in here like nothing is amiss?"

"Jake," Regald tried again. "Listen to me. That wasn't my doing. You know it wasn't. The king gave those orders himself. I didn't even know about it until he was being tied to the table."

"And yet, you stood by and did nothing. I can't believe Mara didn't have your head."

"She almost did," he replied. "And might still yet. But that is her life to take, not yours."

"He is my captain, Regald. That makes it as much mine as anyone's." Jake took a step back, removing his blade from Regald's throat. "Draw your sword, Captain. We will do this fairly."

"Jake!" Garreth's voice cut in sharply as he rounded the corner. "Put down that Arius blade before you do something that cannot be undone! Within these walls Regald is a guest until Edward deems otherwise."

Jake turned back towards Garreth with a firm scowl before proceeding to do as he bid, sliding his silver sword securely back into the leather sheath that hung at his side.

"What brings you here, Captain? If you are here for Nolan, Mara assigned him to Edward's guard, pending a move to the Black Rose."

"I am not here for Nolan," Regald told the older man. "I've come as an escort to our court's future princess." He motioned to the dark-haired woman standing behind him. Dressed in a pair of black slacks and a pale blue shirt, she stepped forward gingerly, her small heels echoing across the gray stone. "Lady Sandra, this is Sub-Captain Jake and Lord Garreth, members of Captain Edward's guard." He gestured to Sandra. "This is the fiancé of the Crown Prince."

"Hmm," Jake replied. "His throat to cut and a hostage to threaten the Arums with. Perhaps he is sorry after all."

"Jake." Garreth's tone spoke volumes.

"Just an idea," he grumbled back.

"Lady Sandra," Garreth said to the young woman. "What may I do for..." Garreth stopped as he took in the girl more fully, staring into her deep blue eyes. It wasn't possible...

"Welcome to the Ciar Court Guard, my lady," Jake said from behind him. "How may we be of service?"

"I would like to see Captain Edward," she replied softly.

"Of course, my lady." Garreth recovered his voice and offered the young woman his arm. "I will escort you to the captain."

"Thank you, my lord," the young woman replied.

Garreth slowly led Sandra down a series of gray stone hallways. It was cold and Sandra wished she had brought a thicker sweater as they ventured deeper into the stone mountainside. "Pardon me, my lady. But I was wondering, have we ever met before?"

"I don't believe so, my lord."

"It's Garreth," he said.

"Garreth," she repeated. "Do you believe that we have met?"

"I don't think so. You just look a little like someone I used to know."

"Oh." She sounded disappointed.

"Here we are." Garreth motioned to a stone door several paces ahead of them. "I will go announce your arrival to the captain." He knocked softly moments before disappearing through the tall door. A few moments later, the door opened again, and Garreth motioned Sandra inside. "I will leave you in the captain's care."

Garreth walked down the long stone corridor before eventually emerging into the cool evening air. "It's impossible." He turned down a familiar dirt path, disturbing the occasional rock as he walked around the royal grounds. He attempted to clear the image from his mind, but could not shake the feeling of foreboding that had begun to descend upon him.

"Those eyes," he said, speaking for the wind alone. "Those blue, blue eyes." He continued his amble, eventually finding himself on the north side of the grounds.

The garden of the Ciar Court was a pale shadow of the grandeur of times past. A few roses had been transplanted from the court's ancestral home, but they had never truly taken to their new environment. Yet, it was to this spot that Garreth inexorably found himself drawn as he thought of times long past. A small spring slid between the overgrown grass, bringing water to the sparse flowers and trees which lined its banks.

"Those eyes," he said again. They were so blue, the eyes of this young girl who had come to see his captain. Garreth searched his memory, but could form no recollection of having ever seen her before. "It can't be," he said again. And yet...it was. A young girl with eyes the color of the sea—eyes that should not exist. "That bloodline is gone," Garreth stated to no one.

Before its fall, the Muir Court had been the second-most powerful in the land. It was a vast empire, the heart of which stood in the form of a silver castle by the sea. The court was ruled by a powerful king who, at the time of its demise, had reigned since the rise of the Roman Empire. He had four sons and two daughters, all of whom possessed the same shade of vibrant blue eyes streaked with white — like waves rising in the sea.

Garreth closed his eyes and could almost see the glint of silver, could hear the clash of swords and the screams of the dying. The cold eyes with which Mara watched the men fall before her with a wrath which knew no end.

He stepped closer to the river, attempting to divine an explanation. Perhaps it had been a trick of the light. Remnants of memories stirred from a long slumber by Mara's recent appearance or Edward's injuries, so similar to those endured long ago. Besides, there was no white in the woman's blue eyes though the color...

He gave a deep sigh, then turned to begin the walk back when something caught his attention. On the far side of the garden was one of the small rosebushes which had been transplanted from its ancestral home. Garreth walked forward slowly. When he reached the rosebush, he fell to his knees before it. Once these ancient roses had bloomed in an assortment of royal colors, but since the moment the Black Rose was formed, they had bloomed only in black.

Garreth struggled to believe his vision as he reached out a hand and found himself caressing the soft, fragile petal of a single crimson rose. Garreth stared at the rose for a long time before his gaze traveled through the garden and he suddenly realized that the roses surrounding him were no longer black, but purple—the color of the royal rose.

"By the Gods," Garreth whispered as the world began to spiral. He turned back to the single red rose and sat there for a long time. When he finally stood, he headed towards his chambers.

Fifteen minutes later when he reached the familiar door, Garreth entered the room and walked directly to the wooden desk in the far corner. He changed into a long-sleeved silver shirt featuring a single black rose, the color of the Ciar Court Guard with the symbol of his former status as a member of the Black Rose. He then opened a hidden panel in the desk from which he withdrew both his passport and a special badge which would allow him to take his sword on his journey. Sliding both into the pocket of his dark jacket, he retrieved his long, silver sword from its place upon the wall and secured it tightly around his waist.

It was not the blade that he normally carried, but instead an Arius blade. A blade made for kings. One so rare and dangerous that from its stroke, even an immortal would fall. There were only a handful of them in the entire world, each one carefully bestowed upon the rules of each court and their most trusted of knights. This blade, silver and encrusted with a string of blue sapphires along its hilt, had once belonged to a prince of the Muir Court. Taken by Mara after the massacre and given to Garreth, who had accepted it reluctantly at her insistence. "It will be safer in your hands than in those of any other," she had answered his protests when he attempted to reject the offered blade. "And the Queen's court must be protected." It was now with a heavy heart that he strapped on the deadly blade.

Garreth walked silently down the long corridors from his room to the palace library. Books and scrolls lined the walls from floor to ceiling. He walked quickly down the rows until he finally reached the back wall where the books were encased behind a thick sheet of glass. This section was temperature controlled, accessed by an electronic panel, one of the only modern additions in the otherwise ancient room. It had been installed only a few years ago when it had been discovered that several of the old books were beginning to deteriorate. Luckily the majority had been salvaged, or at minimum, repaired enough to still be legible.

Garreth pressed his thumb against the electronic panel. After a series of loud beeps, the glass slid sideways, opening for the sub-captain with a loud *whoosh.*

It took him several minutes to locate the book he sought, but he eventually found it, withdrawing it carefully from the shelf before again pressing his hand to the panel. The glass slid back into place as Garreth carefully raised the leather-bound book to his lips and lightly blew a thick layer of dust from its cover. It was very old, over five hundred years, and had been carefully transcribed with quill and ink. The pages were now yellowed and fragile. *Historia Vltima Aulae Marinae.* "*The Final History of the Sea Court,*" he translated aloud. He then moved the book to his side and proceeded to walk towards the outer doors of the ancient keep.

A few turns from the outer doors, he found Nolan walking down the hall in his direction, dressed in an identical shirt of silver tucked into black slacks. "Hi, Garreth," Nolan said with a slight wave.

"Hi," he replied. "Sorry, but I am in a bit of a hurry."

"Oh, where are you off to?"

"Just...I have to go."

Garreth attempted to walk past the younger man when Nolan said, "Forgive me, my lord. I know that something is going on. I saw your face when the prince's fiancée arrived. It...it was the same look that Edward had when he..."

"What? Edward has met her before?"

"Yes. Sandra was the one who threw herself over him while he was being whipped."

Garreth stared at Nolan for several moments, attempting to put the pieces together when Nolan suddenly said, “Let me go with you, my lord. I can tell you about it on the way.”

“You don’t even know where I am going.”

“All the same.”

Garreth parted his lips to say no, but instead found the words, “Let’s go,” falling from his lips.

It was only after they had left the royal grounds that Nolan finally asked, “So, where are we going?”

CHAPTER XVIII

NOLAN READ THE TITLE. "*THE Final History of the Sea Court.* The same one which was destroyed by the Black Rose?"

"Yes. The Muir Court was also referred to as the Sea Court."

Nolan shifted slightly, attempting to find a more comfortable position, grateful that Garreth's sub-captain status had upgraded them to the business section of this exceptionally long flight. "Forgive me, but isn't the story well-known? Mara is famous for the victory, after all."

Garreth regarded him for a moment as though in consideration and then said, "No. It is not."

"What do you mean?"

Garreth stared at the younger man for what seemed a long time before answering, leaning forward to be better heard over the roar of the plane's engine. "Tell me the story you know."

"The Muir Court was an ancient and powerful court lead by a cruel king. Their tyranny may have known no end, if Mara had not taken a group of men against them. She led an attack and dispatched the king, saving the realm and all those under his evil reign. Mara gained eternal glory and the Black Rose became peacekeepers between the remaining courts."

Garreth nodded. "Yes, that is the story they would tell."

"But not what actually happened, I assume?"

Garreth motioned to the book held gently in Nolan's hand. "Do you read Latin?"

"Yes," he replied. "I knew I would have to learn if I wanted to join the Black Rose."

"Open the cover," Garreth instructed, "carefully."

Nolan did as instructed. On the first yellowed page was a single line: *Scripta a Navarcho Rosae Nigrae Custodis Confessio.*

"Written by Mara's own hand?" Nolan asked Garreth with wide eyes.

"You have heard the stories, Nolan. But there is only one truth." He drew a deep breath. "Mara was born a princess. Did you know that?"

Nolan shook his head and Garreth continued.

"Her mother was Queen Clarissa's younger sister. Her father, the son of a powerful lord. It was a politically sound match, but at its core was the rarity of it also being a match created in love. The kind of love Mara asked you if you had ever experienced. A love that becomes your sole reason to draw breath." Garreth drew a deep breath. "But what was a great romance for Princess Mellissa, brought only tragedy for her daughter, Princess Mara."

CHAPTER XIX

900s AD

MARA WALKED DOWN THE DIRT path under a gray sky, pausing occasionally to glance at the tall stones which rose around her in the shape of broken crosses and fallen angels. Eventually, she reached the tall cross which marked the entrance to her parents' tomb. It was a symbolic location of course. Her parents were no more in this silent grave then they were within the mountain spring over which the majority of their ashes had been spread. Yet, there was still something about this place which made Mara feel closer to her long lost parents than anywhere else she had ever known. She knelt before it.

It had been four years since the last of her father's ashes had been placed within the marble structure and two years to the day since her mother had chosen to join him in death. Mara sat before the tall statues surrounding her for a long time, offering silent prayers to the Gods above. Yet these scattered visits always ended the same way. "Why?" Mara asked the question which could never be answered. "Why did you leave me?"

She turned toward the stone which bore her mother's name. "Why? Why did you leave me all alone?" Her hands dug into the dirt, lowering her face to the ground. She sat there a long time as she cried. "You left me," she shouted for the dead alone. Then, someone touched her shoulder.

Her eyes flew open to find Edward kneeling beside her. "I thought you might be here."

She looked at him and the single glance was all it took.

"I'm sorry," he said gently. "There are no answers. I wish I could tell you why, but...I can't."

Mara turned from the tomb with deep bitterness. "I know why. He left her alone and the isolation was unbearable. She was all alone."

Edward reached forward, lifting her gaze. "You speak as though you know."

A shiver slid through her and she spoke in a voice thick with emotion. "Don't I?"

"Princess." His gaze was deep. "What are you saying?"

"She knew that she would never love again. No one—not even me. She was alone."

"But you are not." He moved his hands to grasp her arms just below the wrists, commanding her attention with his touch. "Do you hear me, my lady? You are not alone."

"Am I not?"

"No," he said and pulled her close, wrapping his arms around her slender frame. "I..." He drew a sharp breath. "I don't know what I would do without you." She began to shiver in his arms. "Please, Mara, you are scaring me."

"Everyone leaves," she answered through tears.

"I won't." He rose from the ground, forcing her to her feet. He stared into violet eyes. "I love you, Mara. Do you hear me? I love you and you will never be alone." He pulled her into his arms again, running a hand through her long black hair. "*ego adsum, mea rosa.* I will not leave you. I will never, never leave you."

Mara had been fourteen when Edward had sworn to end the loneliness which consumed her life. And only nineteen when he would embark upon the quest that would force him to break every promise he had ever made, condemning her to the life her mother had chosen death over being forced to endure.

Edward had taken her back to her rooms that night, disregarding every hint of protocol as he laid the princess upon the bed and pulled her to his chest. She clung to him, oblivious to the fact that Garreth had entered the room and taken silent watch in the far corner. "It's okay," Edward whispered, cradling her against him to place a gentle kiss upon her brow. He held her for a long time before her breathing finally slowed to the steady rhythm of sleep.

"What happened?" Garreth asked quietly as he moved to a chair beside the bed.

"She went to see her mother."

"Is she all right?"

"No." He traced a hand gently through her long hair which trailed down her back. "I don't know what to do."

Garreth slowly shook his head. "I wish I knew."

"She is so young. I wish I could take her away from here."

"Yes...but the queen would never allow it. She is still a princess. I try to stay here as much as possible. Though, as a member of the guard, it is difficult."

"Yes." Edward nodded. "We could bring her into the circle for a while. Move her to the chambers between ours."

"A princess of the blood living in a circle of guardsmen? You can't be serious."

"I don't know what else to do. Does she still train with the swordmaster?"

"Every day."

Edward nodded. "I will take over her training myself. I will devote more time. I will..." He tightened his arms around her, fighting to keep his words a whisper. "Garreth...I can't lose her and if we don't do something..." He shook his head.

"Careful, Edward. She is a princess. You could be in trouble for simply lying here like this."

"She cannot be alone. She won't survive it."

Garreth drew a deep breath and said simply, "I know."

That had been the beginning of her official training for the Royal Guard. She was moved from her royal suites into the captain's section of the palace. It was against the majority of protocols, moving her into a chamber of men. However, the queen either had no issue with the move, or did not care enough to offer an objection.

It was here, under Edward's watchful eye, that Mara continued to learn the true ways of the sword and fell into a regular routine. He, along with Garreth and Phillip, worked together to train her not only in combat, but also to instill within her an appreciation for the codes they were sworn to live by.

Honor, truth and valor were among the highest, along with the value of living a life of service. Embracing these core values had, more than anything else, been the key to Mara's will to survive even in the darkest of days—the notion that her life belonged to a purpose greater than herself.

Mara was the youngest to ever enter formal service into any Royal Guard. Garreth had been enraged when, at only sixteen, she had requested formal admittance. "You are too young to know that this is the life you want," he had raged at her. "You're a princess! Think of what you would be giving up. Your title, your wealth, your privilege. For all you know, you might be queen one day. You cannot join the guard at sixteen!"

She spent the next year in a futile attempt to change her cousin's mind. When Edward finally asked her why she was so insistent on joining the guard now instead of waiting to ensure that this way of life was what she truly wanted, she gave an answer from the heart. "I was lost," she told him. "That night you found me by my parents' tomb, I had every intention of joining them. But then you came and gave me a reason to go on living. This guard, this way of life, saved me." She leaned closer to stare into his eyes. "You saved me, Edward, and for the first time, I feel that I have something to live for. I want to fight, to live, to breathe for honor and truth and all the rest of it. I know that this is the only way I want to live."

Edward had not initiated her into the Guard that night. He may not have for many years, except that, only a few weeks later, the queen called her to the royal chambers. "I think it is high time we remove you from those ghastly chambers," she was informed by her royal aunt. "You are a child no longer.

A Princess of the Blood cannot live among the men as you do. It is improper. Finding you a royal match will be difficult enough even without such tarnish."

Mara had held her tears in check until she reached her rooms where Phillip found her. No sooner had she finished repeating the queen's words then he went to find Edward and Garreth.

"For God's sake, just give her the initiation vows," Phillip advised.

"She is too young," Garreth repeated, replaying the same old argument.

"Yet not too young for the queen," Phillip pointed out. "I hear rumors of a Muir Court prince heading our way. Could it be that he is coming for her? If she is old enough to be forced into a royal wedding, then surely she is old enough to choose a different way of life. I fear that if we do not let her choose now, the queen will choose for her." He turned towards Edward. "After all the years you have spent teaching, are you really going to take away her choice?"

Edward exchanged a glance with Garreth before turning to face her. "You are a Princess of the Blood," he said to her. "If you choose to join the guard, it is a title you will bear no longer. You will surrender everything that goes with it—wealth, title, rank and ultimately, your freedom. You will surrender all of it and will be expected to sacrifice everything for those to whom you are ordered to serve. Do you understand, Princess Mara? Your life will not be your own."

She looked him in the eye, reviewing each of his words slowly as she searched his gaze. In a breath barely above a whisper, she said, "The queen would see me locked up alone, in a tower, before giving me to a man of her choosing. How is that life my own?" He parted his lips, but when no words came Mara continued. "You promised you wouldn't leave me alone. Please, Edward, don't let her. I can't bear it. I want to be with you. I just...please."

Edward nodded and took a step closer, shortening the distance between them to a single pace. "If you join the Guard, Mara, it will be a hard life; one of pain and sacrifice, but..." He reached out and caressed the side of her face. "You will never be alone."

"Then please," she begged, "let me take my vows. Before it's too late."

He searched her violet eyes, and for one moment, she thought he might refuse her. Then he suddenly leaned forward and kissed the cheek his hand had caressed only moments before. "Mara Sethian," he said, dropping her title, "welcome to the Royal Guard."

CHAPTER XX

Present Day

LADY SANDRA PAUSED AS SHE stepped inside the dark room, allowing her eyes to slowly work their way across the chamber. A black desk stood against the wall immediately to her right, topped with several piles of neatly stacked papers. In the center of the far back wall was an immense, four-post bed covered in thick wool blankets. Her eyes lingered on each item as she wracked her memory, but she could find no recollection of having ever been there before.

"My lady." The deep, masculine voice forced her attention to the farthest side of the room. Edward stood dressed in all black. His pale skin seemed almost translucent as he stood before a roaring fire. "My lady," he said again, taking several steps towards her. "You're..." He paused as recognition began to dawn. "You're the one."

A slight shiver ran through her. "Please," he said, motioning her closer. "It is much warmer by the fire." She stepped forward until she was close enough to feel the warmth of the fire on her pale skin. As her gaze focused upon the flames, it was not to desolate chambers of torture that her mind wandered, but to a very different memory.

"There once was a magical knight," her mother's voice rose from an all but forgotten dream. "He was brave and strong. He will protect you from all harm."

"My lady?" Edward's voice brought her back to the present.

She turned from the flames to face him. "My lord, I needed to see you. I needed to know that you were..." Her voice again trailed and she asked, "Do you know who I am?"

"No, my lady."

"Have we ever met...before?"

His eyes searched her, tracing their way up and down her body. "Not to my knowledge."

She turned back to the flames and could almost see her mother sitting within them. Her long dark hair, the ruby lips that never smiled. There was so little she could recall of her mother. She was little more than a vague image and an air of sadness which Sandra had been too young to understand. *"A hero with a fierce soul and eyes of night." The long-forgotten words rose from the deepest recess of her memories. "He will protect you."*

"My lady," Edward's deep voice eclipsed her mother's. "Will you tell me your name?"

"Sandra."

"It would seem that I am in your debt, Lady Sandra. What I don't know, is why." He took a step closer to better see her face in the light of the flames. "What would you have of me, my lady?"

"When I was young, I was in an accident. I have very few memories of my past. And of those I have, fewer still exist outside of a few stories." She drew a breath and turned to face the flames, unable to look at Edward as she continued.

"When I was a little girl, my mother told me stories about a hero—a knight in shining armor. Late at night I used to pretend that he was watching over me, guarding me while I slept. I had terrible nightmares, and storms often raged across the night sky. But when my mother told her stories, I always felt safe, protected.

"My mother spoke of a man who knew no fear. Who helped those around him without so much as a thought to himself. A man so strong and brave, he could only exist in the realm of dreams." She drew a trembling breath and forced herself to face him. "Yet, here you stand." She searched his gaze. "I don't know what these memories are or what they mean. I don't know what happened to you that night. But...I have dreamed of you my entire life."

"Forgive me, my lady. I don't understand. Of what memories do you speak?"

She drew a shallow breath. "I...I saw you. Lying..."

"Yes," Edward answered. "You saved me."

"No," she replied. "Not that one, another. I saw you on a bed with a woman." Her voice grew small, haunted. "She held a silver blade and you were..."

No sooner did she speak than that horribly angelic laughter seeped into the room. She shook her head vigorously, desperate to clear the echoes from her mind. "You...you were screaming." Her breath became shallow. "I have seen these visions...nightmares. I..."

"How do you know this?" A touch of anger fueled his voice. "Who are you?"

"I don't know. I remembered nothing, nothing but a few vague images...whispers in the dark. Until I saw you, lying on that table."

"How do you know this?" he asked again.

"I don't know, please..." Tears of frustration and fear filled her vision. "I don't know who you are. I don't know why this is happening. I don't know why I am seeing these things." Her gaze lowered to the floor as tears began to fall. "Help me. Please. I'm afraid." That angelic laughter slid back into the room, growing steadily louder until it was all she could hear, could feel, could breathe.

Edward leaned forward and grabbed her, pulling the young woman against him. Jerked back to reality by his touch, Sandra realized that she had dug her hands into her own arms so hard she had drawn blood, which had prompted Edward to grab her. "I've got you," he said gently.

"I'm sorry."

"It's all right. You're safe."

"Can you help me?"

He stared at her and it was only then, holding her in his arms, that he caught the full weight of her gaze. He raised his right hand from her arm and brushed a long strand of her hair from the side of her face. "Your eyes are so..." He leaned closer. "Who was your mother?"

"I...I don't really know. She died when I was very young and my memories are...scattered."

"Anything you can remember."

"All I know is that she was beautiful. Soft spoken, a gentle touch and...sad. She was always sad."

Edward gave a slow nod. "Her eyes," he asked. "What color were her eyes? Do you have your mother's eyes?"

Sandra's tears ceased. She closed her eyes, attempting desperately to focus upon the long lost memory. She sat at her mother's feet, playing with the edge of her blue, satin gown. *"A hero," her mother whispered, "unmatched with a sword, with eyes dark as night. He will always protect you, my darling—always."*

"She was beautiful," Sandra said with a startling realization. "With long, dark hair and sad, violet eyes."

Chapter XXI

MARA SAT AT THE DESK, poring over the papers spread before her. Multiple requests had arrived over the last few days, everything from politicians to movie stars requesting bodyguards from among the elite of the Rose. Once, kings and queens would have traveled hundreds of miles to beg for such favors, swearing titles, fealty and even kingdoms for help from the famous Black Rose. That was no longer the case in this new world where technology disrupted old traditions and one's solemn promise lasted only as long as the speaker could find another to utter the same words to.

Mara shook her head in disgust before finally putting pen to paper, authorizing the requests of both the American president and a joint request from several members of the European Union. She tossed aside those from the more Hollywood types, whose names meant as little to her as any other member of the nameless billions now populating the world. "I miss the days of kings," Mara said with a sigh. "So easily is wealth mistaken for nobility. These people get the slightest taste of wealth and suddenly believe they are entitled to be privy to the elite of the immortal world! Like buying their way into their own isn't enough. We were Gods when their ancestors were carving their names on cave walls and they think to buy my loyalty with thin strips of paper which they claim to possess the value of gold!" It was an argument she had had frequently with her sub-commanders.

Not that gold was not important, or that the Black Rose didn't have its fair share. As a group, the Rose held titles to the former holdings of the Muir Court. In fact, there was a possibility that her small, elite force had wealth to rival both the Ciar and Arum Courts. The wealth was spread strategically among vaults, and yes, even banks across America, Europe and Asia. Her guard was also paid handsomely for their services, though it was a fact that continually made Mara's stomach churn. This 'false gold' as Mara referred to modern forms of wealth, was a shadow of the respect that was once given so freely to members of her court by the mortal world. "We are no longer Gods," she was continually forced to remind herself. "And one day soon, will be no better than hired guns."

Her rant was interrupted by a knock at the door followed a few moments later by the appearance of Jonathan. He was shorter than the majority of her guard, standing only 5'6", with closely cropped brown hair and matching eyes. He took several steps into the room and then slid to a knee in a time-honored bow before his captain. Mara pushed the papers to the side of the desk and then stood from her straight-backed chair and addressed the man who had served her for just over two hundred years. "Yes?"

He rose from his kneeling position, but was still required to tilt his neck in order to meet her gaze. "I came to ask if you had seen the requests of guardship which had arrived while you were away. But," he motioned to the crumpled papers laying at the foot of her desk, "I see that you already have."

Mara sighed. "Let me guess, there is some new starlet who one of our more recent recruits is just dying to meet?"

"Meryl Streep is hardly a new starlet."

"Who?"

"She's only been nominated for more Academy Awards than any actress in history! You know, the actress?"

Mara stared at him with cold eyes. Jonathan lowered his gaze. "You will take these," she held out the two requests she had selected from among the pile, "to Sub-Captain Brendan. That will be all." Jonathan gave a brief nod and then bowed at the waist before turning to leave the room. He walked quickly down the stone corridor and down several flights of stairs. As expected, he found Brendan seated in front of a desk in the ground floor study. He walked forward and placed the two papers on the edge of the desk.

"Let me guess," Brendan stated without looking up from his papers. "She turned you down on the Jennifer Lawrence request."

Jonathan sighed. "I even tried telling her it was Meryl Streep."

Brendan gave a soft chuckle. "You should have tried Kate Middleton instead."

"Yeah, but then she might have taken it herself."

"Not likely. Elizabeth perhaps, but not Kate."

"Really? Not even for a Princess of England?"

Brendan shook his head. "Sometimes I forget how much younger you are than the rest of us. The last time Mara served on a human guard detail was for Queen Victoria on her wedding day."

"Really? That must have been an honor."

"Actually, she was named Duchess of Argyll and Marquesa of Kintyre. She still may have turned down the request, if a few castles had not been attached to the title. Mara has always had a soft spot for the Scottish coast."

"Look," Jonathan said. "Did something happen? She seems a little..."

"Nothing for you to concern yourself with," Brendan replied. "Just have all queries brought to me for the next few days."

Jonathan paused for a moment as though in consideration. "How can I do my job effectively if I am unaware of what is going on?"

"Leave it alone, Jon." He shook his head. "This is not something you want to become involved with—trust me."

Jonathan gave a nod before turning to leave the room with an air of frustration with which Brendan was all too familiar. Mara had spilled a great deal of blood over the years in order to protect both her charges and the men who served her, but never more than for the protection of the one man she never should have been required to protect.

Brendan had entered the guard a few years after the princess had died. In the centuries between his joining of the Queen's Guard and taking the vow of the Black Rose, he had never seen Edward act in a leadership role. It had been Mara who had placed herself again and again between the ravings of the queen and men who strove to serve her. Mara, whose blood had stained the walls of the palace chambers as she substituted herself in the placement of her men.

Brendan had never understood Mara's endless devotion to the captain. Yet, neither had he been surprised when Mara had fled the castle in the middle of a stormy night to rush to the side of a man whose name she had refused to so much as speak for the last six hundred years. Phillip had once attempted to explain the relationship. "They are two halves of the same soul," Phillip had said. "Without an ounce of light between them."

"But why?" he had asked. "Why would she keep going back to that? What is it about Edward? He's not—"

"It wasn't always so." Phillip reminded him again that he was younger than the others. "When the queen sent him away, he was gone for twenty-five years. On the ten-year anniversary of his disappearance, I attempted to force the reality upon Mara that he would never return. I tried again a few years later, more forcefully, but she refused to believe it. She was right of course, but there was no reason to believe it. It was beyond stubbornness. Yet, to this day, I can't help but wonder if it was not something more...if their souls are not truly intertwined."

Brendan sighed as the memory receded. He had spent half a millennium watching Mara punish herself for events that occurred long ago. He stood silently as she locked herself away from the world, attempting in vain to forget the horrors of those dark nights. Yet, on those rare occasions when she did emerge, it was always to Edward that her infrequent questions would eventually turn. In recent years she would occasionally turn on the news during the royal press conferences, her eyes searching for the man who was always pictured on the camera's edge, just to the right of the queen.

Brendan gave a heavy sigh and then called for the twins, Aiden and Brian. When they arrived, they gave a brief bow. Brendan cleared his throat. "I have two assignments for Guardship. I know that it has been a few years since either of you have left the grounds, so I thought you might want an assignment."

"We would be happy to take it," Aiden replied.

"Sure," Brian said, echoing his brother's sentiment.

"Good, then I am sending you both to Washington, D.C." He handed them Mara's signed Order of Guardship. "You will report to Agent Barstow upon your arrival and then report for secret service detail."

"Secret service?" Aiden inquired. "You mean...for the president?" Brendan nodded. "Seriously? Awesome!"

Brendan drew a deep breath. "I would refrain from allowing Captain Mara to hear you say so. Do we need a lesson on proper etiquette before I send you off to guard the *President* of the United States?"

The brothers turned to each other and exchanged a glance. "No, Captain," they said in an eerie unison that only twins seem to possess.

Brendan dismissed them with a wave. It would be good to get the younger members away from the grounds for a few days. Mara was never in a good mood after an encounter with Edward, and their youthful antics would be sure to keep her there even longer. He returned to his chair and began the daunting task of working through the daily e-mails when Jonathan knocked on the door.

"Forgive the disturbance," he said to the sub-captain. "But Lord Garreth, Sub-Captain of the Ciar Court Guard, is requesting an audience."

Garreth slid his chair to the opposite side of the desk and placed his hand on the black phone. "Put him through."

"No, Captain. He is here."

"Here?"

"Yes, my lord. He awaits you in the foyer."

Chapter XXII

900 AD

THE NIGHT WAS QUIET IN the upper level of the Black Rose castle. On the four-post bed, Mara lay in a deep slumber. Her body moved from left to right, stirred in its sleep by unquiet dreams. It was always like this, seeing Edward. Ever since she was nineteen and the queen had sent him away for all those years.

It had been a rare and beautiful day when Edward had surprised Mara with a knock on her door. "Would you care to join me for lunch?"

"I'd love to," she replied.

He led her from the underground palace and into the sunshine above. "I thought we might partake in the garden."

Mara followed him around the royal grounds until they reached the royal rose garden. Among a sea of purples and red, Edward led Mara to a blanket. Moments later, servants arrived with an assortment of meats, cheeses and wine. Mara had sipped slowly on the dark red liquid, savoring the taste only half as much as the company. They spoke about a play that Mara had seen several weeks before, and a book of poetry which she had recently come to adore. "It's a new tale about a mythical King of Britain, who rules through valor, honor and chivalry," Mara told him, reaching a hand forward to caress the side of his face. "I felt like I was reading a story about you." She offered a smile.

For a moment, Edward retuned that smile, then he stood from the blanket. He motioned to the servants, who collected the remains of their meal and then quickly fled the scene, leaving Edward and Mara alone in the garden. He then offered her his hand, slowly pulling her to her feet. "Take a walk with me, my lady?"

She smiled and stepped forward when he tightened his grip on her hand. She met his gaze as he began to walk her down the path, the sweet aroma of roses perfuming the air. Edward did not speak as they walked, but instead led her forward silently, only the occasional bird disrupting the tranquility surrounding them. When they reached the edge of a stream, the water was so clear that she could see the violet of her eyes reflected in its gentle current. It was here, on the edge of the water, that Edward finally paused. Mara turned to face him and saw confusion in his dark eyes. "Edward?"

He reached his hand forward, caressing her cheek. Her words ceased as his eyes seemed to search hers. "Edward," she said, more softly than before.

It was then, in that moment, that Edward leaned forward and kissed her for the very first time.

The wind blew across the garden, rustling through the leaves and swaying the roses back and forth in its cool breath. Edward pulled back slowly from the kiss. The smile on Mara's face was enough to break his heart. "I'm leaving."

Mara's smile faded as though in slow motion. "What?"

"I came to tell you that I am leaving."

"What?"

"I am leaving," he said a third time. "The queen has ordered me to the east."

The ground seemed to shift under Mara's feet. She took a step forward, but stumbled. Edward placed his hand upon her left arm to steady her. Her heart pounded in her chest. "You brought me here..." She searched for the words. "...to leave me?"

Edward's hand tightened on Mara's arm, his fingers digging deeply into her flesh. His gaze fell to the ground as he said, "I came to..."

"To what?" she snapped, her voice more cross than she had intended. "To make sure you, what...leave my heart in pieces?"

"To tell you that I don't want to go," he spoke softly, unable to face her. "That I don't want...hurting you is the last thing I would ever want to do; the very last thing."

"I don't understand," Mara replied. "You are her captain, the leader of her personal bodyguard. Why in the world is she sending you away? It doesn't make sense. That doesn't fit your job description, unless...is the queen going East?"

"No." Edward shook his head, finally raising his eyes to meet Mara's gaze. "And I can't tell you why I am going or where and," he inhaled sharply, "I cannot tell you when I shall return."

Her voice was aflame. "Well, then, what the hell can you tell me?"

"That I have no choice and that I would stay...if I could."

"And the kiss?" she asked. "What was that? Some sort of..." She searched for the word. "Pity? Guilt? A half-hearted goodbye to make yourself feel better? What the hell was that?"

"A plea!" An unfamiliar strain filtered through his words.

"What?"

"A plea," he said again, shaking his head as his gaze returned to the green grass of the garden floor. "I am asking, pleading, for you, knowing that you owe me no debt nor do I have any right to expect you to say yes. Yet, I ask it of you anyway..."

"Ask what, Edward? What could you possibly—" Her voice tightened in her throat, diminishing to a deep, rasping sound. She swallowed hard. "What would you have of me, my lord?"

"Don't," he said. "Don't do that. I'm not..." He drew a deep breath. "I do not ask this as your lord or captain. I ask it only as a...as a man."

"Ask what?"

"Wait for me." He spoke slowly, as though the words were held somewhere deep inside him and had to be dragged carefully to the surface. "I know that this is unfair, telling you this way and...and I have no right to ask. I know that. But, I am asking anyway. Wait for me, Mara. Wait for me and I will pledge to you my devotion, my heart and my honor." His hand dropped from Mara's arm as he bowed his head. "I know that you deserve more. But, it is all I have. All that I am; and I offer to it to you."

Edward continued to hide his face, staring towards the ground, unable to face the woman for whose heart he pleaded. Mara's thoughts trailed to a world without him. It was unbearable, unthinkable. Edward was her strength, her savior, her love. She couldn't breathe.

Edward leaned forward and pressed his cheek against her left shoulder. His entire body sagged against her. "I'm sorry," he said. "Gods, Mara... Forgive me. *ignosce mihi, mea rosa, mi amor.* Forgive me." His body shuddered against hers and she suddenly realized with a bitter chill he was afraid.

"Edward," she whispered, attempting desperately to gather herself as best she could. "I don't know where your path will lead or what task you have been charged, but," she drew a deep breath, struggling to keep the anguish from her voice, "you are the strongest man I have ever known. You will fulfill this quest."

A tremor ran through Edward's body. "Mara...Mara..."

"I will wait for you, *mi amor*. No matter how long it takes. I swear it to the Gods."

Edward slowly raised his gaze to meet hers.

"I love you, Edward. All I ask is a single promise in return."

He stared at her in silence for several moments, fully meeting the weight of her violet gaze. "Name it," he said in a tone so forceful that it drew Mara's own tears to the burning surface of her eyes.

"Come back," she said simply, her heart breaking with each word. "Please come back for me."

He gave a single nod, never removing his gaze from the woman standing before him. "*promitto. rosa mea immortalis.* I will always come for you, Mara. Always."

She stepped forward slowly and then pressed her lips against his. He wrapped his arms around her. She pressed her cheek against his broad chest, as the first of her tears fell from her violet eyes.

Chapter XXIII

Present Day

GARRETH WAS STANDING IN THE entryway. "What did I tell you?" he said to Nolan who stood beside him, gazing up at the vaulted ceiling. "You just thought the Ciar Court was bleak." Nolan did not answer, but instead gazed around the vast chamber, seemingly mesmerized by the spiral staircases and the towering, red curtains which draped the gray walls, blowing from the cold mountain winds. "Still," Garreth continued, "there is a certain level of power to it."

"Sub-Captain Garreth." Brendan emerged from a pair of wooden doors on the left side of the chamber.

"Sub-Captain Brendan." Garreth bowed his head in greeting.

"Welcome back to the Rose," Brendan stated to his former superior. "What has it been? Sixty, seventy years?"

Garreth nodded. "That sounds about right."

"What brings you to my humble door?

"Came to see the captain."

"Ah. I don't suppose there is any way that this visit might *not* involve Edward?"

"Afraid I can't say that."

Brendan sighed. "He leaves her in the foulest moods. I'm a little tired of the worst of it falling on me."

"I know," Garreth responded. "I remember well."

Brendan nodded. "What can I do for you?"

Garreth motioned to Nolan. "This is Nolan, a member of the Arum Guard, assigned to the Ciar by Mara."

Brendan offered a firm handshake to the younger man. "Hell of a mentor you have there." He nodded towards Garreth. "He was mine, once upon a time."

"And now look at you; second-in-command of the Black Rose."

Brendan smiled. "It's good to see you, Garreth. Miss you around here."

Garreth nodded. "It is good to see you as well. I wish this was a visit for pleasantries."

"But it never is."

"The roses from the Lorcan Court. The ones which appeared when Mara took ownership of the castle. Do they still bloom?"

"Same place they have always been."

Garreth nodded. "Perhaps we should..."

"Garreth!" A feminine voice entered the room. Mara stood at the top of the spiral staircase. She wore a gown of thin silk under an open robe of black velvet. Her hair hung straight down her back, cascading over her shoulders to frame her face. She searched the room, fully appraising the new arrivals. Her eyes narrowed as she began to walk down the steps, her black heels echoing through the room as they stuck the dark stone with every step. When she finally reached the ground, she glided slowly across the faded red carpets. "Did I or did I not, order this one," she motioned towards Nolan, "to remain with the Ciar Court Guard?"

"Technically, you ordered him to serve in the Ciar," Garreth stated. "Which he is still technically doing."

She shot him a glare than had made braver men squirm. "What are you doing here, Garreth?"

"Let me show you. If I am right, then you are going to want to see this."

Mara did not ask, but merely motioned him back towards the outer doors. The group walked together into the brisk mountain air and turned down a dirt path which Garreth remembered well. Nothing seemed to have changed in the four hundred years since he had left the Rose to return to Edward's service. It had been a difficult choice and one for which Garreth knew Mara had never forgiven him. Hurting her in spite of their best efforts not to—another thing that he and Edward had in common.

"I'm sorry," he had told her. "But the war is over, Mara. Her memory is avenged. Maintaining this guard," he shook his head, "I know you say it is for the protection of the realm, but come, Mara; be honest."

"I can't go back," she replied tersely. "You know I cannot."

"Mara," he said. "You have done your job. You avenged her. Please, put it to rest. Come home with me. You don't have to do this anymore. Liza would not want you to..."

"Don't speak her name! Please, just...don't."

"Mara, I can't do this anymore. This living in the past. I..." He drew a deep breath attempting to gather his words. "I need to move forward."

"Then go!" she had shouted. "If you want my blessing, then fine; you have it."

"Mara I can't leave you."

Her eyes closed tightly for several moments, silence filling the space between them. When she finally opened them, her voice was firm and steady.

"Yes you can. You have to." She offered a sad smile. "Just do one thing for me, please."

He stared at her for what seemed a long time and then said, "I'll watch over him, Mara." Those words, spoken so long ago, had now become yet another in a long line of broken promises.

The group continued down the dirt path in silence until they eventually emerged into the garden where not even weeds had been able to thrive. *rosae immortals* survived at every court, though they thrived at few. The Black Rose was one of those few. Unlike the scattered bushes of the Ciar Court, the roses thrived here, as though sustained by the power of the guard which had been named exclusively in their honor and the princess for whom they had appeared. They climbed the taller shrubberies and trees, their thorns piercing deeply into the other plants upon which they clung.

It had always been a dark affair, the black roses upon the deep green vines lying against the gray backdrop of the mountains. Yet as they rounded the familiar corner, the entire party froze.

In place of the familiar black petals, every rose in the garden, was the color of freshly spilt blood. "By the Gods!" Mara whispered. "Is this what you have come to tell me?" She took several steps forward, still not sure if she could believe her eyes. "Are the roses in the Ciar Court..."

"Violet," he answered. "The roses in the Ciar garden are violet."

"They haven't changed color since..."

"The night you took your vows," Garreth finished for her.

"I don't understand..." She forced herself to turn and face Garreth. "What is going on?"

"Let's go inside and talk."

She nodded and the group turned back towards the castle. When they entered the chambers, Mara led them up several flights of the spiral staircase until they emerged into one of the guest rooms on the upper floor. Mara walked to the back of the room where a series of chairs sat before a massive unlit fireplace. Each of them took a seat in the velvet chairs.

After everyone was settled, Mara drew a deep breath and said, "Okay, Garreth. I'm listening."

Garreth began to speak, quickly recounting the arrival of the young girl and his discovery of violet roses along the palace grounds. "Wait," Mara inquired. "You are saying that this young woman shows up and suddenly, the roses begin to change color?"

Garreth nodded. "According to Nolan, the girl threw herself over Edward's body when he was being whipped. Took the brunt of a few blows before they were able to stop, effectively ending his torture. Yet, when Edward was asked why the girl would have done such a thing..."

"Edward said he had never seen Lady Sandra before," Nolan finished for him.

"I don't understand. Why would she do that for a stranger?"

"I am not certain," Nolan continued. "However, the princess did not seem herself that night; not in any way. She seemed lost, confused and when they pulled her away, she started screaming, in Latin no less. I didn't understand much of it, but I did distinctly hear her say the words: *sanguis rosarum.*"

"The Blood of Roses," Mara translated. *hic iacet sanguis rosarum.*

"Garreth had the same reaction, but...I'm afraid I don't understand. What does it mean?"

It was here that Mara grew silent, her posture straightening in her chair. *sanguis rosarum.* "Please, Mara," the young knight asked. "Can you tell me what is going on?"

"It's none of your concern," she answered, anger slipping into her tone. "Garreth, why did you bring him here?"

Wait for me, Edward had pleaded. The red roses... *Why are they returning?* Another form of torment for the woman forever trapped in her isolation. *I will have them torn from their very roots*, she vowed silently. *I will burn them as though they never existed.*

"Mara, we need to tell him about Liza."

She started at the princess' name, rising from the chair to gather her full height. "Like hell I do! He's naught more than a child. A child I specifically instructed you to keep away from here."

"It is too late," Garreth stated. "He is involved now. He's been involved since the first stroke of the whip landed on Edward's back."

She glared at him and then turned to walk towards the glass doors leading to an expansive balcony. She stepped into the cool air, the previously still wind now rising in the form of a chilly mountain breeze. She took a deep breath, trying to drive back the overwhelming emotions which threatened to crawl along her skin. "He doesn't need to know!" she all but hissed at Garreth as he followed her onto the balcony.

"Mara, I'm sorry, but...something is happening here. The roses changing color, the Arum Court moving against Edward, the appearance of this woman; something is not right. You know it is not."

Rage filled her eyes. "I'm assuming that you already started this story?" She turned her gaze upon the younger man. "Did he tell you, Nolan? That is strictly forbidden to speak of such things? To even speak her name! What the hell did he tell you? Some sad story about the captain and the young girl he left standing in the garden? How he left me, broke my heart." She stepped closer, pausing mere inches from him. "Do you pity me now, Nolan? The poor, broken Captain of the Desolate Rose?"

"No!" he said hurriedly. "Not at all. I asked him about Edward. I saw the way you looked at him; the way you risked everything to get him away from

King Mathew. I...I just asked him." He shook his head. "I just want to understand what happened. Please, my lady, please tell me."

Mara drew a deep breath and finally asked, "What has he told you?"

Nolan turned to Garreth, who produced the thick, leather-bound book.

"I see," Mara replied. "So everything, then."

"No. I've only read the beginning. Enough to know that you were orphaned as a child and that Edward initiated you into the guard at seventeen."

Mara turned from both men and moved her gaze to the high mountains where the sun was just beginning to lower itself from the sky.

"Mara." Garreth moved to her side speaking softly. "I know how hard it is for you to talk about this."

"No, you don't." The anger fled her voice, replaced by a deep sadness Garreth knew all too well. "How could you possibly know what it is to live, to breathe, to exist, without your heart? Without your soul? I avenged her; but even that wasn't enough. The price of honoring my vow," her lungs gave a slight gasp for air, "the cost, was his love. I swore, I would never see him again. I would never open that door. But, Garreth," she turned to give him pain-filed eyes, "I couldn't let him die. I couldn't let Mathew...how could Mathew do that? I don't understand. Mathew knows. He saw the fight. Why would he do it? Him and Edward and roses...what is happening?"

Garreth looked at her with sorrow. "I don't know, Mara. But I think, I truly think...that the answer lies in the past as you always suspected it would."

CHAPTER XXIV

"YOU MUST UNDERSTAND THAT I have always loved Edward," Mara stated in a haunted voice. "I loved him when I was five years old and he told me that he would one day teach me to be a knight. I loved him when I was seventeen and he initiated me into the guard. I loved him when he kissed me in the garden. And yes," she drew an unsteady breath, "when he professed his love to Liza, I loved him still." She closed her eyes, a cool mountain breeze nipping at the edge of her gown.

"Anything you can tell."

"Nolan," Mara replied slowly. "I loved Edward as the queen plunged a blade into his chest. It...all of this, comes back to that night. I loved him so much, that I stood by and let him sacrifice himself for Liza. Because I understood, Nolan, the cost of the love that he had for her. The cost of a love that ravages the soul, and breaks every piece of your heart until you know, it will never again be whole. I loved him as he lay upon the bed, shattered and broken. I..." She shook her head, returning her gaze to the sun setting slowly behind the massive mountains from her balcony. "I have loved Edward all my life. I loved him then, I love him now, and I will love him the day I draw my last breath." She gave a slow nod before turning back to meet Nolan's eyes. "Liza died over eight hundred years ago, and I still wake up in the night and hear her screams. They will haunt me until the very last star falls from the sky."

Nolan remained silent, allowing Mara to continue in her own time. "When Liza was young, she had terrible nightmares. Edward was walking by her room one night and heard her cry out in her sleep. He woke her and stayed by her side, promising Liza that he would watch over her while she slept. He was always kind to children, myself included – once upon a time."

A bitter smile crept over Mara's haunted face. "The queen was highly intolerant to her daughter's dreams, so it became a private duty which Edward took upon himself to check on her every night before she went to sleep. When he was sent away by the queen, he made me swear that I would continue to...what is the modern term? Tuck her in at night. He told Liza that I would now keep away her dreams, and I was the best he had ever trained." Mara shook her head. "It didn't matter though. Liza cried herself to sleep every night for a month after he was sent away. It was a sorrow that we shared, and was perhaps the key to the bond we formed."

"What was she like?"

"Liza?"

"Yes."

Mara's lips formed a thin line. "Liza was the sweetest child and most genuinely beautiful woman that ever walked this earth. She had long black hair, moonlit skin, and violet eyes with just the slightest hint of silver."

"Sounds like you are describing yourself."

"Yes, a fact I am reminded of, every time Edward looks at me."

Nolan tilted his head and raised his hand as though wanting to offer comfort, but was uncertain if such an offering would be accepted. Mara stood perfectly still. Nolan lowered his hand back to his side.

"Liza had an innocence about her that was incredibly rare among even the youngest of the courts," she continued. "She saw the best in everyone she met. To meet her was to consider yourself blessed, and it had nothing to do with her royal rank. I suppose that we were all in love with her, in one way or another.

"When Edward was sent east to carry out the queen's plans, there were no phones to call, no letters to be carried. No one knew if he was even alive, let alone of his whereabouts."

"How long was he gone?"

"Nine thousand, two hundred and twenty-four days."

"So that would be..." Nolan paused, attempting to do the math.

"Twenty-five years." Mara answered before closing her eyes.

Wait for me, he had asked. A request she had complied with for twenty-five years. How many nights had she cried herself to sleep, longing to see the dark depths of his eyes just one more time? How many mornings had she awoken calling his name to find that it had only been a dream? Then the sheer horror of learning of all he had been through during those years. The two decades he had spent in...

"Mara," Garreth's words brought her from her memories. "I am sorry, Mara."

She turned to face him. "What do you want from me? Do you want me to say we broke each other's hearts? Don't you see, Garreth? There is no forgiveness. For the years he spent trapped in that hell? For standing aside while he was tortured. For loving him when I should have been..." She turned her neck in a full circle as she drew a deep breath. "I can't relive this. Please, Garreth." He raised a hand as Nolan had done, but where she had rejected the touch of the younger man, she allowed Garreth to gently pull her forward, surrendering herself momentarily to his embrace.

"I am sorry, Mara." He had known this would be hard for her, but he had no idea that the wounds would be this raw, this fresh. It had been centuries since he had seen her so fragile. She pulled away and walked out of the room without another word. When she finally reached her chambers, she slammed the heavy door behind her and then sank down to the floor with her back firmly against it, burying her face into her hands, sliding her fingers into her dark hair.

900s AD

WAIT FOR ME, HE HAD asked. *I will come back.* Yet he had never had. Held in captivity by another court, it had been Mara who had eventually come for Edward, an event after which he had never been the same. Haunted by his endured torments, he would wake in the night, physically shaking from his dreams.

"It is okay, Edward," she would whisper as she soothed him.

"Mara?" He reached out a hand and touched the side of her face. "Mara, is it really you?"

"Yes, my love." She placed her hand on top of his and pressed it more firmly against her cheek. "Please," she pleaded, "talk to me."

"You don't want to know."

"Yes, I do. I want to help you."

"I...it was..." He shuddered against her. "I can't. Don't ask me. Please don't make me."

She moved more securely into his arms, eventually sliding down to settle against his chest. Her heart ached at his pain as he struggled with demons that were not hers to face. The nightmares continued over the many months, though after the first few nights, their meetings became intertwined with the duties required by their rank within the Royal Guard. Theirs was a romance of public discretion, lest the queen decide that she was unhappy with the match.

Blinded by her relief at Edward's return, she barely noticed that she was not the only one overjoyed. Edward's frequent appearances with Liza seemed nothing out of the ordinary. After all, the princess had known him as a child, and seeing Liza also meant seeing Mara. It took the better part of a year before Mara realized that the princess had a more serious crush on Edward than she realized.

Then the day came that she was walking the grounds and heard Edward's deep, masculine laugh. It caught her off guard, as laughter was something not frequently heard from the queen's Captain of the Guard.

He was haunted by his time away, still steadfastly refusing to talk to Mara about what, exactly, had happened to him in those long, twenty-five years.

Yet it was on a spring afternoon in the garden not unlike the day Edward had kissed her that Mara finally realized she had lost him. They were walking around the garden in a sea of red, violet and white roses which formed an intoxicating aroma around the two lovers.

"How is Liza today?" Edward inquired.

"Same as yesterday. Though, I do think that the queen is far more excited about the upcoming ball than our young princess."

Edward laughed. "No, she is not fond of the attention, is she? Reminds me of another princess I once knew."

Mara shuddered. "Can you blame her? Hundreds coming to ogle her like some prize to be won. I would not want her position for all the world."

"She seems to be dealing with it well enough," Edward interjected. "She is certainly not the child that I left behind."

"Yes and no. She is not technically a child, but there is a certain innocence about her."

Edward nodded. "Yes, I'm not sure I have ever seen anyone so willing to see the good in others."

"Naïve."

"Yes, but a naivety that I would not have any other way." A smile appeared upon his normally stoic face and his eyes seemed to glaze over as he stared at a cluster of red roses mingling with a wall of ivy. "She is so gentle and kind; youthful and innocent. I could not imagine trying to change that about her. It would be...tragic. She is everything you and I are not." His smile widened. "It is one of the reasons I love her."

The words were carried on a breeze, and it took several moments for them to reach her. She turned to him in confusion. "Love her? What do you mean?" She expected him to laugh it off, to say he meant it in a clearly platonic way. However, his startled expression told a far different story.

One glance was all it took. "Oh." Her eyes closed as she drew a deep breath then opened them slowly. "You mean you're *in* love...with Liza?"

Edward became so still that one would not have known he was real if he had not been speaking only a moment before. "You're in love with Liza." This time, it was not a question. She stared at him silently for several moments. Then a rough sound escaped her lips—between a chuckle and a choking gasp. "Of course," she said in disbelief. "The young princess whose happiness I am bound to protect." She stared directly at the man before her. "The one woman, the only woman, in the entire kingdom, you cannot have. How could you not be in love with her?"

"Mara."

"No," she interrupted, her laughter ceasing as anger took its place. "No, I waited for you. For years, I waited. For...for *decades*!" Mara's heart began to thump through her body. Her gaze trailed blindly along the garden walls as her mind attempted to comprehend. She couldn't focus. Then, finally the words escaped her lips. "You don't love me. By the Gods." Her body began to tremble as she forced her eyes to travel back towards Edward's. She repeated the statement. "You don't love me."

His lips parted as though to speak, but words faltered as he caught her violet gaze. Her eyes burned, yet no tears rose to cool their surface. She sounded childlike as she asked, "What have I done?"

"Done?"

"To make you not love me? What did I do?" Silence lay between them as she searched his eyes for answers that did not exist. Her body began to shake more violently than before. "I waited... You asked me to wait....I...I don't..." The world spun. Her heart pounded ferociously, physically jerking her body with every beat.

"Mara." Edward found his voice. "I do love you. It's not what you—"

"I don't believe you." Her voice escaped in broken pieces. "You don't...don't..." She swallowed and it hurt. "I did everything you ever asked." Her voice began to increase in volume. "I was a princess. I gave up everything, everything to be with you. You said you loved me! You asked—no—begged me to wait." Her words became laced with bitter laughter which she was neither able to control nor let subside. "*Twenty-five fucking years*!"

Edward had never heard such rage, let alone from the beautiful girl standing before him. He reached out slowly and placed his hand upon her left arm.

"Don't touch me!" she screamed, pushing him away with enough force that he had to step back to prevent himself from tumbling to the ground.

"Mara," he tried again. He could feel the pain radiating from her slender form.

"No!" she shrieked. "No, no, no!" Physically ill, Mara turned from him, leaning her face into her hands before letting out a wordless scream. The sound carried through the garden for any to hear. She did not care.

"Please, Mara. I did not want to hurt you. I would never want to hurt you. I did not mean..."

Mara rocked back and forth, her arms wrapped tightly around her body. She couldn't move, couldn't cry, couldn't breathe. All she knew was pain.

Garreth, who had heard her scream from the opposite side of the gardens, raced around the corner with his hand upon the hilt of his silver bade. He froze at the sight of Mara shivering. "What in the name of the Gods is going on?"

Mara heard him as though from a distance. Edward again moved his hand towards her. "You will hurt yourself." At his touch, Mara broke from her frozen position, turning from him so violently that she lost her footing and would have fallen to the ground had Edward not caught her.

"Damn you!" She attempted to slap him, but he caught her wrist in his strong grasp. "You swore!" she continued to yell, tears at long last blurring her vision. "You swore to love me! You promised." Her words became sobs. "I waited for you. You promised, you promised, you..."

"Mara, please," Edward pleaded. "You must...I never..."

"Let me go!" she yelled as she sobbed. "You don't have the right to touch me." Edward released his grip on her pale wrist which would likely be bruised the next morning. She sank to the ground feeling everything, yet nothing. She fought to draw breath, but could not seem to force the air down her constricted throat.

"What the hell is going on?" Garreth directed the question to Edward as Mara's second-in-command, Davith suddenly appeared by his side. "What..." Mara did not hear his next words. The world spun faster through her blurred vision. She had no idea how long she lay there before a pair of arms slid around her. Mara fought the form which attempted to comfort her, oblivious to the fact that it was now her cousin and not Edward who attempted to gather her in his arms.

"Mara, Mara," he repeated again and again attempting to cut through her hysteria.

"Don't touch me!" she screamed. "Don't you dare touch me!"

"Mara," Davith said, joining her cousin in his attempts to calm her.

"No!" she sobbed before Garreth suddenly stepped back, allowing Davith to take his place. "They won't touch you," he assured her. "Neither of them will touch you."

She had no idea how long she sat there, resisting their offered comfort before finally turning to bury her sobs against Davith's chest.

Beside them, Garreth stared down at the shattered remains of the girl who had grown into one of the strongest women he had ever known, reduced again to that fragile child who had been pried from her dead mother's hand.

From the far side of the garden, Edward looked on helplessly.

CHAPTER XXV

Present Day

REGALD AWOKE TO A SOFT knock on the door. He jerked from the bed, scrambling to grasp his sword from where it lay upon the floor. A second knock made him grateful that he had removed only his shirt the night before as he rushed forward and placed his hand upon the silver door handle. He stood slightly to the side as he opened the door, peering out to find Sandra. "My lady," he stated, opening the door wider.

"Sorry to wake you, but I wanted to know if it would be okay to get some fresh air? Being inside this mountain is a little..."

"Of course. Just give me a moment to dress." He motioned her inside, walking to the closet tucked into the back wall of the room. Having been unaware that he would be away from his court for multiple nights, Regald had not brought extra clothes. As such, he borrowed one of the silver shirts in the closet. The sleeves were slightly short, but otherwise it seemed to fit nicely. He quickly secured his belt and sword around his waist before offering Sandra his arm. She accepted it gladly and he led her down a series of stone hallways before emerging into the entryway of the mountainside keep.

As they stepped outside, Jake approached from their left. "Where are you going?"

"Lady Sandra requested a walk around the grounds," Regald replied. "I offered to escort her."

Jake eyed them for several moments. "You cannot go walking around the grounds, as a guest of our court, without Ciar Guard protection. I shall accompany you."

Regald did not question, but merely nodded. "As you wish, Sub-Captain."

Jake took the lead. "I must apologize, Princess, for my behavior yesterday. I would love to act as your guide, if you will allow."

"Thank you," she spoke softly. "But I am not yet a princess and therefore, should not be addressed as such."

Jake nodded. "May I show you around the grounds then, Lady Sandra?"

"Of course, Sub-Captain. I would be delighted."

The three began their walk along the winding dirt path with Jake pointing out occasional markers along the trail. They took their time, walking at a leisurely pace as the morning sun blazed through an almost cloudless sky. "Most of the court stays in more modern structures on the opposite side of the mountain," Jake informed her. "The queen among them. She had the palace built about, oh...I would say, two hundred years ago."

Sandra gave a soft chuckle, causing Jake to turn and look at her. "Sorry. Sometimes I forget that two hundred years would be 'modern.'" She offered a warm smile which Jake found himself returning.

"Trust me, Princess...sorry, Lady Sandra. It is practically brand new by Ciar standards. The rooms you were in last night were carved from the mountainside nearly six hundred years ago. The underground palace you recently visited with Captain Regald was ruled by our queen for nearly nine hundred years and by her mother for a thousand years before that."

Sandra turned to Regald. "The Arum Court isn't nearly that old, is it?"

"No, my lady. The Arum Court has only been in existence for half a millennium, give or take. King Mathew's uncle, Richard, was the first king, but he was not considered strong enough to hold the throne on his own. Mathew, a member of the Black Rose Guard who had just come from a series of victories, was named his heir. Richard surrendered the throne only a few years after the creation of the court and Mathew has ruled ever since."

"You were a part of that guard as well, weren't you?"

"Yes, my lady. When Mathew left to become his uncle's heir, he offered me a position as his captain. I knew that Brendan was next in line to be Mara's second in command, so when Mara gave me her blessing to leave, I accepted the king's offer."

Sandra nodded as they continued around the winding path. A cool breeze blew across the mountains slowly being warmed by the blinding rays of the sun which now hung high above them. The green grass rolled gently down the hill, the color scheme interrupted by the occasional patch of wildflowers. Sandra slowed her pace and waited for Regald to step beside her.

"It is so beautiful," she said softly. Mountains rose higher in the distance, the tallest of the peaks capped with ice that had been there since the cretaceous period. She stood silently for several moments, taking in the breathtaking views, the wind pulling at the edge of her dark blue gown.

"Regald," she said softly. "What is happening to me? Why will no one tell me?" She turned and tilted her head up in stare into his eyes. Yet even as he met her gaze, she heard the faint echo of that angelic laughter. She closed her eyes tightly against the sound, prompting Regald to reach toward her.

He pressed his palm to the side of her face. "Stay with me."

She turned her head to the right, pressing her cheek more firmly against his hand. She forced herself to open her blue eyes to stare into his pale green ones. His expression was soft, concern showing plainly on his features. "We will help you, Sandra. You have my word."

She drew a deep breath, the laughter pushed back by the sound of his voice. She placed her hand over his and he slowly lowered his arm, his fingers interlacing with hers for a brief moment before he let go, offering her a much more formal grip on his arm. She slid her arm over his, the contact unusual in the borrowed shirt instead of the long sleeves he normally wore.

Jake, who had remained silent during this exchange, motioned in a sweeping gesture in front of them. "Shall we continue the tour, my lady?"

"Yes. Please lead the way, Sub-Captain."

"Jake. No need for formalities."

She nodded. "Then please address me as Sandra. As I said, I am not a princess yet."

Jake smiled and continued the tour. They walked past a series of towering stones upon which lay the names of many heroes who had come before. Past a series of fields where various members of the Ciar Court Guard stood conducting their morning exercises, a few running along the green grass while others faced off with swords in their hands.

However, when they reached the edge of the garden, Jake stopped walking so suddenly that Regald almost ran into him. Jake stared wide-eyed at the garden, his lips parting as he said, "By the Gods."

"I thought the roses never flourished here," Regald said from a few paces behind them.

"They don't," Jake answered. "Or at least...they didn't." He walked forward towards the stream which ran through the center of the garden. Where the night before the garden had consisted of only a few scattered flowers, now the roses lined the entire length of the stream, rising from the ground in a cluster of climbing and intertwining vines that matched the height of the men who walked towards them. They bloomed in royal purple—a color that had not been seen in over eight hundred years.

"It's the same thing that happened on the grounds of the Lorcan Court. The roses changed color."

"I am going to get Edward," Jake replied.

It took fifteen minutes for the captain to arrive. Similar to the two other men, he was unable to keep his surprise from showing.

"What does it mean?" Jake asked from beside his captain.

"I don't know," he answered. "The roses have not changed color since..."

"Mara took the vow of the Black Rose."

CHAPTER XXVI

MARA AWOKE TO A KNOCK on the door, pulling her from the torturous memories depicted so clearly in her dreams. She ignored the sound, but the unwanted visitor opened the door despite the withheld invitation. No one in Mara's own guard would be foolish enough to do so, which narrowed the identity of her intruder to one. "Go away, Garreth." He continued to ignore her, walking slowly across the room until she felt his weight settle upon the side of the bed.

She lay on her side, facing away from him, and he sat still for several moments before his hand touched her shoulder gently. She was not sure what she expected, but the feel of her cousin wrapping his arms around her in an awkward embrace was not it. The feel of another's touch, for which she had so long denied herself, was enough to bring fresh tears to her eyes. She fought them back.

"Mara,' he whispered softly.

Only the voice did not belong to Garreth. She jerked up, twisting her body around to face the man who held her. "Phillip."

"Mara. My brave, brave girl."

She rose to a seated position, leaning more fully into his embrace. "Phillip." She placed her head upon his shoulder and he pulled her close. "I'm dreaming."

"Yes."

"Please, don't force me to wake. "

He stoked her back, running his fingers through the long strands of her dark hair. "I'm so sorry, my lady. But you must."

She shuddered in his arms. "It hurts, Phillip. I don't know how much longer I can do this."

He kissed her brow, and suddenly she could hear the sound of the soft ocean waves. Mara pulled back and was kneeling again on that long abandoned beach. Once, it had been the living, beating heart of the Muir Court. But now, only the ancient ruins remained. It had been here on this beach that Mara had led the Black Rose Guard to their most famous victory.

The Arum and Ciar court had not yet come into existence the day that the Lorcan declared formal war upon the Muir. However, since it was the princess that was being avenged, the honor-bound Black Rose was in charge of the attack. The Black Rose, transformed over the course of nearly two hundred years, stood as an assemblage of the most skilled warriors the Lorcan Court had to offer, save one. They had been charged with sneaking into the ancient keep and opening up the gates. Instead they had slaughtered nearly everyone inside long before the bulk of the Lorcan Court was able to join them.

Mara remembered cascading over the high walls. The entry point upon the wall had been carefully chosen after years of silent observation. The Rose had plotted this night to perfection, right down to knowing the rank of every single guardsman who stood upon the wall. She reached the ground and walked quietly towards the thick wooden door which was all that stood between her men and the inner halls of the palace with Phillip following closely behind her.

A single man stood before the door, wearing the dark blue of the Muir Court Guard. Mara walked directly towards him. The man actually raised his hand in greeting, not realizing who or what she was. When she reached him, she paused a single moment and raised Arius blade - one of the few capable of killing an immortal - in a practiced movement, driving its deadly edge into the side of his neck. Blood splattered her clothes as she proceeded to open the wooden door.

On the opposite side, two additional members of the guard were seated at a table as Mara and Garreth stepped forward, side by side through the wide entryway. It took only three long strides to reach them. Mara slid her blade across the throat of the man seated on the right while Garreth did the same to the one on the left. Blood gushed from the open artery, but the men convulsed with only a slight gurgling sound. The Arius blade Mara carried had once belonged to her father. It had been given to him by King Cathair the day he had married her mother.

She slipped down the hall, leading her men as they killed all in their path: man or woman, it did not matter. When they reached the royal apartments, her men entered the rooms, forcing occupants from their beds and into a parlor which stood in the center. In the center of the group stood King Dacian and Queen Sophia who had stood by his side for over a thousand years. The couple had three sons and two daughters, all with the same blue eyes. But Mara's piercing gaze was fixed upon the Crown Prince.

"Mara." Phillip's voice drew her back to the beach. She was dressed in a thin blue gown covered with thousands of tiny crystals which sparkled in the light of the sun now sinking into the ocean waves. "You are even more beautiful than I remember."

"Liar."

In reply, Phillip offered a sad smile and ran his hand gently down the side of her face. "You look sad, my lady."

"Please, let me stay. I want to stay."

"I'm sorry, my princess. I would give anything to take away your pain. But alas, we both know it is the one thing I have never been able to do." Regret shined through crystal blue eyes. "I am sorry, Mara."

"You did what you thought was right."

"It was wrong. So wrong. I hurt you. I never meant to, but I did just the same."

"Oh Phillip," she said, pursing her lips. "You were scared and that was my fault."

"I would give anything to take it back."

She remembered it all too well. It had been the day they had learned the true identity of Liza's killer.

1300 AD

THE VOW OF THE BLACK Rose was an ancient order from the most powerful of the immortal beliefs. It was tied to a vow of vengeance which Mara, and all those who had left the Ciar Court to follow her, had taken before the Gods of old.

The vow of the Rose: *Rosa Nigra te in vita tueatur teque in morte ulciscatur. May the Black Rose Protect you in life and avenge you in death.* According to the tradition, all subjects within a given immortal court belonged to a single, ancient bloodline. The revelation that the man they sought was a prince of the court could only result in one outcome.

"I can reveal the truth," the priestess had informed her. "But there will be a price."

"Any price."

The priestess gave a single nod. "The blood of roses lies within the waves of the sea."

Mara felt her breath caught deep in her throat. "You mean, someone in the Muir Court...the court by the sea?"

"Of blood most royal."

"No." The word escaped her lips before she could stop it.

The priestess looked at her with great sadness. "Your vengeance will not return her to you, Princess Mara."

She stared at the priestess for a long time, silently begging for it not to be true, but knowing such hopes were futile. When she returned to the ancient castle of the Black Rose, Mara had locked herself in her secluded tower. For days she sat in the darkened chambers, refusing so much as to light the fire in the cold chambers.

For the first few days, Phillip simply brought Mara bowls of broth in silence. She never acknowledged his presence, but merely sat upon the bed, staring at the stone wall.

Her expression remained blank, as though her soul had long abandoned the body which refused to quit breathing. It was a look that Phillip had seen before and with a chill he realized she had never looked more like her mother. By the time the fifth day rolled around, Phillip found himself standing just outside Mara's door, his heart fearful of every sound, yet the room beyond the door remained silent. And it frightened him more than any scream.

It was on sixth evening that Phillip had come, entering the room quietly with a cup of warm liquid in his hand. "You need to drink this," he said softly. From a seated position on the bed, she had reluctantly taken the cup and forced the warm liquid down her parched throat. Phillip sat in silence until Mara had drank the majority of the brew and then took the cup, placing it on the stone floor to the side of the bed.

"My lady," he said as he slid to one knee. "You do not have to do this. You can let others take this task."

"No," she replied but her voice lacked conviction.

"What can I do?"

"Nothing. There is nothing that anyone can do."

"That is not true though, is it Mara?"

She looked at him uncomprehendingly.

"My lady, I cannot leave you here in this isolation. Nothing in this world terrifies me more than seeing you so."

"I don't even know what I am. Nothing, I feel nothing."

"I know...and it scares me."

"There is nothing you can do."

"Perhaps not. But there is one who can."

"No, he can't."

"Mara, listen to me."

"No."

"Mara, this isolation, this anguish—it killed your mother."

Mara stared at Phillip. "What are you saying?"

"You are suffocating. Locked in your tower unwilling to face the world surrounding you." He stared directly into her amethyst eyes. "I know it has been difficult. I cannot even begin to imagine how difficult."

"What do you want from me? What the hell do you want? What more must I give?"

"I want you to live! I want you to leave the tower, before its isolation consumes you completely. I want you to let people into your world, Mara. Please, Mara. I am trying to help you."

"You can't!" she exclaimed. "Don't you understand? You cannot help me."

"Mara." He leaned forward, closing the distance between them.

"Don't." She stood from the bed, moving several paces to her right. "Just don't."

"I know how badly you need Edward," he stated in a low, strained tone, slowly rising from his kneeling position. "If I could change that, I would. I would rip him from your deepest memory and make you forget his very existence." He drew a deep breath. "I know you need him, Mara. But he is not here...and I am."

"So what?" she asked bitterly.

He walked forward and turned her back to face him. He reached forward and touched her cheek before slowly sliding his hand to the back of her neck. She watched in confusion as he suddenly leaned forward and pressed his lips against her own. She jerked back, but he kept his hand firmly on her neck, controlling her until he pulled back.

"How dare you!" she began when Phillip moved a second hand to her back and pulled her forward into another controlled kiss.

This time when he pulled back, it was to give her the full weight of his pale eyes. "I will be damned if I am going to stand here and watch you die."

"Why?" she asked, her voice boiling with anger. "Just think, Phillip. Then the Black Rose would be yours and you could run it however you damn well please."

Phillip moved his hand to Mara's arms and grabbed her just above the wrist. He forcibly moved her towards the center of the room to a seated position upon the bed. "Don't!" she said again, attempting to twist her arm away from him. He ignored her protests and knelt in front of her as he kept her on the edge of the bed, refusing to loosen his grip upon her wrists.

"What do you need, Mara? Tell me what it is that you need so badly that you lock yourself away night after night."

She shook her head.

"Tell me, Mara." He made it a demand.

"What do you want?" she all but screamed. "You want me to say that I need him? That I don't know how to function, to live, to breathe, without him—fine! I'll say it!" Her words began to crumble. "I need him. I love him. But...I can't have him." Her eyes were wide, wild. "What do you want from me?"

"Let me give you what you need."

"I don't understand."

"I will be whatever you need, Mara. Whatever...whoever...you need me to be. Close your eyes, my lady. Tell *me* what you would tell *him.*"

Fear began to climb along Mara's spine. "You are asking me to..." She searched his gaze. "To close my eyes and what? Pretend. Call you by his name and...are you insane? How could you even propose such a ghastly, such a..." She could not find the words she reached for.

"You need to feel something, Mara. By the Gods above, you need touch and warmth or you will not survive this. You just learned the identity of Liza's killer. Yet, you are numb. Completely numb."

"What should I have done? Yell, scream?"

"Yes! Any, all, just...anything, Mara. Anything."

"No. I cannot..."

"Damn it, Mara!"

"I can't! Don't you see? If I do, it will never stop!"

"You are not alone in this," he said, unknowingly echoing Edward's broken promise. "Do you hear me, Mara? You are not alone. You can share this burden with your guard—with me."

"No more lies!" she yelled bitterly. "He lied, he always lies. I am alone. I have always been alone."

Phillip leaned forward until all she could see were the blue pools of his eyes. "But you do not have to be." She felt his warm breath upon her face. "Not here, not tonight." He kissed her and this time, she allowed it, closing her eyes against the world which sought to break her. He pulled her close, running his hand gently through her hair in a familiar gesture. "Mara." He spoke her name softly. "Let me be what you need," he whispered as Edward had done so long ago. "I am here. You are not alone, my Mara. *mea rosa immortalis.*"

His lips claimed hers. She sank into the kiss, refusing to open her eyes as he slowly pressed her down into the blankets. Her voice rose soft and confused as the world began to shift. "I don't...we shouldn't be..."

He pressed a finger lightly against her lips, silencing her protests as his hand slid down her face. "It is okay, my rose," Edward's words washed over her. "*adsum, mea rosa, mi amor.*"

Time seemed to slip away as the strong hands caressed her, exploring her face before moving down her throat to reach the top of her black sweater. He traced the line of the cloth for several moments before reaching down to touch her breasts through the thick material.

She slowly began to give herself over to the sensations—the simple touch—her body longed for. It had been so long since he had held her, caressed her; the mere act of being touched brought fresh tears to her closed eyes.

He moved her as he willed, slowly removing her shirt and pulling it over her head to expose her flawless skin. "*te amo, rosa, mea rosa immortalis,*" he whispered as his hands slid slowly to her breasts, drawing a gasp from her parted lips. Then he moved lower, sliding his hands completely up and down each of her long, pale legs before moving his hand between them. Yet it was here at this unfamiliar touch that Mara's eyes flew open and she found herself staring not into Edward's dark gaze, but into Phillip's crystal blue.

She jerked frantically from the bed, scrambling towards the edge. "What are you doing? We were...oh Gods...No."

"Mara," he said, trying to calm her. "Just listen to me."

"No. No." She felt nauseated. The world seemed to spin.

"Mara..."

"No." She shook her head, dressing quickly as she scrambled towards the door.

"Mara..."

"Stay away from me!" She raced forward into the hallways and down the winding stairwell to the castle floor. When she reached the doors of the ancient keep, she threw them open with such force that they slammed against the stones.

"Mara?" Garreth asked from his position on the opposite side.

"I have to go," she stated without so much as glancing in his direction. "You're in charge."

"Go? Where are you going?"

Mara kept walking straight to the stables. As she entered, she pulled a heavy wool cloak from a hook at the entrance and wrapped it around her shoulders. Then she proceeded to her horse, a tall black stallion who she had named Noir. Without bothering with a saddle, Mara mounted him, gently stroking the horse's neck as she led him from the stables.

"Mara, what is going on?" Garreth inquired. "What happened?"

She shook her head. "I have to go."

"Mara, please."

She dug her heels into the side of her horse and rode toward the front gates, which were opened at the order of their captain. She raced along the dirt path toward the distant mountains beyond, memories dancing in the swirling winds surrounding which refused to be banished.

She rode hard and fast until finally reaching a spring where she suddenly stopped, giving her horse a much needed respite from the long run. She lay down in the spring grass and fell into a deep slumber until morning light, when she rose and again resumed her journey across the mountains.

It took over a week of hard riding before she reached the lush forest she had known so well as a child, and longer still to reach the palace grounds. Still a few hours away, she found herself caught in a ferocious downpour, slowing her ride to a walk as she attempted to maneuver the horse through the pouring rain.

By the time she reached the palace, she was completely drenched. At the sight of only a single rider, guards opened the gates for her, ushering her in from the rain.

"Greetings," a man with light brown hair said to her. "What may I do for you, my lady? Must be awfully important to be out in this storm."

"Captain Mara?" a blond suddenly spoke from her left. "Mara, is that you?"

"Jake?"

"By the Gods, it is you." He turned to the other man. "Let her through, Quinn. She's a friend."

Quinn nodded. "I will leave her to you then."

Jake approached her with a long black cloak. "Here," he said, wrapping it around her wet shoulders. "Let's get you inside and into some dry clothes."

"No," she said. "Take me to Edward. I need to see Edward."

"Yes, I figured as much. I'm guessing you remember the way?"

Jake led Mara down a series of winding hallways which were instantly foreign and familiar at the same time. "Is everything okay?" Jake asked, lengthening his stride in order to match her determined pace.

"I need to see him."

When they reached the doors to the captain's chambers, Mara did not pause to knock, instead throwing open the doors. Edward sat on a sofa on the right side of the room, staring at a stack of papers on the table before him. A pair of candles were lit upon the table, providing much needed light, and a warm fire burned several feet to his left. He glanced up from the papers, startled as the doors flew open. For a moment he simply stared, a voice in his head questioning his sanity as he stared at the woman standing in the doorway. Her dark hair was matted against her face, water streaming steadily from its wet strands. Her wet clothes clung to her body like a second skin.

The scroll Edward had been holding fell to the floor. "Mara?" His voice told a story of disbelief as he slowly rose to his feet. He caught her wild gaze as she quickly crossed the room. "What are you..." he started to say but his words were silenced as she wrapped her arms around him and pulled his lips down to hers. She kissed him deep and thoroughly, pressing against him as though attempting to thrust her soul out of her body and into his.

When she finally pulled back she did not speak, but began to peel the soaking clothes from her body, revealing her pale skin to his gaze until she finally stood nude before him. Then she leaned forward and kissed him again, giving in to a desperate, wild sense of abandonment. "Mara, I don't understand. What is going on?" he asked on the edge of a heated breath.

"It doesn't matter. All that matters is that I love you, Edward. I'm so tired and scared and alone. Please." She forced herself to meet his gaze. "I need you."

Edward looked down at her for several long moments, then he raised his own shirt and throwing it to the floor beneath him, revealing the taut lines of his pale chest. He then reached forward and pulled Mara toward him, kissing her thoroughly. "You are sure?" was all he asked.

"Completely."

He reached a hand to the side of her face and pressed it tightly against her cheek. "I was such a fool. That last day..." His neck twisted in a tight spiral. "Gods Mara, I was such a fool. Forgive me." He drew her to him, pressing her bare breasts to his chest. Then he scooped her into his arms and carried her across the room to the bed. He stared at her for several heartbeats, his eyes roaming her as though trying to memorize every line and curve. Then he stripped off the rest of his clothes and lay down beside the woman who, even after all they had been through, remained the possessor of his soul.

Time seemed to melt as Edward ran his hands over her smooth skin, eternally young despite her centuries of life. He traced his hands down her throat and to her breasts, slowly circling each nipple before moving his lips to enfold their sensitive tips. Mara moaned at the sensation, tracing her hands along his spine.

When his hands finally moved lower, her entire body was trembling and she was unable to suppress another moan as he ran a finger down her legs and up her inner thigh. Very slowly, he slid a finger into her warm depths, causing her to gasp at his touch. At the sound, he moved his attention higher yet again, slowly settling himself above her and leaned down for another searing kiss. "Mara," he whispered. "Are you ready?"

"Please," was all she could bring herself to say, but the single word was enough. He took her, sliding slowly forward as she whispered his name. "Edward, Edward..."

"*ego adsum, mea rosa.* I am here." He kept his voice at a gentle tone even as he drove his body deeper into hers. "*mea rosa immortalis.*" At the sound of his voice, Mara completely gave herself over to the sensations consuming her. The world faded to nothing, save for the exquisite feeling of Edward's body melding into hers.

It was only later, after their passions were spent, that the full range of her emotions came rushing to the surface. Mara rose from where she lay to a seated position on the edge of the bed, fighting to draw a steady breath.

"Mara?" Edward rose from the bed beside her.

She shook her head, still fighting to breathe.

"Mara," he said again, his voice washing over her with more intimacy than any caress, pulling tears from her eyes. He placed his hand on her shoulder and gently turned her to face him. "My lady."

She drew a ragged breath and tried to speak. "You're here," was all she could seem to manage as her left hand moved to touch the side of his face. "You're here."

He moved his hand over hers, pressing her fingers firmly against his cheek. "Yes," he replied softly. "*adsum, mea rosa, mi amor.*"

"You're here," she said again. "I...I didn't know what else to do. I couldn't...all I could think of was getting to you." She closed her eyes against the tears burring her vision. "Edward, I'm..."

He pulled her against him, crushing her in his strong embrace. "Oh Gods, Mara. You can always come to me. I..." He pulled back enough to see her eyes. "Mara..." Her name escaped as a strangled whisper. "*mea rosa immortalis.*" His hand slid to the back of her neck and he lowered his lips to hers.

She kissed him back, pouring her heart and soul from her body and into his as she collapsed into his arms—surrendering all thought, all control everything she was or would be into his powerful embrace. She spoke the words which bared her soul. "I love you."

She lay down beside him, closing her eyes as he ran his hand gently through the long stands of her dark hair, relaxing into his soothing embrace. "I am here, Mara; *te amo, rosa, mea rosa immortalis.*" He whispered over and over. She drifted to a dreamless sleep still listening to the sound of his voice.

It was only later, when she awakened in the dark chambers, Edward's arm draped protectively around her, that the full weight of reality came crashing down upon her. She drew herself slowly from Edward's sleeping form, tears filling her eyes and she forced herself to leave his warm embrace.

She walked quietly into his closet and pulled one of his shirts from where it hung along with a long, full-length black cloak which she tied securely around her. The clothes dwarfed her slender frame, but at least it was dry. She slipped quietly towards the door, but no sooner did her hand reach the silver handle, that she felt a touch on her shoulder. "Mara?" Edward said questioningly before adding, "I expected to wake and find this a dream."

"Forgive me," she said softly. "I have to go."

"What is going on, Mara?" He turned her gently to face him, and realized she was crying. "Gods, Mara, what is it? What?" He spoke more gently than before. "Please talk to me. Are you upset because of what we..."

"No." Her protest rose louder than planned, but she didn't care. "I...I love you. I needed... I couldn't..."

"Mara," he said and pulled her into his embrace. "It is okay. Just, tell me what is going on."

"I know who killed her," she said miserably.

Edward pulled back enough to see her face, a look of uncertainty crossing his features. "Her...you mean?"

Mara nodded. "I know who killed her."

"Liza? You know who killed Liza?"

"Yes."

Edward's lips parted and he drew a sharp breath. "By the Gods."

"They killed her, Edward."

"Who?"

"It doesn't matter. They are all dead. I am going kill them all."

"Mara..." He looked ill. "Are you okay?"

"No." She continued to search his gaze then said, "Come with me, Edward. I don't think I can do this without you. Please. I need you."

"Mara." He drew an unsteady breath. "Oh, Mara. I...I can't. I want to, but I just...I'm sorry."

She shut her eyes tightly. Her words trembled as she forced herself to answer. "I know," she whispered. "I know. I'm sorry."

"Mara, please. You don't have to go. Come back to bed, get some sleep. We can talk about this in the morning."

"No." She shook her head.

"Mara you need sleep."

"No," she said again. "If I lie back down with you, I will never leave. I will stay with you until the end of time and my vow shall remain unfulfilled. I'm sorry, Edward. I...I have to go." She shook her head and more tears fells. "I love you, but I have to go."

"Mara." Something in his voice drew her eyes unwillingly into the depths of his. "Promise me."

Her entire body trembled as she said, "Anything."

"Come back. Come back to me."

She sank her teeth into her bottom lip, drawing a constricted breath and gave a single, slow nod before finding the strength to say. "*promitto.* I will always come for you, Edward. Always. But I have to go now, *mi amor.* I have to go."

With those words, Mara turned and left, leaving Edward alone in the ever darkening room.

CHAPTER XXVII

Present Day

MARA STILL STOOD UPON THE beach, wearing a crystal blue gown that matched the color of Phillip's eyes. He ran his hand down the side of her face, gently brushing her dark hair back. "I'm sorry, Mara. I never meant to hurt you." He pressed his palm against her cheek.

"You were trying to save me. You did save me. You sent me to the only one who could."

"I wish I could take it back."

"You are here now," she answered, the cool breeze blowing gently through the strands of her dark hair. She moved her own hand to touch his face when she suddenly heard a distant thudding. She turned from him to stare at the ocean. For a moment she heard only the crashing of the gentle waves. Then, the sound rose again, louder this time, more insistent. She turned back to Phillip. "I don't want to go. Please, please Phillip—don't make me."

He looked at her. "They still need you Mara. You are not done yet."

"Why?" She shook her head pleadingly. "All I know in this world is death and pain. How can they possibly need that in their lives? It is so peaceful here. Please, Phillip—let me stay."

He stared at her for several moments and then suddenly gave a single nod. "The choice is yours, my princess. But what I stated before remains true; if you stay, Edward will die."

Again there came that awful sound only this time it was accompanied by a faint cry: "Mara."

She stared at Phillip. "It is your choice," he said.

She drew a deep breath, the taste of salt dancing upon her tongue. "Don't leave me."

"I will always be here, my princess."

"Mara!" The cry was louder this time, more insistent than before.

Very slowly, she shook her head. "Captain," she corrected. "Only Captain."

He nodded slowly. "Then I bid thee farewell, Captain of the Black Rose."

She opened her eyes to find Garreth leaning over her. He was holding her by both arms, his fingers digging into her pale skin with physical force. He shook her body vigorously, lifting her upper body from the bed as he did so. "Mara, wake up!"

"For Gods' sake, what is it?" she demanded, twisting in an attempt to get away from him. "You're hurting me."

He moved back, and she was ready to begin yelling at him for daring to invade her privacy, when she suddenly heard a loud clatter, as though something very large had shattered. It was instantly followed by the sound of clashing blades echoing through the stone castle. Her head snapped to Garreth, giving him her full attention, her exhaustion vanishing. Garreth's silver blade lay on the edge of the bed inches from his hand.

"We are under attack."

Mara did not question this, but instead slid into her centuries of training without a second thought. She moved from the bed to where her sword hung on its normal place. She then grabbed her discarded clothes from where they lay crumpled and slipped into them in moments, not caring that Garreth was still standing in the room. Not bothering with the sheath, Mara grasped her naked blade, the familiar weight grounding her. She moved towards the door with Garreth at her heels. "How many?"

"At least a dozen. Maybe more."

She did the math. The castle was only lightly guarded. A majority of her men were out on assignments. No one had been foolish enough to attack the Rose in centuries. *What the hell is going on*? She broke into a full run down the hall but slowed and took the corner to the staircase more cautiously. Fortunately the intruders had not reached the upper levels of the castle. "We will take the back staircase," she ordered. They took the stairs quickly as they dared, pushed forward by the cries of men and the clash of steel. When they reached the ground floor, they emerged into the deserted study and rushed toward the wooden door. "Who are they?" she finally asked.

Garreth avoided her gaze.

"That bad?"

"At least two of them are from the Arum Guard."

Mara drew a sharp breath, thoughts racing through her mind faster than she could follow. Finally she forced her gaze upon her cousin's and simply said, "No mercy."

They burst through the door, swords in hand. Outside nearly two dozen warriors were engaged in heated combat. The intruders wore the dark red shirts that marked them as members of the Arum Court Guard. Her own men wore their signature black, marked by the silver rose embroidered upon their shirts. She moved immediately to the man closest to her left. She plunged the tip of her sword between his shoulder blades before he even knew she had entered the room. He collapsed to his knees with a shriek and she plunged her sword in a downward stroke, inserting the sharp tip between his left shoulder and neck, spilling his blood in a stream as his body collided with the ground.

Without pause, she stepped forward to engage a bronzed-skin man standing to her right. He was several inches taller than Mara and a good fifty pounds heavier. Broad across the shoulders, he should have been intimidating, but Mara walked towards him at a steady pace with a blank, firm expression. Recognizing the famous captain, the man tightened his grip on the weapon in his hand. Mara's sword slashed forward and he rushed to stop her movement.

Mara took a step back and drew a deep breath. Her opponent stepped forward, shifting his weight to back leg before bringing his blade down upon her. She raised her sword, moving both hands to the hilt and bracing her legs as his weight came down upon her. Mara held her ground and for a moment the two stood still, their blades crossed as they caught each other's gaze.

The man pulled back and Mara lowered her blade, thrusting forward suddenly so that the downward stroke cut though the dark material of her opponent's shirt and sliced into his skin. He jerked back with a hiss, but the cut had not been deep enough to end the fight. He then took up a defensive posture. Mara brought her blade to his right side with such speed that he was barely able to stop it. The two blades rose together, metal on metal causing a single spark to flicker between them. Mara spun her body in a tight spiral, and this time her sword forced its way into the layers of his left arm, causing blood to swell to the surface of his skin.

She took advantage of this, moving her blade again to his left. This time he blocked her movement and parried with a stroke of his own, attempting to use his superior strength to his advantage. Mara stepped to her right. His attempted strike struck only air, putting him momentarily off balance. It was all Mara needed. She twirled around him, spinning her body into a full circle as she slid behind her opponent. He attempted to twist to face her, but only managed to make himself even more off balance. Mara moved her silver sword in a single, fluid arc stabbing its sharp edge directly into the center of her opponent's back. He fell to his knees with the impact. Mara followed him, pushing the edge of her blade into his spine.

A glint of light in the corner of her eye caused her to pull back just in time to avoid the slash of her next attacker, who had rushed to the defense of his friend now lying paralyzed on the stone floor.

She moved away from the blade that raced towards her. From the corner of her eye, she caught Garreth facing off with an intruder of his own. Mara twisted, turning her full attention to the new attacker, a tall man with golden hair and eyes the color of speckled gold. His blade crashed down and she fell to her knees, skidding across the floor to avoid the blow, while sliding her blade into her would-be killer's leg. He cried out as the razor sharp edge bit through flesh and touched muscle and bone. Mara continued to roll forward, moving herself several feet from him. He collapsed under his own weight, unable to support himself on only one leg as Mara quickly scrambled away, dragging her blade from the floor to her side.

Her opponent held his sword tightly in front of him even from his awkward kneeling position. She took a circular glance but saw no one else coming in her immediate direction before she turned back to the injured man. "Do you really want to fight me injured?" He looked at her for several moments, then dropped the blade. She kicked it away from his reach. "Stay down. If you attempt to rise, I will kill you."

She turned back to the frenzy around her and realized suddenly that the fighting had stopped. Her eyes flew to Garreth, and she followed his gaze. Near the front of the stairs stood a man Mara vaguely recognized as a noble of the Arum Court. He had short black hair, dark brown eyes and dark, tanned skin. His blade was silver and the sharp edge was pressed against the delicate line of Nolan's throat. "I'll kill him."

Mara took several steps forward, ignoring the warning, when Garreth spoke from behind her. "Wait, Mara don't."

She paused in her movements but did not remove her eyes from the assassin before her. "If I put down this blade, they will kill him anyway."

"No," the man replied in a tight, controlled voice. "You have my word, upon the Gods. Surrender and no harm will come to the boy."

"Jayden." Nolan gave a name to the man holding him hostage. "Why are you doing this?"

Jayden pulled Nolan closer against him, using Nolan's body as both hostage and shield. "No more games." His eyes scanned the room, but his words were meant for Mara alone. "Drop the sword, or I kill him."

Mara forced herself to draw a sharp breath, her eyes recognizing the deadly Arius blade clutched in Jayden's hand. "I have never dropped my sword for anyone, Sub-Captain Jayden. I'm afraid, that I cannot oblige..."

Jayden pressed the Arius blade more firmly against Nolan's throat. A trickle of blood seeped to the surface of his skin; a drop of crimson against a sea of white.

An icy hand seemed to clutch Mara's heart. Instead of resisting, she closed her eyes and welcomed it, allowing the cold to spread over her body like a suffocating blanket. Many claimed that killing was like a fire—something between rage and fierce passion. But for Mara, it had always been the opposite.

With her eyes still closed, she could almost picture herself encased in an icy wasteland on the edge of night. It was a calm world, a place where no fire, no passion, no emotion could hope to survive. It was here she went, to the place inside that Mara had been forced to lock herself inside the night Liza had died. The night Phillip had stepped into the sea. The night she had crossed blades with... Here, was where Mara died and the Captain of the Black Rose was born.

She opened her eyes slowly, giving the full weight of her gaze to Nolan. "I'm sorry." Her voice was quiet, calm. "Nolan, I hereby name you to the

Rose. To die with all the expected honors accorded to one of your title and rank." She met Nolan's frightened eyes, but had no comfort to offer. She began to take the fatal step forward, when a voice rang out.

"No! Mara, don't." Edward's voice poured over her like liquid fire, melting the protective layer of ice surrounding her. She turned as though in a daze to face the only captain she had ever known. "Drop the blade, Mara. Please...do it for me."

Staring into Edward's dark eyes, Mara released her grip on the silver blade. It clattered to the stone floor. She did not speak a word when two of her yet to be named attackers approached her. They took her arms almost gingerly, moving them behind her back and slipping steel manacles around her slender wrists.

Then another voice rose. "What are you doing, Jayden?" Regald asked from a few paces to Edward's right.

Jayden's head snapped towards where Mara stood. "Captain Regald. Did the king send you to make sure we did our job? You can assure him that Viktor," he motioned to a tall man standing beside him with dark brown hair and eyes of liquid gold, "and I have this well under control."

"What are you talking about?" Regald took several steps forward. "What the hell are you doing here?" Jayden's eyes narrowed as he stared at the other man. "It is forbidden to attack the Black Rose."

"I could ask you the same question."

"I am escorting the future princess to see Captain Mara, per Lady Sandra's request."

Jayden's eyes flew to the young woman standing between Edward and Phillip as though he had not realized she was there, and perhaps he had not. "Lady Sandra? What..." Jayden shook his head without removing his blade from the side of Nolan's neck. "I am following the orders of my king, Captain. Will you join us or not?"

Regald gazed around the room until his eyes finally settled upon Mara's still form, the silver blade lying at her feet. "You forget, I was once a member of the Black Rose. I will not betray its captain."

"Then you will be exiled from your court as an oath-breaker and traitor to the king."

"The king himself once served Mara, and was allowed to the throne only with her blessing and power. Something he seems to have forgotten long ago." Regald met Mara's violet eyes. "I stand with the Captain of the Rose."

"So be it." Jayden motioned to another of the men who approached Regald, tying his hands with a thick, coarse rope that bit into his skin as it was tightened.

Regald turned back to Jayden, anger showing plainly on his face. "What about Lady Sandra?"

Jayden turned his gaze back to the young woman, draped in a simple gown of blue crushed velvet. "She will be returned to the court. The king can decide what is to be done with her there."

The young girl looked at Regald with wild eyes. "Do not fear," he assured her in spite of the predicament in which he now found himself. "You are the fiancée of the Crown Prince of the Arum Court. These men will not harm you."

Fear showed plainly on Sandra's pale features as Regald assured her:"I will come for you, my lady. You have my word."

"Silence!" Jayden finally stated. "Take them below. Bring the girl to me."

The three captains, along with other members of the Black Rose Guard, were herded to the stone steps and forced into the bowels of the castle. Though they had not been used in centuries, the dungeons were still in good repair and would be more than capable of preventing the escape of their former masters.

Garreth was moved into the cell first, while Edward was forced into the second. Jayden kept his blade trained on Nolan while another member of his guard who Regald had previously identified as Viktor grabbed Mara, jerking hard on her right arm, turning her to stare into his golden eyes. "The mighty Captain of the Rose," he taunted. "Perfectly prepared to let every single person she has ever known die. Yet a single word from Edward and you surrender all."

He laughed. Mara met his gaze, silently cursing him with her cold eyes. Viktor then reached carefully into his left pocket and withdrew a syringe filled with a clear liquid capped by a plastic cylinder. He handed the protected needle to Mara and pushed her into the cell where Edward already stood against the back wall. Once inside, Mara turned to face him, apprehensively awaiting his next demand.

It was Jayden who spoke. "If you want the boy to live, you will take that needle in your hand and inject its contents directly into Edward's bloodstream."

Mara froze, her mind shifting silently through the list of liquids the syringe might contain. There were only a limited number that could affect an immortal and even fewer with the capacity to cause harm. Anger radiated through her violet eyes as she stared at the man threatening Nolan's life. "Do it, Mara." Jayden moved the blade lower and gave Nolan a shallow cut across his upper chest.

Nolan hissed at the blade's razor-sharp precision. Edward stepped forward, his sleeve already rolled up around his left arm. Mara carefully removed the cap from the needle and turned to face him.

"Here," Edward offered his arm. She maneuvered towards the exposed flesh, but when she attempted to place the needle to Edward's arm, she froze. More names appeared on the list of possible poisons and Mara's hand began to tremble. Cyanide would prevent tissues from absorbing oxygen, slowly causing suffocation. Conium would cause paralysis, while leaving the mind fully capable of being aware its surroundings. Belladonna could cause hallucinations, spasms and painful convulsions which would torment its immortal victim for hours.

Edward reached forward and tried to close his hand upon the syringe, when Mara jerked away from him and stepped back several paces.

"Mara," Edward attempted to assure her. "It's okay."

Mara plunged the needle deep into her left arm. A stinging sensation accompanied the motion as she forced the clear liquid through the layers of her skin, into the veins beneath. The motion was completed before anyone could draw the breath required to utter protest. Edward's eyes flashed in a mixture of anger and fear, then Mara turned and tossed the used needle back through the iron bars of the cell to clatter to the ground at the feet of her captors. "Self-sacrifice," Viktor stated in a mocking tone. "As noble as they say."

No sooner had his words faded then Mara's vision began to blur. She blinked several times, but the sensation grew worse. Cold fingers began to crawl slowly up her back, beginning at the base of her spine climbing towards her neck. She began to shiver, as though someone was pouring ice through her veins where warm blood had flowed only moments before. As the chills trailed up Mara's tall frame, she found herself unable to suppress a gasp as the figment of cold, icy fingers touched her suddenly constricted throat. As her shivering quickly became visible to the naked eye, Viktor gave a cruel laugh before promptly turning and exiting the room.

Edward grabbed Mara's shaking form. "What did they give you, Mara?"

"I don't know," she said through chattering teeth. She had to fight to draw breath then managed to whisper a single word: "Cold."

She drew short, quick breaths as a tightness entered her chest, accompanied by a sharp pain in her left side which would have brought Mara to her knees had Edward's arms not moved securely around her. "Damn it, Mara!" Edward's voice sounded tight with restrained anger.

Mara ignored the frantic statement, concentrating too hard on breathing to respond. Keeping his right hand on her shoulder, Edward managed to shrug out of his long black coat and tossed it to the ground. He lowered Mara onto the woolen fabric, following her to the stone floor.

He lay her body gently upon the cloth and pulled her head against his chest. She scrambled for his hand which she clutched like a lifeline, digging her nails deep into his skin as another painful spasm tore through her left side.

Her vision went from blurred to unrecognizable as she clung to Edward, fighting to breathe. "Hold on," Edward said, but his voice seemed distant, filtered. Then the world began to fade.

CHAPTER XXVIII

NOLAN SAT IN THE CORNER of his cell with his face buried into the palm of his hands. "What have I done?

"You can't blame yourself," Garreth said from beside him.

"But it was my fault. If I hadn't been there, then she never would have..."

"Mara knew what she was doing when she dropped her blade."

"But she wouldn't have done it if I hadn't..."

"Nolan," Garreth interrupted. "That decision was made by the captains. Let the consequences lie with them." Garreth gently touched the younger man's arm, slowly coaxing him to reluctantly lower his hands.

"They are hurting her because of me. She's a hero...my hero. It's my fault they are doing this to her. I am not worthy of such sacrifice."

"I'll say again, Nolan. Mara knew what she was doing when she dropped that blade." He paused before adding, "If it helps, she didn't do it for you anyway."

"For Edward?" Garreth's lack of response was answer enough. "I understand they have this love story. But I don't understand what happened. Why did Edward stay when Mara left? Why have I never even heard of them being in the same room before, let alone in love? I saw the look on Edward's face when she showed up to save him from the Arum dungeons. He looked shocked, like she was a ghost."

Garreth glanced around, but the guards stood on the far side of the room which would make their conversations difficult to overhear. "Mara had not seen Edward in half a millennium."

"But why? I mean, all you have to do is look at them." His gaze trailed to the cell across the room. Mara lay unconscious in Edward's arms. "How could they stand it?"

Garreth sighed. "How far have you gotten in the book I gave you?"

Nolan thought for several moments and then said, "She was invading the court. She had gathered the royal family into the parlor."

"Yes," Garreth replied. "I remember."

1400 AD

THE ROOM HAD BEEN VAST. A fire blazed along the back wall with a series of blue velvet chairs standing before it. Numerous members of the guard lined the wall awaiting orders of their captains who had entered the room moments before. The highest ranking members of the guard—Brendan, Regald, Mathew, Phillip, and Mara—were in matching black cloaks with the silver mark of the rose etched into the dark material. On the opposite side of the room stood the royals of the Muir Court.

King Dacian was a tall, handsome man. He was broad across the shoulders with deeply tanned skin from his many days along the beaches that lined his kingdom by the sea. Sophia, his golden-haired queen of over a thousand years, stood to his left.

Draped only in a thin gown of white silk, the queen stood closest to the fire. The family had been held in this room for several hours while the Rose, along with the army of the Ciar Court, had secured the ground, killing all in their path. Now, only the royal family remained of one court that had been so powerful only hours before.

Mara stood in silence, watching the gathered group for what seemed a long time before she drew a deep breath and began to cross to the opposite side of the circular room. She paused a few paces from them, Phillip and Mathew flanking her on either side.

"At last," it was the king who spoke, "someone in charge. Princess Mara, what is the meaning of this?"

Mara ignored the question, her eyes focused upon the tall man standing to the king's right. "Would you like to tell him, Prince Nicholi, or should I?"

"I have no idea what you are talking about," the prince lied.

Her eyes narrowed. "Then you are even more of a coward then I originally envisioned. Or is it that your father is already aware of your crimes?"

The king's voice cut through Mara's words. "Where is Queen Clarissa? I demand to see her."

"You will not be making any demands today, Your Majesty." She turned her violet eyes upon his blue ones, laced with white like waves foaming in the sea, before turning back to the prince. "I ask again, would you like to tell your father why we are here?"

"Because you're insane," came his response.

She ignored the statement, allowing more silence to slide between them before she took a step back to stand alongside Phillip and Mathew. "Fine, I will tell him." She placed her hand upon the hilt of the blade sheathed at her side. "Prince Nicholi of the Muir Court, I charge you with the murder of

Princess Liza Sethian of the Ciar Court. In the name of the ancient Order of the Black Rose and the captain of her memorial guard, I have come to see her avenged." She drew a deep breath. "Confess your sins, Your Highness, and this shall all be over quickly. Lie and you shall face the wrath of my entire guard."

He stared at her, surprise showing through his features. It was again the king who spoke. "How dare you make such an accusation! I demand to see your queen!"

"With all due respect," Phillip said from beside Mara, "the Captain of the Rose outranks the queen in this matter, as well you know, Your Majesty."

Mara never removed her eyes from Nicholi's. "Do you confess to the murder of our princess?"

"I'll say again, Mara. You are insane."

Mara watched him for several moments, then she stepped to her right and grabbed the arm of the king's middle daughter, Princess Cordelia. She was tall and slender with long hair that was so blonde it was almost white. Mara dragged her several feet across the room while several members of the Rose stepped forward with blades drawn to stand between the royals and their captain. Mara then turned the girl roughly to face her brother, forcing Cordelia's back against her chest. Mara reached her hand forward and grabbed the princess by the back of her neck, directing her line of sight to Nicholi's. "Confess your sins, Nicholi. Confess to the murder of our princess."

"Let her go," the prince replied. "She has nothing to do with this."

"Then tell me the truth. Tell me how you killed her." Mara's voice held a calm that was far more dangerous than her anger. "Why did you kill our princess?"

"I did not."

Mara stared across the room directly into the eyes of the Crown Prince as she raised her silver blade and slit his sister's throat, covering her hand in a gush of warm, wet blood. The king raced forward, only to be met by Phillip who plunged his own silver blade deep into the king's chest. It ripped through skin and muscle, separating bones to pierce the king's lungs. Then Phillip stepped back, jerking his deadly blade from the king's chest as he fell to the floor, unable to breathe. The entire room stood frozen for a moment before the queen let out a scream, scrambling to the side of her fallen husband.

The prince took a step forward, rage burning through his deep blue eyes. Mathew and Regald moved forward as one, grabbing the prince by both arms, forcing him to his knees. They held him there, forcing his arms behind his back, putting their full strength into the movements. His sisters began to sob from several paces behind them, but they dared not move for fear of the seasoned warriors surrounding them. The prince lowered his head as far towards the ground as he could with the hold on his arms, anguish showing plainly upon his features. "They are Arius blades, Prince Nicholi; killer of the immortals. There is no coming back from their strokes." Mara drew a slow breath. "Now tell me, Your Highness. Do you confess to the murder of Princess Liza Sethian of the Ciar Court?"

Nicholi jerked his head from the ground in his kneeling position. "If you are going to kill me, then do it."

She moved left and grabbed the youngest of his sisters. At only a hundred years old, Princess Yara had hair more golden than either of her two sisters. She forced Yara across the room as more men stepped forward, placing themselves between where the prince knelt and where Mara now stood. Mara turned the youngest of the Muir Court princesses in front of her, holding her in a similar fashion as to how she had held Cordelia, placing the princess' back against her chest. Mara then aligned her silver blade with the princess' throat and stared coldly at Nicholi.

"Tell me how you killed Princess Liza!"

"I did not kill her!" Nicholi stated. "My sisters have nothing to do with this. They are innocent, for Gods' sake! Mara, please!"

Yara died with a single stoke of the blade.

Nicholi attempted to rise from the ground, fighting the two men who held him, but it was no use as Mathew and Regald held him tightly. Eventually they forced his torso to the ground so he went from a kneeling position to lying flat. The prince made a sound that was neither sob nor scream but something in between, full of anguish at watching his family die. "Your brother is next," she stated. "Confess and I will put you in his place.

"Damn you!" Nicholi shouted. "Curse you! By the Gods of old I curse you, Mara Sethian. You killed them! Innocent girls!"

"Then may the Gods curse us both," she replied. "As it is no more than you once did to our princess. The girl, the child, whose body you sliced into bloody strips until we could barely even recognize her. You sister did not suffer half of what my princess endured as she fought to draw her last breath." Her eyes fell upon the remaining siblings, a younger brother and his eldest sister, both golden-haired. "Is that what I should do? Shall I slice through their pale, flawless skin? Slip my blade into the sockets of their sea-blue eyes? Shall I tear their bodics until not even you can recognize their remains? Is that what I must do, before you will confess?"

"No, please." Nicholi's voice was frantic, fearful and left no doubt that he believed that Mara would carry out her threat.

Mara bent down to her knees in front of the prince who was still being held in his helpless position. "Confess," she demanded. "Confess."

The prince drew a ragged breath and finally said, "Okay. I killed her! I killed Princess Liza."

Mara drew a deep breath, a relief pouring through her from a tension she had not known had existed. Her voice came out enraged and unsteady, her calmness of moments ago vanishing in a single word: "Why?"

"Because I had come to make her my bride only to find that she had been sleeping with the captain of your guard. Tainted, spoiled, ruined! So I cut her, one piece at a time. Oh how she cried out as we cut into her skin. She called for you, did you know that, Mara? She called your name as we stabbed our blades through her chest and cut her skin into long, bloody ribbons." Mara felt her hand tightening on the blade against her will. "Two princesses ruined by the same man. Tell me, Mara, did you stand guard while he fucked her?"

Mara brought her sword down with all her strength. The blade sank through his neck, severing his spinal cord, leaving his head attached to his body by only a few strands of skin. Blood spurted, splashing over the two men who held the prince, causing them to jerk back in surprise.

Mara again brought down the blade, the two remaining siblings standing in shocked silence. More blood splashed upon her dark cloak. A third time and Nicholi's head was completely removed from his body. A fourth, fifth, sixth...Mara lost count, bringing her sword down in a rage which knew no end.

It was Garreth who, finally stepping away from his place by the far door, touched her shoulder. She whirled around, causing him to side-step her wild turn of the sword. He grabbed her arm, forcing it down to her side. "It's over, Mara. It's over." Her body trembled. Her face and both of her hands were crimson, covered in blood most royal. "It's over."

She stared at him for several long moments before her eyes trailed past him, and she realized that Edward had, at long last, arrived. She stared into his jet black eyes and said, "Kill them."

She did not turn to look at the rest of the slaughter, only listened silently to the screams as the last prince, princess and finally, the Queen of the Muir Court were slaughtered by her men. When the last scream had died, Mara Sethian, Captain of the Black Rose Guard, walked across the room and took a formal bow before Edward, bending at the waist, without ever removing her violet eyes from his dark ones. "Behold the murderer of Princess Liza," she stated in a voice with all emotion long spent. "May the Black Rose protect you in life, or avenge you in death."

She then straightened and issued an order to the men standing behind her. "Burn it. Burn it all."

Then she left the room without another word, walking past Edward into the halls beyond.

Present Day

"EDWARD NEVER FORGAVE HER." GARRETH'S voice was a mere whisper across the dark cell in which he sat beside Nolan, his eyes trailing to Mara's still form, cradled in the circle of Edward's arms.

"For avenging the princess?"

"Yes...and no."

They sat still for a long time. "Wait," Nolan suddenly said. "Something's not right."

Garreth forced his attention back to the younger man.

"You named three princesses, the Crown Prince, and one younger brother."

"That's right."

"But in the book, Mara said there were three princes. Three of each, I'm almost sure of it."

Nolan suddenly seemed even younger, a child raised in a time of peace. "Yes," he answered. "There was another: Prince Dorian. He was four years old. The nursery was in a different part of the castle. His maid managed to hide him along the edge of the beach before members of the guard found her." Garreth's words trailed off again.

"What happened to him?"

"You don't understand, do you, Nolan? The oath of the Black Rose which you have attempted to take in such ignorance? It is an ancient oath, one to supersede all bonds of friendship, fidelity and love. An oath taken before the oldest and most powerful of the Gods of old. Mara swore to destroy the line which killed our princess." Garreth gazed up at Nolan with an expression he did not understand. "You asked what happened to the child, the last Prince of the Muir Court?" His gaze trailed again to where Edward sat, his back against the thick metal bars of his entrapment. "Mara killed him. A sin for which she has never been forgiven."

CHAPTER XXIX

MARA AWOKE TO FIND BOTH arms encircled with thin, silver chains which held her securely to a silver chair. She was disoriented, the world out of focus as though the injected drug had not completely worked its way through her bloodstream. The light was harsh upon her eyes and it took several moments before she was fully able to examine the scene around her.

Edward stood near the center of the room bared to the waist. His arms were forced above his head in thick, silver chains, pulling his body taut. She continued to trail her gaze across the room to find it nearly barren, save for a single black table to her right upon which laid an array of cruel-looking instruments meant for a single purpose. Beside the table, holding a thin silver blade, stood Viktor.

"Well," Viktor said, "it would seem our Briar Rose has awakened. Welcome, Mara." Viktor stepped closer to his seated captive, holding out the blade as though for her inspection.

She looked at him fearlessly through the slowly lifting fog, leaning forward in her chair. "I'm ready."

"Fearless," Viktor responded. "I was told it was one of your many faults."

"Deadly," she replied, "would be another."

He moved the tip of the sword closer, stopping mere inches from her skin.

She looked up at him with cold eyes. "If you touch me with that blade, my young, young lord," she paused to let silence emphasize her words, "I will kill you." She forced her body forward, pushing her chest lightly against the blade. Viktor pulled his arm back before blood could be drawn. Mara continued to glare coldly into Viktor's golden eyes as realization slowly dawned. The curve of his lips began to harden to a straight line, the spark of laughter faded, and yet still, Mara continued to stare silently upon her would-be torturer.

Viktor straightened his posture and turned slightly toward where Edward stood chained in the center of the room. He put the tip of the blade to Edward's chest and dragged the blade lightly over Edward's skin. "Well," he said slowly, "since it seems that you are prepared to welcome your fate, let's say we start with him."

The sight of the blood running down Edward's chest drew Mara's gaze as a moth to a flame. She watched it well to the surface and slide slowly down his pale skin in slender streaks. Her eyes followed the crimson trail, so striking against his white skin.

Edward did not offer a repeat of Mara's threats, but instead remained silent as Viktor pressed the blade into his left shoulder, against his collarbone. Viktor moved down Edward's shoulder before returning to his chest. He pressed lightly, just enough to draw blood. He slowly moved the thin blade in long, vertical strokes. Mara watched Viktor's movements, unable to remove her eyes from the lines of blood which were slowly beginning to change the color of Edward's skin from white to red.

Memories poured through her, increasing in their intensity. As she watched, the skin began to split, the cuts growing wider until Edward's chest was a mass of blood, the cuts becoming inseparable as his chest transformed into a single, gaping wound.

Mara blinked. When her eyes opened, the cuts were again thin, shallow marks. However, moments later, they began to widen as though living things slithering across his chest. Her heart rate began to increase, thrumming through her body as bile rose in her throat. She tried again to clear her vision, but this time it was to no avail. She stared at the injuries that continued to widen, exposing bone and muscle. As the blade again struck his collarbone, this time above his right arm, a slight hiss escaped Edward's lips.

A high-pitched, feminine laugher entered the room at the sound of Edward's gasp. Mara's body jerked involuntarily and she pulled against the silver cuffs.

She thrashed, throwing her weight against the chains, which cut into her wrists, causing them to become slick with blood. She ignored the pain, pulling even harder, but the chains did not budge.

The blade slid down Edward's right side, slipping into his ribcage, drawing another hiss from his lips. "No!" Mara's voice came out against her will. "No, no, no!" She jerked her left arm so hard that she cursed from the pain. "No!" she repeated as panic began to grip her. "Don't please, don't!" She again threw her body to the left, letting out a sharp cry of pain as she pulled her left arm from its socket.

Viktor paused his ministrations and turned to stare at Mara with a sense of bewilderment. "No, no, no," she said again, only this time her voice rose in a shrill scream as the laughter that had faded long ago danced throughout the dimly lit room. The blood that seeped from Edward's shallow wounds began to cascade down his body, forming a pool of blood which raced across the floor as though it possessed a living, breathing purpose. It spread through the room, climbing up the walls as Mara let out an ear-shattering scream.

"What the hell?" Viktor asked. He stepped briskly across the room towards the writhing girl. When he touched her arm, she began to shriek.

It was Edward's voice which cut through her panic. "Mara," he called. "Look at me!" The vision receded slightly at the sound of his voice. "Please, Mara."

She forced herself to find his gaze, as she had all those years ago. She remembered his screams, kneeling in a pool of wet blood, the metallic taste...

"Mara!" Edward called again.

"No!" she sobbed, pleaded, begged. "No, no...Edward! Please don't make me. *minime, precor.*" Tears streamed down her face. She again thrashed against her chains, this time letting out a sharp scream at the jarring movement of her dislocated shoulder and the chains which had begun to cut through to the tendons of her wrists. "Please, Edward; *minime precor.* I cannot watch her do this anymore!"

"Her? What is going on?"

"Don't make me. I cannot! Edward, please no. Do not make me watch her hurt you again." She shook her head, the blood from her vision refusing to recede from the floor.

"Mara..."

"No, no, no!" Her body gave way to great, heaving sobs.

Mara was unaware when Viktor unhooked Edward from his chains, nor was she aware when the man she loved raced forward, unshackling the bonds which held her prisoner. She scrambled away from him, avoiding his touch, unable to recognize that it was Edward whose hands were attempting to calm her. She tried to slide across the stone floor when he finally grabbed her, drawing her body slowly towards him in spite of the blood still trailing down his chest.

"Mara, it's me," he said to the hysterical girl in his arms. "It's Edward. Please, Mara." He kept his voice in as soothing a tone as possible. She struck out against him with her good arm, but he forced her closer, clutching tightly while attempting to avoid further damage to her injured shoulder. "Mara," he said again. "Oh, my sweet rose." Her body was wracked by great, heaving sobs as he tightened his arms around her slender frame. "Mara, it's me. It's Edward. Do you hear me? I'm right here. Right here."

"Please," she whispered through her tears. "Don't let her do it. I can't survive it. Don't make me. Please, Edward. Don't make me."

"She's not here, Mara. Open your eyes, Mara. The queen is not here."

Mara clung to the sound of Edward's voice as fiercely as his arms held her physical form. "*minime, precor,*" she begged through inconsolable tears. "Don't leave me alone. I can't...can't." She began to choke on her sobs, pulling at the deepest recess of Edward's soul. "I'm sorry. I couldn't save you. I'm sorry, I'm sorry, I'm sorry. Don't leave me. Don't go."

"Shh." He again tried to calm her. "I am not going anywhere, do you hear me? Not anywhere." Edward held her. Held her as he had when she was a child and he had been forced to inform her that her father had been killed; and again a year later when her mother had chosen to follow him into an immortal grave, leaving her daughter kneeling a pool of immortal blood.

"Mara." He again spoke her name gently, conveying a mix of sorrow and love which, despite everything, had always been reserved for Mara alone. "I am here," he assured her again and again. "My Mara, my rose...I am here."

Her sobs began to quiet as he held her in his arms. Her trembling lessened. He continued to soothe her. "*te amo, rosa, mea rosa immortalis.*" He spoke in the language of their childhood, holding her tightly in his arms. "*tuta es: te tuebor, adsum, mea rosa, mea dulcis, mi amor.*"

You are safe with me. I will protect you. I am here, my rose, my sweet, my love.

CHAPTER XXX

EDWARD CRADLED MARA IN THE circle of his arms until long after she had spent her tears. With her head against the right side of his blood-caked chest, Edward ran his hand lightly along the edge of her dark hair, listening to the steady rhythm of her breathing. She seemed almost peaceful lying against him, her soft hair flowing in layers down her back, framing her flushed cheeks. His mind trailed back to one of the last times she had lay in his arms, equally exhausted from the trauma she had been forced to endure at the hands of the queen. His heart ached at the realization that she was once again being forced to endure the effects of that night long ago.

He continued to stroke her hair as his memory traveled back even further, to the twenty-five years he had been forced away from all he knew. All those cold, winter nights where his only warmth was the memory of Mara's arms, the fire that burned in her eyes saving him night after night, yet always fading with the first rays of the morning light. Those endless nights rose from the past, crashing against him in a suffocating wave. He stared down at the sleeping girl, who suddenly seemed so fragile in him arms.

"*ignosce mihi, mea rosa immortalis, mi amor,*" he whispered. "Please forgive me. I am so sorry, *mi amor.* How I have wronged you." He continued to lay there holding her close, a part of him wondering if he was ever again going to be able to let her go. "I am not going anywhere," he repeated his earlier promise. "*adsum, mea rosa, mi amor.* I am here."

Edward was unsure how long he sat there holding her. Sporadically her body tensed, but each time he would wrap her more tightly in his arms, soothing her with tender tones. She had screamed as he had forced her arm back into place, and had spent several hours in and out of consciousness as it healed. She let out another soft moan. "It's okay," he said gently.

"Edward," she whispered. "Please don't go." If her words were actual pleas or the reminiscence of dreams, he was uncertain. When the echo of approaching footsteps sounded, Edward attempted to move Mara to the floor, but froze when she began to stir. He paused, deciding to allow her those last few moments of rest before their captors returned.

To his surprise, the man who rounded the corner was not dressed in red, but instead in the dark garb of the Black Rose. Brendan walked quickly to the gate and addressed Edward. "I came down through the side passageway. Mara had it boarded up a few centuries ago, so our 'friends' were unaware of its existence." He pulled the blade from his side. "I can break the lock but they might hear..." It was at that moment that the man's gaze fell to where Mara lay in the protective circle of Edward's arms. "What happened?"

Edward ignored the question, instead raising his hand to Mara's cheek, waking her as gently as possible.

"Edward?"

"My lady, your men are here." He proceeded to assist her into a seated position, turning her towards the man standing on the opposite side of the cell.

"Brendan."

"Yes, my lady," he said and gave a slight bow. "Jonathan went to release Nolan, Regald and Garreth. They are being held together in the next hallway. Only two intruders have been seen on this level, but there are at least eight more upstairs."

Mara stared forward, but did not respond to the question. Instead, it was Edward who took charge. "Get us out of here," he instructed. "We will join the others at the stairs from which you came. Then we will deal with the rest of the men."

He stood, pulling Mara to her feet. She stood unsteadily, her arms limp at her side as Edward guided her towards the door. As they reached the exit, Edward turned her back to face him. "Mara," he said firmly. "We are about to go upstairs in the middle of a fight. A fight we cannot win without you." He drew a deep breath. "I know you are tired. I know you are hurting. But right here, right now, we need you." He stared directly into her eyes. "I need you."

Mara gave a slow, reluctant nod and then turned back towards the bars where Brendan stood waiting. She echoed Edward's commands. "Get us out."

"Yes, Captain." Brendan walked to the lock and withdrew a key from the pocket of his black slacks. Moments later, Brendan slid open the cell door. "Come," he directed them. "I believe we successfully incapacitated all the men at this level, but I am not certain. We should move quickly."

"Lead the way," Edward said to the sub-captain, who turned and walked down the left side of the dimly lit corridor.

Two minutes and three turns later, they found themselves standing at the bottom of the previously hidden staircase. Waiting for them were the other members of their party; Regald, Garreth and Nolan stood beside their rescuers, Jonathan, Aiden and Brian.

Mara drew a deep breath and turned to face her second in command. "I don't suppose..."

"Right here," Brendan said, anticipating her request and holding out a thick silver sword which he offered to his captain hilt-first. The familiar weight of the blade helped to steady her. Then Brendan turned and handed an additional blade to Edward. "Your personal blades are upstairs," Brendan informed the group. "But these should suffice."

Edward gave a single nod as Brendan moved towards the stairs. "These will lead us into a side room," he informed the others, "which opens through a stone door into the front entryway of the castle." Edward nodded in acknowledgment before Brendan turned and began to ascend the long, winding staircase. Edward and Mara brought up the rear. As they reached the top, Mara began to exit the stairwell when Edward grabbed her arm. He pushed her against the side of the dark stone wall.

"Edward?" Mara asked uncertainly.

He took a step forward, closing the distance between them. "There is a fight outside these doors—and the men are deadly, Mara."

She shook her head. "Your point?"

"Look at me."

"I am."

"Look me in the eye. Tell me you are going to make it through this fight."

Her violet eyes ignited. "I am the Captain of the Black Rose Guard."

"No," he challenged. "This morning you were. But right here, right now, you are not."

"How dare you!"

"Mara," he said, cutting through her words. "You are not the Captain of the Rose today."

"What the hell are you saying? I am most..."

"You're shaken and ignoring that could cost you your life."

"Why do you care?" Her anger increased with each word. "What the hell do you care? You haven't cared in centuries!"

Edward stood motionless as Mara met his dark eyes in challenge. She scoffed in a disgusted tone and began to push past him. She had taken little more than a step before Edward reached forward and forced her back against the wall. She parted her lips to curse him when he leaned forward and offered a deep, bruising kiss.

By the time he pulled back, she was breathless. A mix of emotions rose through her too quickly for her to feel any of them. She then forced herself to slowly, carefully draw a deep breath before closing her eyes.

Mara dug deeply to that cold, wintery wasteland she knew all too well. As the familiar ice began to wrap securely around her, she opened her eyes.

"I am the Captain of the Black Rose. And every single man standing outside those doors," she spoke the next words slowly, "is going to die."

Edward did not answer, but instead stepped to the left, allowing Mara to walk past him and through the door.

They emerged into a well-lit room crafted from the same dark stone which formed the rest of the ancient castle. The other men were standing in the center, awaiting the arrival of their captains. Mara's gaze flew to where Garreth stood beside Nolan and then she addressed the younger of the two. "Are you injured?" she inquired.

"No, my lady," came the reply. "None of us were harmed."

Mara gave a nod in their direction and then turned to address her sub-captain. "We do this quickly. Give me the report."

"Eight confirmed men on the premises. Not sure on the original intent, but for the last few hours it has seemed as though they have been awaiting instructions. And," he drew a quick breath, "I can personally confirm that at least four of the seven—Viktor, Jayden, Fynn, and Alicia—are members of the Arum Court Guard."

Mara's eyes flew to Regald.

"They all are," he confirmed. "But I swear, upon my honor as a former member of the Rose, I have no idea of either their mission or intentions." He turned towards Brendan. "There was a young woman who arrived with us—black hair, blue eyes—do you know what they did with her?"

"I saw her," Aiden interjected from Regald's left. "They put her in a car right after the fight. Is she a hostage?"

The question brought a pause of consideration, then Regald shook his head. "That remains uncertain. However, she is the Prince's fiancée, and therefore likely in no immediate danger. Let us deal with the men outside, and then I will fill the rest of you in on her story."

"All right," Mara answered as she again surveyed the room. "We have multiple captains here. However, this is Black Rose territory, thus rules of combat dictate that all other courts yield the chain of command. Any objections, speak now." She paused for several seconds, but no one chose to challenge this standard rule of battle. "I'm in charge, Brendan is second and Garreth, as a former sub-captain of the Rose, is third. Edward, I expect you to keep Nolan by your side during this battle." She shifted her eyes to the younger man. "You are to stay with Edward at all times. This is not a request and if you don't agree, then you shall not be permitted in this battle, no matter how badly your sword may be needed. Understood?"

"Yes, my lady."

"Good." She nodded. "Last thing. These men invaded Black Rose territory. They threatened our lives and implemented dishonorable tactics in the highest degree." She swept the room, briefly catching the gaze of each individual standing before her. "The Black Rose," she stated, "knows no mercy in this matter—only vengeance." As the room fell to solemn, Mara motioned towards the door.

The door in question was tall and made of thick, dark stone. There was no way to open it quietly, so instead they forced it open in one swift motion.

Swords drawn, Garreth and Brendan led the way, leaving Mara a thirty second window to take in the layout of the room beyond. The majority of the invaders were gathered in a group on the opposite side of the room at the bottom of the stairs while two more were standing closer to the doors. The startled men began to draw their blades, but unfortunately for the two standing by the door, were not fast enough. Brendan and Garreth raced forward, Brendan slipping his blade deeply into the neck of the first man, while Garreth slashed expertly through the second man's chest. The wounds would not be fatal due to the ordinary blades being used. However, it would be more than enough to incapacitate them for the remainder of the fight.

A quick glance showed that Brendan's estimate had been correct; six men remained, now armed with drawn blades. Without pausing to issue either demands or threats, Mara moved forward with the men alongside her.

The invaders began to cross the room to meet them. "Viktor's mine," Mara informed the others as she centered herself to meet the identified man.

There was no pause or ceremony, merely the clang of metal as six sets of silver blades collided. Mara was grateful for the two-handed grip on her blade as the cold steel clashed against Viktor's, who easily had sixty pounds on her. She took a single step back, separating their blades. Viktor lunged forward. Mara side-stepped the attack, then swung her sword sideways, narrowly missing the line of his back.

Viktor turned quickly to face her, holding his blade close to his chest, awaiting Mara's next movement. "I would advise you to lower your blade," Mara stated. "However, I seem to remember promising to kill you, and, as you know, I have a reputation for never breaking a promise."

"Says the woman," Viktor retorted, "who cannot stomach even the merest sight of blood. All those tough words, yet a few shallow nicks with the blade are enough to send you screaming. I wonder if these men would still follow you if they knew the truth?"

Mara stared at him, the protective armor she had fought so hard to keep in place beginning to vanish. Jarred by his words, Mara was unprepared when he again lurched forward, guiding his blade into a downward stroke towards her lower stomach.

She jerked back, turned left, but not quickly enough to avoid sustaining a cut on her left arm. She let out a slight hiss and took several steps back, but Viktor pursued, pressing his momentary advantage.

Brought back to the fight by the sting of her arm, Mara parried Viktor's next downward stroke. She then stepped back and drew a deep breath, refocusing her full attention on the man standing in front of her. She again raised her blade, swinging it towards Viktor's left. The swords slammed against each other and Mara used the momentum to spin her body in the opposite direction. She aimed high as Viktor rushed to stop her, then switched the blade to a downward angle at the last moment.

The blade sank into Viktor's right hip. He cried out in pain as it tore through flesh and muscle to touch the bone. She then jerked back and aimed towards Viktor's left. He blocked the first stroke with some difficulty. She struck again, pouring all of her strength into the movement. The force of the swing knocked her opponent off-balance. A third swing and he began to fall, his injured leg unable to support his full weight. She followed him towards the ground with her weapon, finally able to slide the sharp edge into Viktor's left side.

He howled in pain at the contact, his own sword clattering to the floor. She again brought down her blade, this time cutting down the center of his chest, causing blood to spray on her hands and arms.

She brought the sword down one more time, leaving him writing in pain then turned to her left to assist Aiden, who was fighting a man she did not recognize. He was several inches taller than her, but this mattered little to the experienced captain. She placed herself between Aiden and his blond-haired opponent. "Go help the others," she instructed the lower-ranked member of her guard.

He did not speak, but instead turned to assist his brother who was engaged in his own fight a few feet to their right. She squared off with the new opponent, again gripping her thick blade with both hands. Her attacker struck first, moving his blade toward Mara's left. She easily sidestepped the movement, turning back with calm eyes. This time he moved in a downward stroke. Mara raised her own sword to directly meet the movement, stopping the cutting edge mere inches above her vulnerable form. She then moved quickly, slicing her sword left and then right, favoring speed over strength. Her blade again lunged to her opponent's left side. He was slow to follow her movement and received a deep slice to his left arm.

She again swung left, this time with three strokes in quick succession, then switched to his right. He was unprepared and her blade bit into his right side. He cried out in pain, the sword faltering in his hand, when she spied Edward from the corner of her eye. He had been disarmed by his opponent and now stood at the mercy of Jayden' silver blade.

The sight made Mara's blood run cold. She rushed forward, abandoning her current opponent in what amounted to a mad dash across the stone floor. But it was too late as Jayden moved the edge of his Arius blade to the side of Edward's throat and turned to face Mara, who froze as she met his gaze.

"I am going to ask you a question, Captain."

Mara took a moment of silence before giving a single, steady nod but was unable to slow the frantic beat of her heart.

"What is he to you?" Jayden nodded towards the man he held captive. "What, exactly, is Edward to you, the Captain of the Black Rose? Answer quickly."

She forced herself to meet his gaze and went for truth. "The other half of my soul. Please, Jayden, take me if you must, but...let Edward go."

"You love him," Jayden stated, through whether for clarification or repetition, Mara was uncertain.

"All my life."

"He was the one you rejected the king for. The one you let Phillip die for, and killed the young prince."

"Yes," she answered. "Yes."

Jayden continued to stare before finally stating, "It's true, isn't it? You would really trade your life for his."

"Without hesitation," she replied in a voice mixed with fear. "Is that what you want, Jayden? My life for his, here I am—take it. Please, take my life. Just don't...don't do this. I can't survive it."

Jayden cut his gaze to Edward and then back to Mara. "So it is all true. The dead princess, the forbidden love, the queen's vengeance. All the stories whispered on a dark night, are true." Mara gave him open eyes and it was all the confirmation he needed. "My Gods."

"Please, my lord. My life for his."

Jayden drew another breath and then, to the surprise of both captains, lowered his sword. "I am not worthy to kill the Captain of the Black Rose nor to take that of the man she gave her life to protect."

Her heart still pounding far too fast, Mara gave a nod and was careful to avoid Edward's eyes as she addressed Jayden. "Are you here to take the oath of the Rose? Or will you return to your king?"

"My oath lies with Mathew, my lady. I was sent after you, but have been deemed unworthy. I shall return to face the king with news of our defeat."

"Then go, my lord. With my thanks, but...not my mercy."

Jayden gave a single nod before turning to leave the castle grounds.

Mara turned to survey the damage surrounding her. Nolan stood in the far corner appearing exhausted but physically unharmed. Brian and Aiden were standing to her left, blood dripping from Aiden's forearm. Her eyes continued to search the room, a sense of relief beginning to settle upon her. Then she caught sight of Garreth.

He was kneeling on the floor, his blond hair matted against his forehead. Brendan was lying at his feet in a pool of blood. Mara blinked several times, wondering if this was another flashback. Then, realizing it was not, she rushed forward, crossing the room in a few quick strides. She hit her knees on the opposite side of Garreth and leaned forward to assess his injuries. There were two long gashes in his chest, one on each side. His breathing came in a faint wheeze, the damaged lungs unable to breathe as his blood continued to stain the floor.

"It will be all right," Mara assured the man who had fought by her side for more than half a millennium. "We will take you upstairs and it will all be..."

Her words faded as she caught sight of Garreth's face. It should have been flushed from the exertions of the fight, but was instead white, as though the color had been drained from his cheeks. His eyes were wide. Something in them sent a chill through Mara. "Garreth, what is it?"

He looked at her as though startled by the question. "Mara," he began in a timid voice.

"What is it?" she asked again, but was distracted by Edward, who appeared beside her holding out a relatively clean shirt. "I sent Nolan for bandages, but until then, use this." She took the shirt gratefully and pressed the dark cloth down upon the open wound.

"Mara," Garreth's voice again interrupted her as Edward moved to Brendan's other side.

"What?" she demanded. "What the hell do you want?"

"It was an Arius blade, Mara."

She gazed at him slowly, her brain refusing to comprehend the meaning behind his words. "It was not Jayden who did this and the king would never have given a non-captain an Arius blade."

"He took it from Regald," Garreth replied in a hushed voice. "When we surrendered our swords."

She stared at her cousin with an air of defiance. "We were in the middle of a fight, Garreth. Everything happened so fast..." Her eyes searched the room, though for what, she was uncertain. Then she returned her gaze to Garreth's. "How the hell do you know what blade he used? How dare you!"

"Mara," Garreth again said her name, this time with more conviction. "It was Regald's blade."

Mara's gaze again travelled to where her sub-captain lay. The cloth Edward had managed to tie around the injuries were now red with blood. She touched her fingers to Brendan's neck and listened for his heartbeat—it was erratic and began to slow under her touch. "Brendan," she said, unable to hide the disbelief which seeped into her voice. She moved her hand to cup the right side of his face. His eyes closed at her touch, then opened again slowly. She saw fear in those deep brown eyes along with a look she knew all too well. He was dying.

Mara's teeth bit into her lower lip as she forced herself to draw several deep, slow breaths. Then she unclenched her jaw, tasting blood from where her teeth had pierced. Nolan had arrived and was now assisting Edward in his attempts to slow the bleeding.

Mara drew another breath and quickly glanced around the room until her eyes came across Brendan's sword which lay slightly to her right. She reached across the floor and picked up the ancient blade before turning to Edward. She wondered for a moment if he would challenge her, but instead bowed his head and slid back from Brendan's injured form. Mara then turned to where Nolan knelt across from her.

"Nolan," she said gently. "You can stop now."

He turned towards her with a look that lacked understanding. "But we have to stop the bleeding."

"Nolan," she said again. "It's time to stop."

He looked at her with a confused expression. "But, he'll die."

A slight tremor ran up Mara's body, but she did not lower her gaze from the young man kneeling beside her in a pool of Brendan's blood. Then, Garreth moved to Nolan, and placed a hand upon the younger man's arms, gently pulling him away.

Mara took the thick, silver sword and placed it upon Brendan's chest, then moved his left hand to the hilt, while taking his right into her own. She leaned down and kissed the hand which clutched the blade before turning to stare into his brown eyes. "It was an honor," she said quietly, though her voice carried like a scream in the silence of the room. His eyes said what he could not speak. "I know it hurts," she told him gently, then drew another deep breath.

"There is a young woman who walks along the edge of the sea, soft waves foaming at her feet. Her eyes are violet, her smile gentle and her laughter—the sound of angels." Mara offered a false smile that she had given far too many times. "She is waiting on you, my lord. Go to her and be at peace."

A few moments later, Brendan stopped breathing. Mara reached forward and gently closed his eyes before leaning down and kissing his brow. "May the order of the Black Rose protect you in life, and avenge you in death," she said, speaking the ancient words before slowly rising from the dark stone floor.

She scanned the room, finding her desired object lying just a few feet away. Walking slowly across the floor, Mara knelt down and grasped the hilt of Regald's Arius blade. She turned and walked to where Viktor lay, his chest exposed in a similar fashion to Brendan's. Without hesitating or speaking, Mara raised the blade and sank it deep in the center of Viktor's still beating heart. He gasped as the blade slid home then began to gurgle as he choked on his own blood. Mara gave the blade a violent twist before removing the ancient blade from the dead man's chest. She turned, and without speaking a word, handed the blade back to the Arum Court captain before ascending the main staircase, leaving the room in silence.

CHAPTER XXXI

MARA STOOD UNDER THE scalding water as the last of Brendan's blood poured from her thick hair to cascade down her body before sliding across the white tiled floor and vanishing down the drain. The blood at her feet made her queasy and she was forced to steady herself against the wall. The fear that had flashed through Brendan's brown eyes as he lay dying upon the cold, stone floor would remain with her until the day someone closed her own. It was exactly the way he had looked during their first encounter, nearly nine hundred years earlier.

1100 AD

SHE HAD BEEN SITTING IN her room, speaking with Garreth, when she was interrupted by a loud knock. She moved to rise from her chair, but the door flew open before she could even call for the person on the other side to come in. "My lady, my lord," stated a young guard who immediately flew to one knee before the two sub-captains.

"What is it?" Mara asked, rising quickly to her feet.

"My lady. It's Andrew and Brendan, two of the recruits who joined the guard in the last initiation. They had been assigned to the guard detail for Lord Bersid, who was called in to see the queen this morning. Brendan, he..."

"Stand up, Raymond," she instructed the younger man. "Take a breath and tell us what happened."

He stood quickly, brushing his coat as he did so. "I am unsure of all the circumstances which lead to..."

"Just cut to the point."

"The queen was angry with the lord and somehow, I'm still not sure, her anger fell upon Jon. Brendan spoke in his defense and the queen..." Mara's heart began to sink. "She has ordered them both to the torture chambers, ordering Brendan's punishment to be carried out by Jon's own hand."

Mara shook her head. "In other words, she has found a way to punish them both; one for contradicting the queen and the other for defending him." She gave a deep sigh. "And you expect me to do what, exactly?"

"I-I-I," he began. "I don't know, my lady. I was told to come to you."

She paused, silently exploring her options, but arriving at no answers. "Raymond," she said, "take us to the chambers the queen sent them to. Quickly."

Raymond led Mara and Garreth from the room and rushed down a series of hallways and stairwells, diving into one of the deepest parts of the castle grounds. They eventually emerged into a dimly lit room of dark stone. In the center of the room was a black stone table upon which Brendan lay. His arms were chained to either side, binding him tightly to the stone. His shirt had been stripped away, exposing his flesh to the waiting punishment.

A few feet from him stood another young guard with short brown hair and olive skin. Clutched in Jon's hand was a long black whip.

Jon looked up as the two new visitors entered the room, but turned back towards Brendan when neither of the newcomers spoke. Mara's mind continued to race through her options, attempting to determine anything that could stop what was about to happen. Contradicting orders given directly from the queen was out of the question. She exchanged a glance with Garreth, who looked as helpless as she felt. Her eyes again traveled to the bound man. Brendan was only in his late thirties, barely an adult by immortal standards.

Jon had been in the same initiation class, and from what Mara could remember, was only a few years older. He was now standing before his friend with a whip clutched tightly in his hand. He moved the whip with unpracticed hands, sliding it across the stone floor and flipping it in an unsmooth arc. He smacked the whip against the stone floor, the sound reverberating through the room and it struck the ground once, twice, thrice. He again glanced at where the two sub-captains stood and again, they remained silent.

Mara's eyes trailed over Brendan's still form as she stepped around the room to see his face, which was turned to the left as he lay upon the stone table.

He seemed young in comparison to those of the higher guard. It was more a look than anything physical. A mixture of fear and confusion; the eyes of a man who was unaccustomed to seeing the more horrific parts of life. Mara's gaze then returned to the man with the whip. He looked almost as scared as the man lying on the table.

Jon again struck the floor with the long black whip and then finally drew back his arm to rake the sharp metal ends against Brendan's exposed flesh. It was at that moment in which Mara called out the only thing she could think of. "I demand the Right of Substitution."

Jon froze at her words. "Forgive me, my lady, but this matter does not concern you. There is no reason for you to do this."

"He is a member of the guard in which I am his superior," Mara answered, taking several steps closer to the young man clutching the whip. "Jon, Brendan is little more than a child. He had no idea what they were doing. You know that carrying out this punishment is not right."

He looked at her with uncertainty. "I cannot change the queen's commands."

"No, but we can save him from what you are about to do."

"My lady," the man stated, "please, I don't want to harm you. Everyone respects what you are trying to do for the guard and for what you have done for the men. You are leading us with honor."

Mara nodded. "Then you can understand why I need to do this."

He shifted uncomfortably. "My lady, I'm not...I'm."

She offered a shadowed smile. "Just tell me."

He sounded timid and unsure. "Please, there is no one considered as highly respected as you. You've been leading...I mean, helping the captain to lead...I mean," he drew a sharp breath, "and you're asking me to cause you harm. Please, my lady, do not ask me to spill your blood."

She looked across the room at Garreth who instantly said, "No." She continued to stare, the weight of her gaze fully settling upon him. "Mara, don't even think about it."

"Garreth, don't allow these young ones to be punished for this. They do not deserve it, and you know what it will do to them." She offered a tight smile that did not reach her eyes. "Look what it did to us."

Garreth finally dropped his gaze to the floor before walking slowly across the floor and placing his hand upon Jon's arm. "I will take it from here," he said in a resigned voice. Then he turned slowly back to Mara, who knelt beside the chained man and released Brendan from his bonds. "It's okay."

He looked at her with unmasked eyes. "I am sorry. I never meant to upset the queen. I don't understand what I did. I was only trying to..."

"I know you didn't. It is going to be okay."

She then motioned him away before turning to face the stone slab which stood in front of her. She drew a deep breath and then turned back to Garreth, the whip now clutched tightly in his hand. It was a long whip hosting three thick strips of leather each tipped with thin pieces of silver metal with jagged edges which would bite into Mara's delicate skin. He took several steps forward and placed his hand upon her right cheek then trailed his fingers to her shoulder. "Mara, you don't have to do this."

A shiver passed over her as she forced herself to meet her cousin's gaze. "Do it quickly. I will try to stay quiet."

He looked at her with such sadness. "Oh, my lady, my beautiful, beautiful cousin. You will scream." He shook his head, then returned his gaze to hers. "You will scream and scream and scream."

Mara's teeth sank lightly into her bottom lip as she drew a deep breath. She gave a single nod. She removed her outer jacket along with the golden chain which was clasped securely around her neck. She handed both to Garreth, who placed the discarded items against the far wall. Mara turned again to face the stone table and slowly lowered her body across it. She gripped the edges; it was cold to the touch.

Garreth drew another deep breath. The sound of metal striking stone filled the room as Garreth flicked his wrist, testing his grip on the whip. A long moment of silence filled the room before Garreth said, "Forgive me."

Moments later the first stroke of the triple pronged whip buried itself into the flesh of her back.

CHAPTER XXXII

Present Day

THE WATER CONTINUED TO CASCADE over her body as she forced herself from those dark memories long ago. "Dammit, Brendan!" She slammed her hand against the tiled wall.

When she had formed the foundation of the Rose, Brendan, along with nearly a hundred other men, had taken the oath by her side. He had been young and untested—not unlike Nolan was now. Mara initially had little time for the youth. In fact, she would have dismissed him outright had Phillip not decided to take Brendan under his wing, training him in both the ways of the sword and the ancient traditions which, even all those centuries ago, had already begun to fade from the courts.

It was nearly fifteen years after his arrival, at the end of a particularly nasty run-in with several members of the Muir Court, that Mara finally agreed to grant him a position of rank among the guard. With valor unwatched by all but few, he rose swiftly through the ranks to achieve the title of sub-captain. When Philip finally died nearly two hundred years after his arrival, Brendan had seemed the natural choice for Mara's second in command.

Though she never expressed much affection, Mara had come to care deeply for the man who had fought so bravely by her side. With great courage and unquestioned loyalty, Brendan had somewhat managed to cling to a sense of hope for the world which Mara had lost long ago. The realization that he would never again stand by her side was almost unbearable.

Mara turned the temperature of the water even higher. Hissing against the heat, she put all of her concentration into forcing herself to remain standing in the spray of the near-boiling water. She pulled at her hair, nails digging into her scalp, as though trying to scrape away the memories along with Brendan's blood.

It was not until the last hint of warmth had vanished from the water surrounding her that Mara finally turned the golden knobs and removed herself from the shower. She glanced into the mirror studying her beet-red skin, long matted hair and hollow eyes. She then wrapped the towel around her body before reaching mechanically for the brush lying on the vanity. She combed through her hair methodically, starting at the end of each group of collected strands and working towards her scalp before moving on to the next piece.

When her hair finally lay in straight, smooth strands, she walked to the closet, where she pulled out a satin nightgown with thin straps. She pulled a matching robe of satin around her shoulders, but did not fasten the black buttons, instead opting to leave the robe open as she turned to walk back into the bedroom. Standing in the doorway was Edward.

Showered and dressed, he leaned back against the side of the closed stone door. His borrowed shirt was loose along his arms, the top buttons open revealing the contrast of his pale skin against the dark material of the shirt. His hair hung straight, still damp from the shower.

Mara drew a deep breath and gathered her emotions as tightly as she could. She forced her features into a cold, blank expression before slowly moving to take a seat on the edge of the bed. She then adjusted her robes, fidgeting until the material finally lay comfortably around her, blending with the dark covers beneath her.

Only then did she raise her gaze to meet the dark eyes awaiting her. She did not know what to expect when she finally met his gaze—anger, arrogance, pity. Instead, she saw none of these things. In their place was a mixture of love and tenderness so raw, so real that it shattered every defense she had worked so carefully to put in place. A look that, she had been certain, she would never see again.

He spoke her name, the sound carrying across the room like the breath of a gentle caress, and Mara began to cry, sobs tumbling from her pale lips. Her long fingers dug into the black cloth of the cover lying beneath her, and her thin frame shook visibly from the force of her tears.

Edward crossed the room in three quick strides "Mara," he said softly, kneeling before her. He reached forward, gently running his hand down her left arm. When he reached her hand, Mara slowly uncurled her fingers from the cloth and slid them through Edward's.

"I can't," she whispered through gritted teeth. "I am so tired."

Edward leaned forward, pressing his forehead against her chest. She raised her right hand and laced her fingers into his hair. "Mara, I..." She felt him draw a deep breath and try again. "Mara."

She tightened her grip on his black hair and gave it a hard jerk, forcing him to stare up into her violet eyes. Her tears ceased as she gazed down at the man kneeling before her. Then slowly, deliberately, Mara leaned down, closing the distance between them. She pressed her lips against his. He kissed her back, softly moving under her caress. She stared down at him with an intense expression then suddenly moved her hands to the collar of his shirt. She ripped it open, exposing the smooth perfection of his skin, almost completely healed from the shallow cuts inflicted by Viktor's blade.

She ran her hands slowly down his chest, as though verifying by touch what she could not trust through vision, then moved further onto the bed. He followed, rising from his knees as she guided his upper body towards her. Pulling him onto the bed, Mara leaned back into the soft black blankets. Edward lay beside her and she placed her head upon his chest, his arms moving to close gently around her.

"What do you need, Mara? Tell me what you need."

Several moments of silence followed, then in a hushed whisper. "To drown them out. To have one, single moment where I don't remember...anything."

He slid her from his chest, moving back enough to see the silver in her violet eyes. Then he kissed her. "*mea rosa immortalis.*" His voice was deep, his eyes intense in their captivating gaze. "I will drown out the dreams."

"Memories. Never dreams."

He stopped her words with another kiss, this time more passionately with a sense of desperation which drove all other thoughts from her mind. For one moment, she melted into that kiss, then pulled back. "No," she said, disentangling their bodies as she moved toward the edge of the bed.

"What is it?"

"This is wrong. You don't want this. You don't want me."

"That is a lie. I have always wanted you, Mara."

"Once. A long time ago."

"Mara," he interrupted. "Do you believe I don't love you?"

Her body jerked at the question. "Of course you don't. How could you possibly love me, when you have spent the past eight hundred years hating me? The one responsible for her death."

Edward moved his hand to the side of her face. He stared as though attempting to force his way past her violet eyes and into her soul. A look of pain crossed his features that caused Mara's breath to catch in her throat, her heart pounding so fiercely she thought it might burst.

His fingers climbed higher to dig into her long black hair. "*te amo, rosa, mea rosa immortalis.* I have always," the words were tight, slow and strained, "always loved you. And tonight, I am going to chase away your pain."

He paused, allowing his words to firmly settle over the woman seated before him. "All these years and I have never once done what is right for you. I would tell you that I am sorry for what happened, but it would not be enough. It will never be enough. So please, Mara. *mea rosa, mi amor.* Let me give you what you ask. A single moment's peace."

She stared at him in heartbreaking disbelief. Tears burned the corner of her eyes, but did not fall. "All I want is to forget. To not remember. To not...

Edward, what the queen did to you. I couldn't watch. And I couldn't not watch. And I can't forget. *ignosce mihi, mi amor.* I am so sorry. I am..."

"Oh, Mara." Edward shook his head slowly. "You didn't do that, Mara. It was our fault, Liza's and mine. Not yours."

She moved her hand to his chest and slowly traced her fingers down his skin. "But I watched, Edward. I watched her split your skin. I watched her paint the ground with your blood. I listened to your screams. I watched her destroy everything I had ever believed in and did nothing. Nothing!"

"Stop it, Mara. It was not your fault, do you hear me?" His tone became more intense. "It was not your fault."

He leaned down and again kissed her, driving her body back towards the bed. He pushed her down, pressing her deep into the blankets. Every protest, every thought, vanished under the weight of Edward's body pressing against her own.

CHAPTER XXXIII

MARA AWOKE STILL WRAPPED securely in the circle of Edward's arms. Her head against his chest, Mara pressed her check closer to his skin. His heart beat strong and steady. She closed her eyes, listening to the gentle rhythm of his breathing, allowing it to soothe the turmoil in her mind.

She was unsure how long she lay there in the warmth of his embrace. How many nights had she dreamed of this, only to find herself alone with the first glimmer of the sun's rays? Edward seemed peaceful in his dreams. It was with the greatest of difficulty that she finally managed to pull away, moving slowly so not to wake him. As she moved to the side of the bed, Mara turned back to stare down at the man lying beside her. His pale chest seemed almost ghostly against the black sheets. His long dark hair covered the right side of the pillow which cradled his head.

She continued to stare down at his peaceful form for several minutes. Then, she rose from the bed and stepped quietly to the closet where she slipped into a clean gown of black satin with a matching robe. Draped in these fresh clothes, Mara walked past the still sleeping Edward and stepped quickly into the stone corridor beyond. Insulated by a thick, black rug, her steps were nearly silent as she turned right and walked down the full length of the hallway. She eventually reached a side stairwell which she slowly began to ascend.

There were twelve flights of stairs between the captain and the uppermost tower of the ancient castle. When she finally reached the top, it was to find herself in a small room with a single window. It was to this opening she walked, where the first glimmer of sunlight had begun to seep into the room. Under the window was a golden chest upon which lay one of the last existing enchantments the world would ever know. Covered in a layer of dust so thick that it was almost white, the chest stood in the same location where it had been sealed nearly six hundred years before. She knelt before the chest and blew softly across the front. Dust scattered through the air, revealing the ancient warning: *hic iacet sanguis rosarum. Here lie the blood of roses.*

Beneath the inscription was an impression in the shape of a rose. Mara ran a finger slowly over the indented words, inscribed all those years ago for the specific purpose of preventing anyone from ever again withdrawing its sacred contents. Carefully, Mara raised her hands to her throat and unclasped the silver chain from around her neck. In the center of the chain lay a single white diamond which had been carved into the same rose-like shape which stood embedded into the side of the golden chest. She removed the rose from the chain and held it gently in her hand. She closed her eyes as she traced the familiar lines of the hollow diamond.

She could still picture the joyous expression which had graced Liza's face the night her mother had given her the pendant, hanging on the end of a thin, golden chain. Liza had been five, or perhaps six at the time of receipt; it had been her first truly royal gift. A necklace which had once been worn by the queen's mother—a grandmother shared by both Liza and Mara. Twenty years later, the same pendant would be seen as the only identifiable element upon Liza's otherwise mutilated body. Found three days after the queen had tortured Edward, a night which would become known from that moment on as the night of 'forbidden love.'

"Here lie the blood of roses." She again traced her finger over the memorized inscription. She had cried herself that night as Edward struggled to comfort her. Broken and emotionally exhausted from being forced to endure in silence as his torture had been drawn out to the queen's pleasure. Mara should have been watching over the princess that night, but instead found herself unable to force herself from Edward's side.

940 AD

IT HAD BEEN LATE IN the night when the stone doors to Edward's chambers had flown open, jarring her from a deep and dreamless sleep. "Mara!" Phillip's voice caused her to rise from the circle of Edward's arms. "Mara," he repeated. "I need you to come with me—right now."

"Why?" she inquired.

"What is going on?" Edward asked from beside her, though he was still too injured to do little more than raise himself into a higher position upon the pillows behind him. Mara stood from the bed, hastened by something in Phillip's voice which she could not quite place. Without answering Edward's question, Phillip left the room, motioning for Mara to follow him.

"I'll find out what is going on," she informed her captain.

"Mara," Edward called, causing her to pause and meet his eyes.

She forced a smile. "I just need to see what is happening."

He looked at her with an expression between confusion and apprehension. "Just be careful."

Mara gave a slight bow before turning to chase after Phillip, who had paused outside the doors but again began to walk forward at a brisk pace when she emerged from the captain's room. "Follow me," were the only words he offered as he led Mara down a series of long hallways before they finally found themselves standing inside the specific corridor leading to the private chambers of Princes Liza. Standing in the hallway, all but blocking their path, was Garreth.

"Mara, I am so sorry," Garreth stammered upon seeing their approach. The words tumbled from his lips in a manner that drew Mara's full attention. Garreth's eyes were wide with panic, his words spoken too quickly. His blond hair was disheveled upon his glistening brow.

"Garreth, what is it?"

Philip moved to stand beside Garreth before turning back to face her. Mara looked from one man to the other, then finally asked, "What the hell is going on?"

"Mara, I...I don't know what...I don't know how..." Here Garreth paused and it was Phillip who continued. "Mara," he said, "my lady, it's—it's not good."

"What happened?" she asked again, suddenly afraid of the answers that might await her.

Phillip knelt before her. "My princess." He addressed her by the rarely used title. "I regret to inform you that Her Royal Highness, your cousin, Princess Liza of the Ciar Court, was murdered tonight. Along with eight members of the Royal Guard who were charged with her protection over the past three days."

Mara's eyes flew to those of her cousin's in a mixture of shock and horror. One glance was all she needed to know that the nightmare that had begun all those years ago when Edward had been sent away was not over, but instead—only beginning.

Mara walked down the hall toward Liza's suite. The bodies of the men who had spent their lives protecting the royal family lay sprawled upon the ground in deep pools of noble blood. As she passed her fallen friends and comrades, the numbness began to spread.

Fredrick and Lars lay strewn together as they had once stood in life. Cousins, they had joined the guard nearly four hundred years prior with a sense of loyalty that was beyond compare.

A few feet from them lay Karrie, one of Mara's closest friends and a longtime sparring partner. Her heart lurched to her throat as her body moved forward as though of its own accord.

When she reached the silver door which guarded the entrance to the private chambers of the princess, she found the door splattered with blood. Mara forced herself to draw a deep breath and then regretted it, fighting not to gag as she was assaulted by the smell of death. It was overwhelming and she found herself frozen before the chamber's entrance as she struggled to gain control of her composure. She drew several shorter breaths and again attempted to cross the threshold when Garreth grabbed her arm.

He jerked her back, roughly pressing her back against the cold stone wall of the corridor's outer chambers. "No," he stated flatly. "No."

Mara looked at him unsure how to respond. She felt cold, as though a thick layer of ice had formed around her, both protecting her from the emotions which threatened to tear her apart, and preventing her thoughts from penetrating its icy grip. She attempted to speak, but no sound escaped her lips. She had to force herself to draw another deep breath before saying, "Garreth."

"No," he said again. "You do not need to see this, Mara. She was my sis..." His voice cracked on the word, but he forced himself to continue. "My sister and she is dead. That makes you the closet thing I have left and I am telling you, Mara—you are not going in that room."

"Garreth," Phillip's voice cut into the conversation. "Let go of the sub-captain."

"She does not need to see this."

"That decision is up to her."

"No, it is not."

"You were Liza's brother," Phillip interjected. "But Mara was the captain of her guard."

Garreth turned to face Phillip, anger blazing in his eyes. "After what she went through with Edward, she is in no condition to..."

As they argued, the chill surrounding Mara began to seep into her veins. Her voice sounded hollow as she spoke, her words silencing the men standing before her. "If I cannot walk through those doors then I never deserved to be..." A shiver danced upon her spine. "I will regret it forever."

"Please, Mara," Garreth pleaded.

"I have to," she answered. "Please, Garreth. Let me go." The moment stretched into a battle of silent wills before Garreth finally released his grip on Mara's arm and took several steps to her right. He met her violet eyes as he stated, "Be strong, Mara. You have to be strong."

She did not respond, instead focusing all her strength on forcing herself to step past the two men and into the room beyond. The chamber was made of the same dark stone that formed the rest of the castle, the chamber lit by a fire on either side along with several torches that lined the walls.

Three bodies lay upon the stone floor. The one closest was the three-hundred-year-old Erik, whose sword still lay clutched in his hand where he had fallen. Mara became grateful for the seeping cold protecting her as she forced herself to move forward, searching for the courage to face the last two bodies.

They lay beside each other on the right side of the bed. Davith was in front of the princess, as though protecting her even in death. With over a thousand years of experience, Davith could have easily been the captain of Liza's guard, but had assented to Edward's request that Mara receive the coveted position. It was argued that given the extreme youth of the princess that Mara, as both young and a woman of royal blood, made a more suitable match. Davith's presence had always been a welcome addition to Mara's inner circle and had proven to be a guiding light upon which she had come to rely upon heavily, especially during the years that Edward had been away.

Now he lay upon the floor, his short blond hair stained red. His neck had been slashed open, spilling his arterial blood across his pale skin and covering the floor surrounding him. His golden blade lay beside him, never to rise again.

Mara stood there for a long time, and the others allowed it, averting their eyes. It was only as her body began to shake that Garreth stepped forward. He did not attempt to pull her back, but instead clasped his hand around her arm and gently led her forward.

They paused a mere step outside of the crimson pool at their feet and Mara finally forced herself to face the fallen princess. A gasp escaped Mara's lips as she realized that Liza had not simply been killed – she had been mutilated.

Liza's light blue gown appeared a dark brown, saturated with blood. Her arms had been skewered, a blade run along the inside of both forearms, creating deep, horizontal incisions in both wrists. Her face appeared as though clawed, covered with deep, long gashes that opened her flesh to a point that she was barely recognizable. The bones of her right cheek protruded through what was left of her skin. Her lower jaw was broken, hanging from its hinges at a most unnatural angle. The sockets of both eyes had been punctured, leaving gaping masses of blood where they should have been.

It was at this moment, staring into the remains of Liza's ruined eyes, when Mara finally reached her limit. She turned her head quickly to her left and bent at the waist, lowering her head just in time to avoid vomiting all over herself.

Garreth leaned forward and held back her long hair. When she finished spilling the contents of her stomach, Garreth wrapped his arms around her, pulling her unsteadily to her feet. She felt lightheaded, suddenly unable to stand on her own. She again stared at the ruins of the princess' eyes. It was an image which even now existed as clearly in her mind as it had the first moment she had looked upon it that night long ago.

Mara did not scream, but had merely collapsed into Garreth's arms. He carried her from the room down a series of long hallways into her own chambers. She clung numbly to her cousin until he lay her down on the bed. She would never remember reaching the room or the details of the next few hours. However, it was still night when her sanity finally decided to return. She was lying on the edge of the bed with Garreth speaking softly beside her. It seemed as though he had been speaking for a long time.

She drew a deep breath and moved herself to a seated position and Garreth's voice fell to silence with her movements. She pushed a gulp of air down her sore throat. Her eyes burned with tears which refused to fall. She finally managed to force herself to face her cousin. "Garreth." A thousand questions raced through her mind, but only one passed her lips. "Does Edward know?"

"Mara, you don't need to worry about that."

"Garreth," she stated again as something deadly seeped into her voice. "Has Edward been told?"

He stared at her for several moments, then said, "No."

Mara gave a slow nod. "I shall inform him."

"That is not your job."

"Yes," she said flatly, "it is."

"Mara, please."

"I was the sub-captain in command of her guard. I was the one, charged by Captain Edward, to protect the Princess of the Ciar Court."

"We were all charged with..."

"It was my job!" Mara stood from the bed and walked across the room to the closet which stood on the right side. Not bothering to close the door, she chose a simple black gown and quickly changed into the selected garment. It was a full-length dress that reached her ankles with long, loose sleeves. It hung slightly off the shoulders, with a scooped neckline. She had just positioned the gown into place when Garreth appeared behind her. He reached for the corset laces of the gown and began to cinch the dress around her slender frame. When he was finished, Mara turned towards the mirror leaning against the vanity and took a seat in a wooden chair. Picking up a silver comb, Mara brushed through the long strands of her hair until it lay in soft, straight layers along her back. Then she finally put down the comb and addressed the man standing beside her. "Tell Phillip I am ready to receive him."

Garreth did not break the room's silence, but instead turned and walked to the entrance of her chambers. As expected, Phillip was standing on the opposite side of the door, awaiting Mara's invitation to enter. He entered the room slowly, acknowledging Mara with a slight bow of the head. When he finally stood only a few paces from her seated position, Phillip knelt down. "My lady."

"What happened?" she asked tersely.

Phillip cleared his throat. "A group entered the grounds. How they did so has yet to be determined."

"Are they dead?"

"No, my lady. No sign has been found of the killers."

Mara closed her eyes attempting to sift through the turmoil in her mind. *Concentrate*, she thought before forcing herself to open her eyes. "The queen?"

"She has ordered a search of the grounds and has contacted the Muir Court."

Mara nodded then turned from both men and walked slowly to the far side of the room and stepped inside of a closet. She moved to one of the shelves and gently pulled back a series of black cloths wrapped around a silver blade. Rubies were embedded in both sides of the black hilt while a string of silver roses were etched into the metal on either side of the blade. She rarely carried her father's Arius sword. She withdrew the blade with great reverence and turned back towards the men standing behind her.

It was Garreth who spoke first in recognition of one of the few blades in existence which held the power to kill an immortal. "No, Mara. This was not your fault."

"It was my job, Garreth," she said, repeating her earlier statement.

"Yes. To see her protected, which she was. The ground is littered with the bodies of those who died protecting her."

"I made a vow to protect her, Garreth. I failed."

"Yes," Phillip said, entering the conversation. "But it was my job to keep intruders from entering the grounds. Here, within this palace, she should have been safe. Therefore, we all failed."

"You cannot do this," Garreth added. "We all..."

"It is not your judgment to cast, Garreth. It belongs to the captain alone."

"Then I am going with you."

Mara did not argue but simply gave a reluctant nod and began to walk towards the door. As she entered the outer chambers, her pace began to increase, terrified that even a moment's pause would cause her to lose the last shred of courage which she was fighting to protect. It was not until she reached the stone doors of the captain's chambers that she stopped, allowing Garreth and Phillip to reach her side before knocking on the door.

At the sound of Edward's voice, Garreth and Phillip reached for the doors, parting them as Mara stepped inside the dark chambers. A roaring fire provided the only light, casting the room in dark shadows as the three sub-captains stepped forward.

"Mara, Phillip, thank goodness! You had been gone so long I was starting to worry."

Mara stared at his relieved expression and all but collapsed to her knees. Garreth raced towards her, but froze with a warning glance from Phillip. Garreth stopped, torn between the anguish of Mara's kneeling form and the silent command of his superior. He eventually drew a breath and dropped to his knees a few feet from where Mara knelt.

"Mara?" Edward asked, struggling to a seated position upon the bed. "Mara, what is it?"

Her breathing became a tight wheeze, and she lacked the oxygen required to speak.

"Mara?" Edward asked again. "Oh Gods, what has happened? The queen, did she hurt you? What did..." He switched his gaze to the man still standing. "Phillip?"

Phillip took a step forward, placing himself directly across from Mara. He also took a knee. "Captain," he said to Edward formally.

"What is going on?"

"Captain," Phillip said again. "I..." He found himself unable to continue. Then, much to his chagrin, Mara found her voice.

"Captain," she stated, trying desperately to form the words, but what came out instead was, "I'm sorry. Edward, I..." Her voice trembled. "I am so sorry. I couldn't... It's...it's my fault. I am so sorry."

Edward sat still for several long moments. "What are you talking about, Mara? You sacrificed yourself to protect Liza from the queen. You saved my life. I never would have survived without you. I don't understand. You saved me. You saved Liza."

At his words, a harsh sound bordered between a gasp and a sob escaped Mara's lips. "Don't, Edward. Please, I didn't. I didn't..."

"What?" He gazed at the three kneeling figures.

"Captain," Phillip tried again, this time managing to raise his gaze from the floor to meet Edward's. "I am so sorry, my lord."

"What are you talking about?" Edward demanded, frustration entering his tone.

"My lord," Phillip continued, "a group of unidentified men entered the palace grounds tonight."

"What? What are you talking about?"

"We don't know how many," Garreth added. "But they were highly trained. I've never seen an attack so expertly executed."

"The queen, is she..."

"The queen is fine, my lord. But..."

"And Liza?" An edge of fear entered his voice. "Phillip, where is Liza? Is she okay?"

"My captain," Phillip answered. "Twelve members of the Royal Guard were killed tonight. Lord Davith was among them."

"Davith?" Edward asked, fear transforming to panic. He tried to stand, but was still too weak to do so without his hand upon the bed for support. "Davith is dead?"

"Yes," Phillip replied.

"Where is Liza? Where is the princess?"

It was Mara who finally broke the silence by taking her father's deadly blade and holding it out, offering it to the man seated upon the bed. "I swore a vow to protect the princess, unto my death." She finally forced herself to gaze up from the floor. "I failed, Captain. I failed. And I offer you my life in payment for this gravest of crimes."

She met his gaze head on, her pained expression leaving Edward no room to doubt her words. "I am so sorry, Edward."

He took a step forward, forgetting his injuries, and collapsed to the floor, his legs still not strong enough to support his weight. He fell facedown, leaving the three kneeling sub-captains unsure of how to respond. The silence stretched on and Mara finally turned towards Phillip. The two sub-captains exchanged a helpless glance. She turned back to Edward as the hush continued to fill the room. Edward's body began to shake against the cold, stone floor. All three sub-captains remained kneeling, afraid to break the silence of the room. Then, Edward's breathing became loud and unsteady.

Mara again turned, this time towards Garreth, whose eyes were glued to Edward's broken form. Tears rose in the corner of Mara's eyes, at long last threatening to fall when suddenly, Edward gave a single, heart-wrenching scream before uttering a single word: "Mara."

She rushed forward, her father's blade clattering to the floor. She touched his shoulder and he rose from the ground. He threw himself into her arms, clutching her close as he buried his face against her chest and great, heaving sobs wracked his body. Mara wrapped her arms around him tightly, rocking him gently in the circle of her arms. "Mara."

"I am here," she replied, finally losing the battle with her own tears. "I am here, Edward. I've got you. I've got you."

"Please, Mara."

"I am not going anywhere, *mi amor. ignosce mihi, mi amor.*"

Chapter XXXIV

940 AD

It had taken both men to move Edward back onto the side of the bed. He clung to Mara as they moved him, and she whispered in the language of their youth, attempting to soothe him as best she could. Afterwards, she lay beside him, his head tucked against her chest, his arms clinging to her until long after his tears were spent. She did not tell him it would be okay or offer any assurances of the days to come. Instead she simply held him, occasionally quieting him from troubled dreams. Garreth stood outside the door, barring all from entering while Phillip had reported to the queen, citing the extent of Edward's physical injuries as his reason to assume temporary command over the Royal Guard.

Mara remained in the chamber for days, refusing to leave Edward's side. On the third morning, he rose to attend the funeral. A funeral which, dictated by the long-standing tradition that ruling members of royalty could in no way be associated with death, the queen was unable to attend. Mara and Garreth stood in her stead, along with other members of the royal family. Liza's body had been shrouded in layers of black silk and veiled to hide her disfiguration from those gathered. Garreth and Mara stood on either side of Edward, guiding him to the funeral pyre where he eventually fell to his knees, collapsing under the weight of his grief. By tradition, each member of the funeral party was permitted to lay a single rose upon the fallen princess. This began with the lowest ranked, yet still noble, members and proceeded up to those highest in rank.

Mara watched for a long time, awaiting her turn. Lower ranked members of the party would place black roses upon the side of the funeral pyre. When it was finally their turn, Mara and Garreth each offered Edward an arm and walked toward the shrouded form. Leaning between them, Edward forced himself to step forward enough to place his rose beside the clasped hands of his beloved. When the black rose touched the princess' hands, it turned violet—a symbol of the royal rank which Liza bore in life, and would now relinquish in death. A gasp arose between those close enough to witness the enchantment.

Edward's body again began to tremble, and Mara stepped in front of him, forcing him to meet her gaze. "Not here, Edward," she stated in a low, commanding tone. "Just hold on. Hold on." A sharp tremor raced through him, but he managed to nod in spite of this. Mara turned and offered a low bow before the fallen princess and placed her own rose beside Edward's. "Forgive me, my princess," was all she could manage before being forced to once again focus her attention back upon the broken form that had replaced the once powerful captain of the guard.

They managed to escort Edward back to his chambers before he again collapsed in inconsolable grief.

CHAPTER XXXV

Present Day

FROM THAT MOMENT, EDWARD WOULD spend the next century as captain only in name. The three sub-captains gathered around him, forming a protective shield, preventing prying eyes from learning the truth; that the Edward they had known, trusted and loved no longer existed. It would be nearly two hundred years before even the slightest glimpse of him would be seen again, and it would take an act of betrayal to force him to return.

Others would spend their lives swearing that Mara's abandonment was not a betrayal. They said it was for the good of both the men she vowed to protect and for the good of the captain who would never again lead as long as he stood within her protective shadow. But Mara knew the truth. She had betrayed him as assuredly as he had once chosen Liza over her. She had chosen to protect the men who followed her to the Rose over the man whose side she had sworn never to leave.

Yet here they were a half-millennium later, still struggling to find a place between the lines of love and hate, loyalty and betrayal. It seemed to be their eternal fate to contend with such issues, which is why Mara now found herself in the uppermost tower of her ancient castle, prepared to open the chest she had once vowed to never open again.

The rose-shaped diamond was still held gently within her grasp, her fingers tracing the lines she knew so well. She cast her gaze to the window where the sunlight had begun to shimmer along the top of the snow-covered mountains visible upon the horizon. The room was absolutely silent, as though even the birds living in the nearby trees knew to avoid this ancient tower.

Drawing a deep breath, Mara ran her left ring-finger along the diamond stem of the white rose. The end of the stem curled slightly, leaving just enough space to slide a single finger between the end and center of the stem. Placing her left ring finger into this hollow, Mara pressed her skin against the sharp, pointed end, pricking her finger. Blood bubbled to the surface almost instantly and Mara turned the rose upside-down, pressing it more deeply into her skin.

The blood seeped from her hand into the hollow veins of the pendant, transforming the white diamond to ruby. Once the transformation was complete, Mara removed her finger from the tainted rose and gazed at the golden chest lying before her. *Put aside the anger*, the plea of the young enchantress who had sealed it long ago echoed clearly within Mara's mind. *Inside, lies a darkness that, if ever unleashed, shall destroy all it touches.*

Mara reflected upon these words now as she considered what she was about to do. Then, fighting through her sense of dread, she moved the bloody rose forward and slid the pendant into the indentation on the golden chest.

The piece slid effortlessly, acting as the key, and a loud *click* sounded as the ancient lock released from the inside. Then Mara placed both hands upon the lids and ran her fingers across the cold, dusty surface. "Forgive me, Liza," she whispered to the long-dead princess. "Forgive me for the sins I must now commit." She moved her hands forward as though caressing a lover and then slowly, carefully upon the top, exposing the contents of the chest to the early morning air for the first time in over six hundred years.

The chest was lined with black cloth. She reached forward, her hands shaking as she slowly lifted the dark silk which held its carefully guarded contents. Within lay two Arius blades. Both were silver, differentiated only by their intricate hilts. The first was black with a line of silver roses running down both sides of the hilt. Two rubies were embedded in both sides of the handle, far enough away from the center that they would not hinder the grip of its holder. The second featured a golden hilt, adorned with black and white diamonds. The blade marked with roses had been Mara's personal blade carried into the battle of the Muir Court. The second had been taken from Edward on sands of the Muir Court.

Mara dipped her hand deeper into the chest and lightly caressed the hilt of her ancient blade. The silver metal was cold against her fingertips as she ran her hands along the length of the sword. Entranced, she pressed her palm against its tip, hissing as the sharp edge sliced through her thin layer of skin. She raised her hand.

A thin stream of blood trickled down her snow-white skin from a wound which Mara knew, would take a long time to heal. She closed her eyes tightly and drew a deep breath before placing her hand back inside the golden chest. This time, she lay her hand flat against the silver, then slowly curled her long fingers around the black hilt. She tightened her grip, her fingers gliding into each nook and crevice as though she had held the sword only yesterday.

She stood slowly as she lifted the familiar blade, a sense of completeness washing over her that she had not felt since she had last held it in her hand, at the edge of an endless sea. She closed her eyes as she raised the sword, drawing it before her in a slow, graceful arc. With this sword, she had saved the lives of her men. With this sword, she had avenged the death of her princess. And with this blade, she had nearly killed the man she loved. With this blade, she had...

She could see the young boy standing barefoot on the sand. The last living Prince of the Muir Court, mistaking his killer for his savior. The little boy, not five years old, staring up at her with a trust which would haunt her for eternity. Those deep blue eyes streaked with white lines like waves upon the ocean – the last eyes to ever hold the sea.

Yes, child, her words echoed through the silent tower, *I am going to make the bad dream end. All you have to do is close your eyes.*

It was this sword which she had pulled in silence from its leather sheath, the enchanted blade that would never betray its deadly purpose. Mara's hands had trembled as she reached to pull it from her side, but steadied the moment her fingers had clasped its dark hilt. The boy's eyes never opened as she raised the sharp blade high for a downward stroke, her body easily moving into the familiar gesture even as her mind recoiled from this most heinous of sins. The blade came down as the clash of striking metal rang through the air, racing down the beach in the powerful ocean winds.

Mara shook her head, recoiling from the memories of that night long ago. She turned to glance out the window leaning her head into the opening, allowing the cold mountain air to clear her mind. She placed the sword upon the ground before reaching down and removing the diamond from its place in the golden lock. She slid the blood stained-diamond back onto its silver chain and secured it again her neck. Then she moved back towards the chest.

Lying beneath the second sword lay two leather sheaths which had been crafted to fit each blade. Mara's, much like the sword it was created for, was interlaced with a line of silver roses while Edward's had several black and white diamonds running down the center.

She pulled both sheaths from among the folds of black cloth and carefully placed each blade in its case. She then gathered both swords in her arms before beginning the long descent down the stairs, leaving the tower to eventually emerge into the same hallway where she had begun.

Mara entered her chambers to find Edward still asleep, his body only partially covered by the sheets and blankets. She walked forward silently and eased herself onto the edge of the bed. She gazed down upon him for a long time before reaching forward and brushing the long strands of his hair back from his cheek. When he did not wake, she kissed his brow before standing from the bed, placing his Arius blade in the spot where she had lay. She turned and retrieved her own blade before exiting the room as silently as she had entered.

Mara walked down the hall, requiring only a single left turn before coming to the door of Brendan's room. Resisting the need to knock, she opened the door slowly as it made its familiar *creak* before fully revealing the room beyond. Everything was in perfect order as Mara stepped into the room.

The bed was made with practiced precision, the thick wool blankets pulled tightly in place. His books were aligned by their coordinating size along the wooden shelves against the wall. A pile of papers were stacked neatly upon his desk, with a single pen lying across them.

Even the fireplace which, Mara knew, was used on an almost nightly basis, was remarkably clean, clear of the ash and soot which one would expect to find. No pictures covered the walls, save for a single calendar opened to a scene of a setting sun dipped into an ocean so blue, serving as almost the only proof that Brendan had ever lived within the room's barren walls.

She moved closer to the calendar as her eyes trailed toward to the desk. Upon it lay the only other proof that a person had lived within these walls—a single portrait. It was small, hand-painted with its age clearly showing, yet it was there just the same. Mara stepped to the desk and reached forward, raising the portrait encased in a silver frame gently in her hands.

She remembered the day they had commissioned the portrait. It had been Brendan's request, the single gift he had been granted upon receiving the rank of sub-captain. They stood there together, Brendan, Mara, Phillip and Mathew. They were standing in front of their mountain setting, the portrait having been painted on the balcony of the room in which Mara currently stood. They were smiling in the portrait, each expressing a rare moment of companionship which was never destined to last.

Still clutching the portrait, Mara moved to the left side of the room and pulled back the curtains which shrouded the entrance to Brendan's balcony before opening the glass door. She stepped out to find that the glimmer of early morning sunshine had vanished.

The sky had transformed to a dark gray, causing the distant mountains to appear almost ominous in the gathered shadows. Mara's black velvet cloak blew gently behind her in the breath of the cold wind as she moved closer to the balcony's edge.

It was carved of stone and lined by thick pillars. From this side of the castle, Mara found herself staring across at the very staircase she had climbed to the tower. She leaned against the black stones that composed the balcony's edge. She pressed her forehead against her palm and fought back a fresh round of tears, clutching the portrait as she shivered in the cold breath of the mountains.

She might have spent days on that balcony had a voice not startled her from her thoughts. "Mara," the strong voice called as she looked up to find Garreth standing between the swirling curtains of the glass doors she had failed to close. Caught off guard, she did not have time to suppress neither the pain in her expression nor the tears gathered in her eyes. "Mara." He spoke her name more gently than before.

"What is it, Garreth?"

He moved from the curtains and walked towards the rail, her long dark gown trailing down the balcony's edge to almost touch the ground.

It was not until he reached her that Mara realized he was not alone. Nolan trailed tentatively behind him, unsure as to what degree his presence would be welcomed.

Surprised by this unexpected presence, Mara's eyes flew to her cousin's, silently awaiting an explanation for the additional intrusion. Then to her further surprise, Garreth knelt before her, reached forward and took her hands in his own, turning her body away from the mountains to face him. "My lady."

"Yes?"

"My lady," he stated again. "I need to speak with you about subjects which I know you would rather be left unspoken. About events which I know you would rather leave in the darkest corners of the past. Yet we need to speak of them just the same."

She looked down at him with a sense of foreboding, pulling her hands from his grasp. "I'm afraid you are going to have to be more specific, my lord. There are several moments of my past which I would just as soon have forgotten."

He gave a slow nod. "Yes, it is true. Yet, despite all the darkness which we have experienced, there is only one which is forbidden."

Anger began to seep into Mara, stiffening her stance and creeping into her voice. "No." She turned, walking back through the swirling black curtains.

She was caught off guard by the roaring fire which was now burning brightly inside the room, but paused for no more than a step before proceeding towards the door. However, before she could reach the hallway, Garreth had reached her side, grabbing her arm in his powerful grip. She whirled around, but froze when she saw the look of concern in his golden eyes. "Please, Mara," he pleaded. "Just listen, that is all I am asking."

She drew a slow breath before pulling her arm free of his grasp then walked silently towards the light of the fire's golden flames. It was not until she stood close enough to feel its warmth upon her cold skin that she finally spoke. "Why, Garreth? We both know what happened that night."

"Yes," he replied. "But Nolan does not."

"This has nothing to do with him. He is just a boy."

"Boy or not," Garreth replied, "he is a part of this now."

Mara turned back to face him. She wanted to say he was lying, that the boy could still be saved, that he could still escape their shared and inevitable fate. Yet, she could not seem to form the lie upon her lips.

"Mara," Garreth said gently. "You need to tell him."

She visibly stiffened.

"Mara, everything that has happened, everything that is happening, ties back to that night."

"No." She attempted to sound firm, but was unable to mask the strain of emotion. "No."

"My lady," Garreth tried again.

"It is forbidden."

"He needs to know."

"No," she said venomously.

"Liza's death..."

"Do not speak *her* name!" Mara felt her hand sliding towards the Arius blade tucked securely against her side. She drew a deep breath and forced herself to stop mid-motion.

Garreth's gaze followed her hand, his eyes widening in recognition of the blade she had sworn to never carry again. He then returned his eyes to her violet ones before slowly shaking his head. "It's staggering," he finally stated in a quiet, reserved tone.

"What?" she asked through clenched teeth.

"The depth of your pain and how little the years have lessened it."

Her breathing became shallow as she said, "You weren't there. You didn't see."

"I saw every—"

"You didn't see!" She took a step forward, closing the distance between them. "I was bathed in blood that night, Garreth...were you?" Her body trembled as she spoke.

"Mara." He spoke her name with such tenderness it threatened to break through her angered resolve. "How can I help you?"

"I don't need your help," she answered, but her voice quavered. "Just, please. Don't say her name."

Garreth shook his head. "We were so worried about Edward, about..." He paused. "About *her*. No one even thought to look to you. I am so sorry, Mara."

"I was not the one on the table that night."

"No," he replied. "But you were—"

"Stop!" she all but shouted. "Please, just...don't. Please. I can't...I just..."

"My lady," Garreth interrupted. "I know this hurts. And you are right. I was not in the room, not when the worst of it happened." He paused, allowing his words to settle over her as Mara attempted to collect her emotions. Then he continued, "But, whatever happened last night—whatever the king is plotting, it has something to do with that night." He drew a deep breath. "You know it is true."

Mara closed her eyes tightly and turned away from Garreth to face the crackling fire which seemed to dance before her. She opened her eyes slowly, keeping her gaze fixated upon the swirling flames. "Okay, Garreth. Tell him...how she died."

CHAPTER XXXVI

"I WAS ONCE A FAVORITE of the queen's," Garreth said quietly. "She was my stepmother, you see. And somehow she managed to find a tender spot in her heart for me; though it was likely due to her love for my father who was also Liza's father. Whichever the way of it, she would, on occasion, listen to me when she would heed no other."

Garreth gave a heavy sigh. "So it was little surprise when I was called to the door of the queen's chambers the night that she had Edward on her table."

"What had happened?" Nolan inquired anxiously. "What do you mean, on her table?"

"An expression," Garreth replied. "It was worse; he was actually on her bed."

"Her bed?"

Garreth nodded. "When I walked into the room, I didn't even notice him."

"What do you mean?"

"My sister, Princess Liza, was lying on the ground with blood running from a cut across her head. Her dark hair was matted across her face. A man was kneeling beside her, jerking her head up with a tight grip on her long, black hair." Garreth cleared his throat softly. "When I walked into the room, it was as if she was all that existed. My vision zoomed in. I was halfway across the room before I realized that she was not looking at me."

Garreth paused, staring into the blazing fire as though he could see the past playing out within its golden flames. "I turned towards the front of the room, where I found the queen lying upon the bed, with a man's bloodied form lying beneath her. It seemed like a long time before my mind reconciled the fact that the man lying there was Edward. It was..." A shiver seemed to run through Garreth, who took a step closer to the fire before continuing. "His chest was in ruins, the skin of his left side completely removed, scattered in blood strips along the sides of the bed; the muscle lay bare beneath. It was the first time in my life that I truly realized the horror of our immortality—the extent of what we can live through."

CHAPTER XXXVII

940 AD

GARRETH REACHED THE DOOR, BUT was met by a pair of men wielding their swords by the stone door to the queen's private chambers. "The queen is not to be disturbed," he was informed in a cold voice by a guard whom Garreth barley recognized.

"I was summoned," Garreth replied. Then a high pitched scream shattered the stillness surrounding them. Garreth's hand instantly slipped to the hilt of his blade at the sound.

"What the hell is going on? The queen—"

"Gave specific orders," the guard on the door spoke again.

"Look," Garreth tried to reason. "I received a message to report to the queen immediately. I have to—" He was interrupted by another scream. "What the hell is going on?"

The door opened. Mara appeared from the other side. Her bloodshot eyes were open wide and her face was streaked with tears. She stepped between the two men guarding the door as Garreth moved forward.

"Mara?" he asked in confusion. "Mara, are you hurt?" She took several steps forward, staring down the dimly lit corridor with a blank expression. She stepped past Garreth who gently grabbed her left arm. Mara jumped at his touch. He stepped forward, guiding her several steps to her right and into his arms. He raised his arms to either side of her, and again spoke her name. "Mara? Mara, have you been hurt?" His eyes searched her shaken form.

"No," she finally answered.

"What is going on? Who is...is it Liza?" His heart pounded harder.

Mara lifted her head slowly as a series of shivers began to run up and down her body. "You need to get in there," she managed to reply, her voice barely rising above a whisper.

"They said the queen..."

"Changed her mind." She drew another shaky breath and forced herself to face the two men. "The queen wants to see Garreth."

"But we were ordered..."

"She wants, Garreth, her stepson, in the room," Mara instructed. She drew another breath.

"But..."

"Stop!" Anger flared into her voice, helping to clear her head. She snapped her gaze from Garreth to face the man speaking. "I am a captain of this guard; you are not. I am a Princess of this Court, niece to Her Majesty, Queen Clarissa. This," she motioned toward Garreth, "is another captain and the son of your king." She took a step closer to the lower ranked guardsmen, grateful to be feeling something other than fear. "Step aside. That's an order." The man who had spoken lowered his gaze and reluctantly stepped aside.

"Garreth," Mara said to the older man.

"What is going on?" he asked again. "I do not understand."

She turned to face him. "Don't ask questions." She kept her voice as firm as she could manage. "Just...try to get her out of there, Garreth. He would want us to get her out of there." She gave a hard swallow. "Go, I will be right beside you."

CHAPTER XXXVIII

"Have you ever seen one of those diagrams of muscles? The kind that are put up in the walls of a biology class, where all the skin has been stripped away, revealing nothing but pink, veiny muscle beneath?"

Nolan nodded.

"It was nothing like that."

940 AD

EDWARD'S CHEST WAS A RAW mess. The sheets were saturated in his blood, which had begun to run from the bed and formed a dark pool across the floor. Thin strips of skin lay on either side of his body. Garreth took an involuntary step forward and had to resist the urge to speak the captain's name. Instead, he turned his gaze back to his sister, who stared at Edward with a slack expression.

Garreth took several steps closer to the table, stopping just shy of the slowly widening pool of blood. The queen glanced up from her victim to turn those dark eyes upon him. "My queen." Garreth attempted to keep his voice steady as he dropped to one knee. "Your point has been made." He drew a deep breath, then regretted it as the smell of blood assaulted him. "Please, my queen."

"They must understand." The queen's angelic voice slithered across the room.

"They do," Garreth replied. "Your punishment has been inflicted. The lesson has been learned." He had to resist the urge to turn his gaze from the bed. "Please, my queen...let me take my sister from this room. Please, Your Highness. Let me take her."

The queen eyed him as though considering his words, then began to shake her head. "They must be punished."

"They have been." Mara's voice joined Garreth's pleas. "But if you feel further discipline is needed, then allow me to take your daughter's place." Mara moved several paces forward and dropped to a knee before her sovereign. "I am her captain; it is right that I be punished in her stead."

"Are you stating, Captain Mara, that you encouraged my daughter to be with this man?"

"No, my queen."

"No." She spoke the word as a hiss, drawing out the syllables into a sinister sound. "You loved him yourself, after all."

Mara fought not to falter at the queen's dark tone. "Please, Your Majesty. Let your daughter go."

It surprised everyone, even Garreth, when the queen nodded her consent. "Take her."

Garreth began to rise at the queen's words, when his eyes caught those of his captain's. He froze mid-motion, captured by the horror of what was taking place. He stood there for several heartbeats.

Edward stared across at Garreth and then, very slowly, raised his uninjured right hand. His fingers shook as he extended them in a single, wave-like motion. His lips parted, but he uttered no words. Edward again made the slight motion, and Garreth turned back to where Liza lay on the stone floor.

The guard released his hold upon Liza, who continued to stare blankly in Edward's direction. Garreth knelt beside her before placing his hand gently on her shoulder. She flinched at his touch and a soft whimper escaped her lips. "Liza," her brother spoke as softly as he could, though his voice carried in the silent room. His sister gave no response. Garreth drew a deep breath and gathered the young woman into his arms.

He stepped forward slowly with the room in silence. He was almost to the door before Liza suddenly gave a shrill scream. It startled Garreth, who had to struggle not to drop her from his arms. She began to fight him, seemingly oblivious to the fact that it was her brother's arms in which she was being held. Garreth found himself turning to his left as he fought to control her writhing body. He caught sight of Edward's blood-soaked form and again asked the silent question. Edward waved him away. Garreth tightened his grip on Liza, restraining her as best as he could. The black doors opened before him and he forced the broken girl from the room.

As the black doors closed, Liza began to cry great, heaving sobs, shattering pieces of Garreth's heart with every sound.

CHAPTER XXXIX

940 AD

WHEN THE SOUND OF LIZA'S cries faded from the room, the queen turned her eyes back to where Mara still knelt upon the stone floor. "I do not require your blood, Princess Mara." The queen addressed her by her seldom used title. "Only your eyes."

Mara's heart began to pound in her chest with a deafening ferocity. "My...my eyes?" she asked, unable to mask the fear in her voice. The queen raised the blade she was still clutching in her hand, and turned it sideways. It was drenched in blood.

"Come here," the queen commanded. Mara stood on trembling legs and stepped slowly across the stone floor. The smell of blood grew worse with every step, assaulting her senses as she approached the side of the bed. The left side of Edward's chest was completely missing its skin. The bones of his ribcage lay partially visible in sawed, jagged pieces. Blood had saturated the bed and was now spilling down the side of its stone base. Mara froze a single step outside the pool of blood which surrounded the bed.

"Kneel, niece. Let me see those pretty, pretty eyes." Mara began to lower herself towards the ground when the queen, clad only in the blood of the man lying beneath her, said, "I cannot see your eyes from there."

Mara straightened and eyed the bed as her heart continued to pound. The queen noted the hesitation. "If you like, I can have Liza brought back and she can—"

"No!" Mara said quickly, stepping forward into the pool of blood. When she reached the edge of the bed she forced herself to kneel, Edward's blood soaking into the dark fabric she wore to wet the skin beneath with a surprisingly cool touch. She lowered her eyes towards the floor when the queen moved a finger to her chin, raising her gaze. "Such pretty eyes," the queen said as she ran a finger along Mara's high cheekbones, smearing her face with Edward's blood. "A hint of silver—so rare among the courts. They were my mother's eyes. Did you know that?"

Mara attempted to answer but was unable to find her voice. The queen continued to run her hands over Mara's face, tracing a finger along her lips and slowly down her throat. "My mother was a harsh woman, Mara. You were fortunate to never have known her." A slight tremor ran through Mara's body as the queen stared down at her. "No," she said. "My mother was not a nice woman at all."

Her blood-soaked hands moved back to Mara's cheek and pulled lightly on her bottom lip. Her lips parted as the queen whispered, "Taste him." She slid a finger over the edge of Mara's lip before slipping deeper, smearing Edward's blood across her white teeth and along the tip of her tongue before slowly withdrawing her finger.

Mara's mouth became saturated with the metallic taste of Edward's blood. Her stomach churned. Her gaze trailed to Edward's against her will. *ignosce mihi,* she begged silently. *Please forgive me.*

She swallowed, fighting the urge to vomit as the crimson liquid lined her throat. Her spine twisted in a violent shudder and a thin stream of blood seeped from the corner of her mouth.

Edward's head tilted and his eyes bore into hers. *I'm sorry*, he said without words. Mara clung to his gaze like a lifeline and as the moments passed, the tremors which wracked her body became less violent. The racing of her heart began to slow. *Hold on*, she prayed.

Then the queen moved her hand back to Mara's cheek, forcing her gaze from the man she loved. "Are you ready, Mara?" The queen raised the silver blade clutched tightly in her right hand.

Fear became a living thing as she watched the blade descend. Blood splattered her face as Edward began to scream.

CHAPTER XL

940 AD

TEARS STREAMED DOWN MARA'S FACE, mixing with the blood that was beginning to cascade down her neck to soak through her shirt. Edward's cries continued in a cycle of low moans to full-fledged screams as the queen found new ways to twist her blade into her victim's flesh. As more blood splattered her, Mara's body began to shake uncontrollably and her heart pounded so hard she thought it would burst from her chest; yet even the constant pounding was not enough to lock out the sound of Edward's anguish.

Hail Eleos, Goddess of mercy, Mara prayed. *Shine your light upon the heart of our queen. Temper her rage with your gentle hand, in the name of those who strive to serve her. Hail Eleos, Goddess of mercy. Lay your hands upon the heart of our Queen. Hail Eleos. Hail Eleos.*

The blade sliced up and down Edward's body in a series of shallow and deep strokes, no two ever quite the same. The queen raised the crimson blade yet again and this time, Mara could not stop herself from praying aloud. "In the name of Eleos, mercy!" Her voice increased in volume as she spoke. "Hail Eleos, Goddess of mercy. In the name of Eleos, mercy! Mercy!"

The queen paused in her tender attentions and turned her eyes slowly upon Mara.

"Please, my queen, I implore you. I beg of you...stop this! Can't you see you're killing him?" Desperation filtered through her voice which quickly manifested to an uncontrollable sob. "Please," she begged, seeing the line and crossing it anyway. "Aunt Clarissa, for the love you bore my mother, your sister, I beg of you, stop this madness!"

The queen rose slowly to a kneeling position upon the massive bed and stared down at Mara, kneeling in a pool of Edward's blood. She took the blade in her hand, and never removing her gaze from Mara's, plunged the point of the now crimson sword into Edward's left side.

"No!" Mara's shout eclipsed Edward's own cry of pain. Her voice reverberated throughout the room before finally fading to a profound silence, shattered only by the shallow gasps of Edward's attempts to draw breath.

When the silence finally fell upon them, the queen stood from the bed, Edward's blood cascading down her body. Dressed only in blood, she walked across the room, leaving a trail of footprints behind her. Without pausing for a robe, the queen turned towards Mara and said, "He's all yours, niece," before turning and leaving the room.

Mara was unsure how long she remained violently shaking in the pool of blood before she finally managed to whisper. "Ph-up...Phil..."

"Forgive me, my lady," said a masculine voice from behind her. "Did you say..."

"Ph..Phi...up." Mara forced herself to draw a deep breath and attempted to clear her throat.

Unconsciously, she pressed her teeth against her bottom lip and had to fight the urge to vomit as the taste of Edward's blood danced upon the tip of her tongue. She forced herself to swallow and again tried to speak, this time managing to gain enough control over her voice to say, "Get Philip. Run!" She did not need to speak twice, as the young guard to her left sprinted towards the door.

Struggling to recall her training, Mara turned her eyes upon the rest of the room. "You," she motioned to a tall, dark-haired guard whose name she could not seem to recall. "Guard the door. Let no one in except Philip. Do you hear me? No one else."

"Yes, Captain," came the singular response as the man began to move towards the door.

Mara's eyes turned slowly back towards the broken form of the man lying upon the bed but spoke to those standing behind her. "Not a word of what you saw tonight." She issued the warning in as strong a tone as she could muster. "If anyone so much as breaths a word of what they saw tonight, I shall personally cut out the tongue that formed them. Is that understood?"

All three of the remaining men voiced their consent, but Mara did not acknowledge them, unable to tear her gaze from the blade protruding from Edward's chest.

His breaths came in short, wheezing gasps. She knew that the sooner the blade was removed, the sooner that he would be able to heal. She knew that she should remove the blade. Yet she remained motionless on the floor, unable to move as her pervious tremors returned to her body with a force of their own.

"My lady," one of the nameless men said. "What can we do?" Mara knew she should answer, but found herself frozen; the world around her seeming unreal as she continued to tremble upon the floor. "My lady?" The guard touched her right shoulder, causing her to jump, slipping deeper into the pool of blood.

"Mara?" This time it was Philip's voice. She turned towards him quickly, splashing more blood upon her already covered form. Relief filtered through her as she spun to find the tall man with sandy brown hair standing behind her. A member of the Royal Guard for more than eight hundred years, Philip had been promoted to second in command of the Queen's Personal Guard shortly after Edward had been promoted to captain. He stood in silence for several moments, taking in the gory scene. Then he turned his light blue eyes to where Mara knelt. "What? I..."

Her senses swirled in momentary relief at the arrival of the far more seasoned captain. "The blade..." She drew a short breath. "We have to take it out."

"Mara?" he asked, "what in the name of all the Gods..."

"Blood," Mara stuttered. "Too much blood." Philip walked across the room and helped Mara unsteadily to her feet. His eyes searched her body. "It's not mine," she managed to answer in broken words, "not mine."

"Take a breath, Mara. Try to breathe."

She obeyed and a few breaths later, the tremors running up and down her spine began to slow enough for her to turn back towards the man lying upon the bed.

Slowly, Mara walked towards Edward. The right side of his face and arm had been left untouched. She was relieved at this, realizing that even in her rage, the queen had not dared to risk injuring the captain's dominant hand.

One of the men Mara had threatened re-entered the room carrying several strips of cloth which he began to tear into various sizes. Mara wondered if Philip had ordered him to do so. If he had, she had completely missed the orders being given. "Thank you, Merin," Philip said softly, confirming Mara's thoughts.

Edward's glassy eyes looked into hers, his lips forming the shape of a repetitive question which his voice seemed unable to ask.

"Liza is safe," Mara answered him. "She is with Garreth." She leaned closer, being careful not to touch his skin. "Do you hear me, Edward? Liza is safe." A touch of relief seemed to filter through his eyes before he again gave a low moan. Mara drew a deep breath that proved only slightly steadier than the one before. "Listen, my love. You have a blade in your chest," she said to him slowly. "We have to take it out."

Panic returned to his eyes. Mara bent back to a kneeling position by the side of the bed. She took his trembling right hand in her left. She then leaned partially over him, positioning her face in his direct line of vision, blocking his view of the blade as Philip moved towards his other side. "Edward," Mara said from her awkward position, "I know you are hurting and I know you are scared."

"*Please,*" he managed to whisper.

She fought against her tears. "Edward. Look at me, *mi amor.*" He turned his dark gaze more directly into hers. "I am so sorry. I love you, and I am so very sorry." She drew a deep breath. "But we have to do this. I am right here and I promise you that we will get through this. I am going to stay right here, by your side." Edward's hand tightened on her own. "Forgive me."

Without warning, Philip pulled up on the crimson blade.

CHAPTER XLI

940 AD

FOR THREE DAYS MARA STOOD guard before his door, her right hand clutching the hilt of her sword. She neither ate nor slept. When at last she was too tired to stand, Garreth reached for her arm. "I can't." She shook her head.

"Mara," he replied. "I will not move from this door. You have my word." He motioned behind him. "Go see him."

Mara stared into Garreth's green eyes. "After what was done to him. After what I saw... After..."

"After what you saw," Garreth interrupted. "He needs you more than ever."

"Needs me? How could..." But her words lay constricted in her throat.

Garreth leaned forward and kissed her cheek. "Be strong, my lady. He needs you to be strong."

Mara drew a deep breath and nodded slowly. She turned her exhausted body and entered the room over which she had spent the previous days standing guard. The captain's injured form lay on the bed on the far side of the room, covered in thick wool blankets. When she reached the edge of the bed, Mara bent to one knee, fighting exhaustion to hold the expected position. She stared at the dark stone beneath her when Edward moved his hand forward, and touched the side of her face. "Captain," she said in a hoarse whisper. "Captain, I am... I can't..."

"Mara," Edward said, moving his hand to stroke her hair. "Mara, look at me."

A shiver ran through her body as she forced herself to raise her gaze. Words tumbled from her lips. "I'm so sorry. I...tell me what to do, Edward. I'll do anything. I should have..."

"Mara," he said, drawing a shallow breath. "There was nothing you could have done. Do you hear me? Nothing."

She shook her head. "Tell me what to do. What can I do?"

"Mara," he said gently as he continued to run his fingers through her long black hair. "My brave, brave Mara. You look so tired."

She shook her head.

"I need you to sleep, Mara."

"No. I have to stay by your side. I must guard...I must stay."

"Then stay, my lady. But you must sleep." He slid his hand to Mara's right arm, careful to avoid her injured hand. He pulled her forward to the edge of the bed.

"I tried to take care...I sent for Garreth. I tried to..."

"You did everything right; everything. You got the princess away from the queen. You got us out of there." He spoke more fiercely. "You saved me."

"I tried. I couldn't...I..."

"You saved me," he said again, brushing her hair back gently before pressing his palm against her left cheek. "But you need to rest now. You are no good to anyone like this. And...I need you."

"I'm afraid," she confessed. "I am afraid to dream."

He moved his hand back to Mara's arm, pulling her across the bed, causing her to fall beside him. "If you dream, I will wake you." He caught her gaze. "Let me hold you, Mara." Her heart beat against her right temple as Edward guided her head against the uninjured side of his chest.

"I should be guarding you."

"You have, Mara. You saved us. Now, I need you to rest. Please, *mea rosa*, lie here with me." She drew a deep breath, listening to the strong beat of his heart. She closed her eyes as he continued to stoke her hair. It was the last time she had ever known peace.

CHAPTER XLII

Present Day

"LIZA DIED THAT NIGHT," GARRETH continued, his voice filtering through the dimly lit room as the dancing flames pushed back against the biting cold that had begun to seep into the room. "Afterwards we...well, we..."

"We were never the same," Mara finished for him. "But Edward, he," she drew a quick breath, "it was like he had disappeared. Everything he was, everything he had been, vanished before our eyes. And without him, we struggled—struggled to maintain the guard, to protect the men under our charge, to stay true to our vows, to protect the captain from those who would have taken advantage, to...to."

"It was difficult," Garreth added. "Edward had always been the strength of the Guard."

"Yes," Mara agreed. "And without him we were broken, shattered, lost. And to be perfectly honest, he was gone for a very long time. We all suffered without him, but then after what had happened to him and to Liza no one could blame him. None of us were truly 'all right' until long after and a few of us would never be okay again."

"I don't understand though," Nolan stated. "I know that she was killed, but I don't know what actually happened. How did she die?"

Garreth and Mara stared at each other for several moments but it was Mara who finally answered. "They didn't just kill the princess; they mutilated her. They sliced open her face into strips of split flesh, gouged out her eyes until she was all but unrecognizable even after the blood had been cleared from her once beautiful face. And when Edward found out, he just...he was absolutely—" The words died upon her lips as Mara's gaze slid towards the back of the room and she found herself staring into Edward's enraged eyes. She stood from the chair in a single, fluid motion.

"How dare you!"

"Edward, please," Mara pleaded. "You don't understand."

"Go to Hell!"

"Edward," Garreth interjected, rising to stand beside Mara. "She's right, you don't understand. Please let us explain."

"How dare you talk about her! How dare you speak her name to someone who was not there! How could you? How dare you!"

With those words Edward turned and stormed from the room. Mara raced after him.

Nolan moved to follow, but stopped when Garreth grabbed his arm. "Let them go," he stated as the stone door closed behind Mara's fleeing form. "Only they can help each other now."

Mara followed Edward down the hall, being forced to break into a full-fledged run in order to catch up to his furious pace. "Edward, stop!" she screamed as she finally reached his side. "Stop, please stop.

He finally acquiesced and slowly turned to face her with a mixture of pain and anger, his hand holding tightly to the hilt of his Arius blade. "Why?" he demanded. "Why would you?"

"Because," she replied. "Once long ago, you, Phillip, Garreth and I made a choice and we have paid for it dearly. We have, our men have, and everyone we have ever known has. But, Edward, it was a choice. A choice we made."

"So, what are you saying, Mara? That he should know because it might cost his life?"

"No, Edward." Pain filtered through her voice. "Not his life—his very soul." She paused, allowing the words to fully settle upon him. "We gave our souls for something we believe in—believed in with the very fiber of our being, with ever beat of our heart. How can we now ask this young man to offer the same sacrifice without telling him why?" She shook her head. "If it were his life, that would be one thing, but it is more than that."

"What do you mean?"

She stared directly into his dark eyes. "I am not worried that he will die Edward; I am worried that he will live. If he does this, if he joins our ranks and chooses to attack the court into which he was born, the men he served alongside, and the king he once swore his life to protect, he will never be the same." She inhaled deeply.

"It will shatter a piece of his soul that no amount of time will ever heal. He will be like us, broken for the rest of time. So yes, Edward, he needs to know. He needs to know the consequences of such a choice and what it did to us." She drew another breath. "I cannot take responsibility for any more shattered souls, Edward. Can you?"

He took a step closer before answering. "Did it, Mara? Cost your soul?"

Her body began to tremble as she reached forward and placed her hand gently against his chest, pressing her fingers lightly over its center. "My soul is where it has always been, Edward. Right here, with you."

He reached to cup the side of her face with his left hand then said, "Mara," in a voice so fierce that her body jerked at the sound. He leaned even closer, shutting his eyes tightly as he drew an unsteady breath before again turning his dark eyes upon her. Then he kissed her. When he finally pulled back, it took several moments for Mara to find her voice.

"What do you want, Edward? What do you..." She drew a constricted breath. "Please tell me. I will do anything you ask."

"I have no right to ask anything of you. I have no..."

"You have the only right! My soul, my heart, my life—they belong to you. They always have. Please, my love, tell me how to help you."

He reached forward, forcing her back against the wall of the corridor. He grabbed both her wrists with a single hand, drawing her arms above her, trapping her against the cold stone. He kissed her again, molding her lips against his own, as the world began to spiral. Mara had no concept of time as he held her there, equally unwilling and unable to resist as he possessed her. When he finally drew back, Mara stared into his familiar dark eyes and recognized a mixture of emotions she knew all too well: fear and desire, horror and desperation, anger and love—all blended into one, singular moment.

"Six hundred years," she said without thought. "I've waited six hundred years. And now you...you."

"I know," he replied, refusing to loosen his iron grip on her slender wrists which he still held above her. "I know I never do right by you. I know I have hurt you and that you hate me for it. I know this isn't right. I know that..."

"It's the only thing that *is* right! And I never hated you. Not when you left, not when you told me you loved Liza, not when you fell apart and not even when we crossed..."

Her words faltered. She could almost hear the sound of blades clashing, could see the glint of steel that seemed to shimmer in the dying light of the setting sun; the sharp, sudden pain. "Even then I could not bring myself to hate you, *mi amor*. I love you." She shook her head. "I did not want to tell him what happened. I did not want...I did not. But he has to know."

Edward jerked her from the wall and pulled her close, wrapping his arms around her, creating the only stability in her crumbling world. "I am sorry," he said softly. "When I saw the blade lying on the bed, I knew what it must have cost you. I thought you were gone, that I had lost you all over again. *ignosce mihi*. I was so..." He could not bring himself to say the words, and instead buried his face against the side of Mara's neck.

She remained silent for several minutes, allowing him to cling to her, before finally forcing herself to speak. "Edward," she said softly. "I need to help Garreth finish the story. I need to tell him about the battle of the Muir Court. Garreth, he...he can't do it alone."

Edward dropped his arms from around her and stepped back enough to nod. "Okay, Mara. I will go with you and we will finish the tale."

"You don't have to do that."

"Yes, I do," he replied. "You asked me what I want?"

Mara nodded.

"I don't ever want you to be alone again. I want..." He searched her gaze. "I want to save you."

His words threatened to bring fresh tears to her eyes. "You can't. I was damned a long, long time ago. But Nolan, and this young woman they have taken, we still might be able to save them. Please, Edward. Help me save them."

"How? Tell me how."

"Stand by my side." She paused. "Stand by my side, until I ask you to step aside. Then allow me to do what must be done."

CHAPTER XLIII

"WE TOOK TURNS RUNNING THE Guard—Garreth, Phillip and I—revolving constantly around Edward's chambers to maintain the appearance that he was still the one giving the commands. Eventually he came out of his room, but as little more than a silent guardsman. We protected him from challenges only by the basic principle that to become the captain, challengers first had to defeat the sub-captains, and as you are aware, Nolan, with a blade we had few equals.

"We tried to protect the youngest of the Guard from the queen, but were not always successful. When we failed, we paid the price with flesh and with blood. Some say our screams still echo down those dark halls."

Her words trailed, prompting Nolan to gently ask, "Do they?"

Mara drew a slow breath. "The screams...are not mine." She could almost hear the sound of the whip crashing down upon exposed flesh. "Never mine." The smell of blood that faded long ago permeated the air; the metallic taste of it. She could feel the weight of the leather gripped firmly in her hand as she again brought the metal tips down upon Philip's exposed back, dragged the jagged metal down along both sides of his spine with practiced precision. He screamed as the teeth big deep into his skin. She jerked her arm back and could hear the sound of ripping flesh as the metal fought to remain firmly embedded. Then she again moved the whip down, drawing a fresh set of screams.

1200 AD

"PHILLIP," SHE SAID, EXHAUSTED. "I think..."

"Finish it," he commanded through a harsh breath.

"I..."

"Damn it, Mara!"

She nodded reluctantly and continued the session, tearing again and again through the layers of Phillip's skin until it was stripped away enough to bite into the exposed muscle beneath. Forty long, careful strokes with a three-pronged whip for a sin he had never committed. When she finally stopped, she moved to the stone slab upon which Phillip lay and sank to the ground beside him. She tightened her grip upon the handle of the whip and threw it across the room with what little strength remained. Then she buried her face into the palm of her hands and let out a muffled scream.

"Mara." Phillip tried to reassure her, but his voice was hoarse and he was too injured to even reach out a hand to comfort her. After several moments of suppressed sobs, Mara turned and reached for Phillip's hand, touching the tips of her fingers to his. "I..." She shook her head. "Phillip, I can't do this for much longer." His hand was trembling in hers from the intensity of the pain. She leaned down and placed her face against his hand as though a child seeking comfort. "I'm sorry," she whispered. "Philip, I am so sorry."

"Shh," he shushed her through a shallow breath. He moved his fingers to brush a strand of hair from her left cheek. "You did only what was required, Mara. Nothing more."

"Forgive me."

"Freely," he replied. "This is not your fault, Mara. You—" A sharp intake of breath showed his continuous level of pain.

"Why does she do this?" Mara asked, the words muffled. "I can't do this much longer. I am not the captain, I am not supposed to be. I cannot keep pretending that I am."

"It's okay." Phillip continued to stroke Mara's left cheek. "Breathe, Mara. Just breathe."

She did as he commanded, closing her eyes as she drew a series of deep breaths, feeling her heart begin to slow. Then she climbed unsteadily to her feet and called to the men guarding the outside doors of the chamber. "Help the sub-captain," she ordered. They came in quickly and assisted Phillip to his feet before beginning the long climb to his chambers. Every moan that escaped his lips struck another blow to Mara's exhausted form as they moved the injured man up a sea of seemingly endless stairs to his private chambers. They called for the healers and settled him as comfortably as they could on his bed. After the injuries were properly dressed, one of the healers moved toward Mara. When the woman's pale hand reached for her left cheek, Mara jerked back.

"Forgive me, my lady. I was attempting to assess your injuries."

"My what?" It was only then, as her hand moved to the side of her face, that Mara realized that her skin had been splattered with Phillip's blood. "It's not mine."

An hour later, Mara was walking down the ancient halls to the hidden hot springs which the courts had been built around. As this particular spring had been set aside specifically for those of the highest rank, Mara was relieved to find it deserted. She removed her saturated clothes and stepped into the searing water, which turned pink as she sank into its depths. She slowly scrubbed her pale skin, cleansing away all remnants of her betrayal. She leaned down, dipping her long hair into the water, wringing more blood from the strands. She kept her face in the searing heat until she could stand it no longer and arose gasping for air.

She moved to the side and seated herself on the polished stone as the colored water began to clear. Her body shuddered in spite of the hot water and she sank further down until she was immersed to her neck. She had no idea how long she sat there longing for the silent tranquility which she knew would never come.

Then the moment was broken as a young girl entered the chamber. With mousey brown hair and green eyes, the girl curtsied as she paused by the pool. “Forgive me, my lady,” the child said. “Captain Edward has summoned Lord Phillip to his chambers. I was told that the order was to be given to you instead.”

Mara nodded before motioning to the pile of cloth lying on the opposite side of the pool. The girl grabbed one from the top of the pile without being asked and brought the cloth to Mara.

She rose from the water, wringing as much from her hair as possible. She then ran the rough material over her body for several moments. Having planned to retire for the evening, Mara had brought only a thin, low-cut gown of dark silk which clung to her damp skin. She ran a comb quickly through the wet strands of her hair, not bothering to pull it back as was her custom. Pulling a matching silk robe over her shoulders, Mara walked from the chambers and into the cool night air.

It was a short walk to the captain’s chambers. When she arrived it was to find Brendan standing in front of the doors. “I’ve been summoned,” she informed him.

Brendan opened the door without question and announced her arrival. She stepped through the doors and walked quickly towards the center of the room where Edward stood a few paces in front of the bed. “Mara?”

“Forgive me,” she stated, “but Phillip is indisposed at the moment. He asked me to answer you in his stead.”

Edward did not question this, but instead gave a single nod. “Members of the Royal family from the Muir Court will be calling upon the queen next week.”

“Yes,” Mara replied. “I am aware of the upcoming visit.”

“We need to increase the queen’s security while they are here. Ensure that one of the sub-captains are with her at all times. Perhaps we could add one or two of the newer members as well? It would give them a chance to be on a royal detail.”

"No," Mara responded too quickly. "I do not believe that we need to add any more new personnel to the regular guard detail at this time. Those assigned can handle the royal visit."

"Are you sure it will be enough?"

"Yes," she replied, a hint of anger beginning to slide into her voice at having her assessment questioned. "The queen's regular guard detail should be more than adequate." How could Edward possibly even consider suggesting placing anyone else within the queen's line of vision?

"And you or Phillip will remain with the queen?"

Aren't we always, she thought. Aloud she said simply, "Yes."

"At all times?"

Her anger returned more fiercely than before. "Unless you would like to take a shift for once?"

"What?"

Mara attempted to rein in her words. She closed her eyes to clear her head, but instead found herself standing in the torture chamber, bringing the whip down upon Phillip's back, tearing the flesh from his bones. Her eyes opened and gave in to her anger. "I said, unless you would like to take a shift for once."

Edward straightened and his eyes began to narrow. "I do not care for your tone, Mara. Do I need to remind you that you are speaking to your captain?"

"Exactly!" she interjected. "My *captain.* Yet you want *me* to re-organize the guard. Me to guard the queen *you* are sworn to protect. When is the last time you placed yourself in a role of leadership, Captain?" She drew a breath but the words continued to tumble forth. "This guard is crumbling. The men are screaming for leadership and everyone can hear them but you! They are calling for you, begging for you, spilling the very blood from their veins to keep the queen from wondering where you are." Anger pushed her forward. "Why don't you take the shift yourself!"

"How dare you!" Edward shot back. "I am your captain and you will treat—"

"Then be the captain, Edward!" she all but screamed. "Be the captain! Open your eyes and lead them!"

"I am doing the best I can."

"Not good enough!" Mara took a step closer, narrowing the distance between them. "They need you to lead them, Edward, because I cannot. I am not the captain, you are. These men—your men—need you now. I'm sorry." Her voice grew softer. "I'm sorry she died and I'm sorry I wasn't there when it happened. I will carry her death to my grave. But, Edward, I cannot do this anymore. I need..." She drew a ragged breath as her anger faded to a plea. "They need you." Her body began to tremble. "I need you."

He reached forward and placed his hands just below her slender wrists, taking them firmly within his grasp. He pulled her forward, moving her to a seated position upon the bed. He towered over her.

"Edward..." But her words fell silent as he reached down, placing a finger under her chin and raising her gaze to meet his. His eyes searched her features with a haunted expression and she felt her words become trapped within her throat. "Please," she managed to whisper. "Help me."

He moved his hand to the side of her face, running the tips of his fingers lightly over her pale skin. "Edward," she whispered his name. His fingers traced their way slowly down her cheek and, brushing back several strands of her dark hair before tracing the outline of her full lips, parting them slightly as he continued to stare down at her.

Then his hand slid lower, down her neck to pause at the hollow of her throat and Mara wondered if he could feel the frantic beat of her heart. She closed her eyes as his hand slid even lower, reaching the edge of her silk dress. He traced the silk edge to her shoulders where he suddenly jerked the outer robe from her shoulders, exposing even more of her pale skin.

"Edward, don't," she protested, but her voice was lacking the conviction she had hoped to convey. He froze at her words, but did not pull back.

He searched her body with nothing but with his gaze, which slid slowly up and down her body as she sat motionlessly, the light of the flames illuminating her pale skin. He reached forward, capturing her slender wrists in his hand and pushed her down on the bed with such strength that Mara knew she would need to forcefully resist to break his hold. She allowed him to push her down, the satin of her gown sinking into the thick blankets.

"Please." Her voice again arose soft and insecure. "Edward," she whispered, not knowing if she was pleading for him to stop, or to never let her go.

He moved his hand towards her left cheek and traced her features with the tips of his fingers. Her high, blushed cheeks, her sharp chin, the hollow of her throat. His fingers explored her possessively as his gaze bore through her violet eyes, directly into her soul.

Mara's heart was beating frantically under his possessive touch. His finger dug against the racing pulse in the side of her neck, all the while, keeping his other hand wrapped tightly around her wrists which fit easily inside his grasp. She gazed as his other hand trailed lower, sliding along the edge of her low-cut gown.

Resisting the overwhelming urge to completely abandon herself to Edward's control, Mara parted her lips to protest his invasion of her body, when his hand dipped lower to cup her breast through the thin, satin material.

She gasped at the touch, nerves awakening which she had previously thought long dead. Her heart increased its already rapid pace as his hand slid under the dress, slowly ripping the material that had clung to her body.

Mara squirmed at the sound of the ripping material, causing Edward to increase the pressure on her wrists to a point that pulled a slight cry of pain from her lips. She attempted to rise, but Edward was having none of it, and ripped her gown further, completely exposing her breasts to his wild gaze. There was something primal in his movements, a need which bordered upon desperation, and one which Mara was unable to refuse. Every protest was driven from her mind as Edward's hand explored her exposed flesh, his fingers sliding in circles around the soft tissue before enclosing upon her hardening nipples.

Her body jerked at his touch, her nerves set aflame by the touch of his skin against her taut flesh. His fingers tweaked the nipple of her right breast, drawing a gasp from deep in her throat. He slid his body further on the bed, pressing his weight against her own, trapping her more firmly against the bed. He dipped his head and pressed her mouth against unresisting lips before finally releasing his grasp on Mara's wrists. She raised her arms to wrap them around Edward's neck as he leaned forward and offered a deep, passionate kiss.

Her breathing became labored and her body tightened. She kissed him harder, pulling a low moan from the man laying above her.

Then Edward pulled back enough to stare into her violet eyes. In a deep voice that was tinged with the promise of all that was to come, Edward spoke a single word: "Liza."

CHAPTER XLIV

1200 AD

THE SOUND OF LIZA'S NAME brought Mara's passion to a halt. Of course Edward would want to take her to his bed—Mara, the spitting image of a dead princess. How could she have thought for a single moment that it was not for her but for Liza alone to whom Edward had ultimately given his heart? Liza, who his fingers had once held so tenderly. Liza, for whom his very heart had once beaten.

Edward's hand slid back toward Mara's full breasts, but all the passion that had flowed through her so magnificently only moments before had vanished. Edward paused and looked down upon Mara's now still form as realization dawned. Mara saw the look as one of confusion that quickly turned to horror as his gaze travelled from her bruised wrists to her torn dress. He shook his head as though in disbelief and finally said, "Mara?"

Mara's heart broke even further at the confused tone which emanated from Edward's voice. Tears threatened her eyes, but she did not allow them to fall. Instead she drew a deep breath and said, "Yes, Edward. It's me; it's Mara."

"Oh my Gods! What did I almost—" He searched her gaze.

"It's okay, Edward," she said softly, moving her hand to his left cheek, gazing up at him from where she lay. "It is okay."

"No." He shook his head, the frustration slowly filtering through his voice. "Why...why am I constantly hurting you? Why?" He drew a ragged breath. Mara moved her arms around his shoulders and pulled him down against her. His weight was almost crushing, but she ignored this, instead holding him tightly.

"It. Is. Not. Okay." He spoke through clenched teeth. His body trembled against hers. "She's gone. She's just..." He drew a deep breath. Mara twisted her arms to the best of her ability to run her fingers through the edge of Edward's dark hair.

He pulled back at her touch and rose to a seated position on the side of the bed. He gazed down at her, his eyes pouring over her exposed flesh. "Oh Gods, what have I done? I almost..." He found her gaze. "Mara, I..."

Mara sat up beside him, pulling her gown up high enough to cover her breasts. She placed her hand on Edward's upper arm. "Please, Edward," she spoke firmly, "don't apologize."

"But I hurt you. I am always hurting you."

She felt her lips tremble as she stared into Edward's broken eyes. "Not half as much as you will hurt me if you apologize for what just happened."

"But I forced—"

"You did no such thing!" Mara rose to her knees, moving both hands to opposite sides of Edward's face. Struggling to control her voice, she focused her attention to the man in front of her.

"She is gone," Mara said slowly. "Liza is gone. There is nothing in the power of men or Gods that can return her to you. I would give my blood, my life, my very soul to bring her back, but I can't, Edward. No force in this world can. But, Edward, I am here." She paused, forcing herself to draw breath as she lost her battle and tears began to gather in the corner of her eyes. "I love you, Edward. I love you, but you're not here." Her hand caressed his cheek in an involuntary act. "You're gone and it breaks my heart every time I look into your eyes." She leaned forward and kissed him. "You once said that you would always come for me, Edward. Now, I am begging you, please, my love. Come back to me."

She stared at him across a vast abyss that could not be seen, only felt. She stared through several deep, trembling breaths before finally speaking in a resigned voice. "I will wait," she finally stated, "until I draw my last breath." She gathered herself from the bed and walked slowly towards the stone doors.

CHAPTER XLV

1200 AD

A FEW DAYS LATER THE royal entourage arrived. Mara rode with Garreth on the five hour journey to the edge of the kingdom where they awaited the arrival of the Prince of the Muir Court. There were fifteen members of the guard in their welcome party, and would be joined by members of the prince's own honor guard upon their arrival. Meetings such as this one tended to occur once every five years. It was a way for the two courts to appear on good terms while privately scheming to overthrow each other the moment the meetings were over. It was a game they had been playing for over a thousand years.

The line between kingdoms had been drawn along the edge of a lush forest. It took a half hour before the other party materialized, emerging from the tall trees. Astride black stallions, Mara and Garreth moved their respective mounts several paces ahead of the general entourage. From across the field, two members of the Muir Court did the same.

The Crown Prince of the Muir Court was easily recognizable. Tall with blond hair and deep blue eyes touched by the sea, he portrayed a level of power not easily mistaken for anything but one of royal blood. Astride a white horse, the prince was garbed in a black, long-sleeved shirt under a full-length dark blue coat with silver trim. Beside him rode his captain, Erik, in a blue shirt which was a perfect match for the black outfits worn by members of the Lorcan Court Guard. The riders slowed their pace as they approached the center of the field, eventually pulling their horses to a complete stop.

"Greetings, Prince Nicholi," Garreth said to the royal.

"Greetings," the prince replied, eying the two riders. "I see the captain did not see fit to come himself."

"The Captain of the Queen's Guard belongs by her side," Mara answered quickly.

Nicholi gave a nod. "Well, at least he sent his prettier half. How are you, Princess Mara?"

"That is not a title to which I answer, Your Highness. As you are well aware."

"Ah, but it could be." Nicholi gave a small chuckle. "Or even a queen if you prefer, once I am seated upon my father's throne."

"Sub-Captain or Lady will suffice."

The prince stared at her intently for a moment, then he shook his head with another laugh. "As stubborn as ever. The man between your sheets must be a lucky one indeed."

"Luckier than you." She offered a tight smile.

"Ha! Yes, indeed."

It was then that Garreth interrupted. "Shall we move this conversation closer to the palace? There is still a bit of a journey ahead of us."

"Of course, Sub-Captain," the prince replied. "Let us not keep your queen waiting."

Mara turned her horse and took a position just to the right of the prince, her rightful place as one of the chosen royal escorts while Erik and Garreth rode on his left.

They rode at a steady pace for several hours, reaching the palace grounds as night was just beginning to drown out the colors of day. They were then greeted at the door by Phillip who informed the tired party that refreshments had been prepared for their arrival and that the guest chambers had been prepared to receive the courts visitors.

"Good," Nicholi smiled. "I am much too exhausted to deal with matters of state tonight anyway."

"Yes," Phillip replied. "The queen imagined that might be the case. She has asked that you enjoy yourself for the night and said to inform you that she shall call at first light."

The prince nodded and moved toward an escort who was to lead him to his prepared chambers, when he suddenly stopped and turned back to where Mara stood several paces to his right. "Care to join me?" he asked with a crude smile.

Mara remained silent.

"Well, you know where I am if you change your mind." Then he turned and, soon after, vanished into the hallway beyond.

"Bastard," a voice said unexpectedly. Mara turned in surprise to see it was the prince's own captain who had spoken. "It's true. If you had any idea..." He shook his head. "Steer clear of him, Mara."

"These hallways have ears," she cautioned him. "But then again, I have a feeling you already know this."

"Still, my warning remains the same. Be careful, my lady."

She drew a deep breath and then stated. "Thank you, my lord. I have no intention of doing otherwise."

Mara rose early the next morning, before dawn, and went to find Phillip. However, when she finally reached his chamber doors, it was to find him still in bed. "Phillip," she called, entering his chambers without bothering to announce herself. "Did you oversleep?"

"What?' he mumbled groggily. "I'm not on duty today."

"What do you mean? The Prince of the Muir Court is here. Edward ordered us to stay by the queen's side at all times."

"Hmmm." He forced his eyes open. "Did he change his mind again?"

"His mind?"

"Edward told me last night that he was going to take the shift himself."

Mara's heart skipped a beat. "He what?"

Fully awake, Phillip rose to a seated position. "Edward said he was going to watch over the queen today."

Mara stared at him incredulously

"I know, it surprised me, too. But, well...he is the captain." He leaned closer to where Mara stood. "What is it?"

She stared at him for several moments and finally asked. "Do you trust me?"

"Of course. Mara, what is going on?"

"Get dressed," came her response. "Stand on the guard detail anyway."

"I knew it! Something happened when you went to see Edward. Brendan said he thought he heard you yelling."

"Brendan should learn not to report on his superiors," Mara answered curtly. "Are you coming or not?"

"Well, since I am already awake."

Mara turned to leave the room when he called after her. "I'll only ask this once. I don't know what you did to get Edward out of that room, but...are you okay?"

She stared back at him and finally said, "No," before stepping quickly from the room.

Chapter XLVI

1200 AD

LESS THAN AN HOUR LATER, Mara was standing along the outer doors of the queen's private chambers. Normally, she would be inside receiving last minute instructions, but today that task was Edward's. "Strange, isn't it?" Phillip asked from beside her. "To not be the one bound to her side. Almost feels like a demotion."

"A relief is more like it," she replied for him alone.

"Then why don't you look more relaxed?"

"Do I not?" She attempted to concentrate, but her mind kept flickering to the last time Edward has been brought before the queen

"Mara?" Phillip interrupted her thoughts.

"Sorry. What did you say?"

Concern crossed his features. "My lady, why don't you take the day off instead? I will help Edward with the queen and there is no need to have three captains in the room. Two will more than suffice."

"No," she answered far too quickly. "I am fine."

He searched her eyes. "I am not certain that you are. Should I make your dismissal a command?"

"Don't." She drew a sharp breath. "Please, Phillip. I need to be here. I have to."

He considered her for a moment, then nodded. "All right, but watch yourself today, my lady. The queen will be on her best behavior with the prince here. Everything will be fine. I..."

"Don't promise. Just...don't."

"Okay. No promises."

They turned to silence as they waited until, finally, the door opened and Edward emerged. "Phillip." He addressed the older man first. "I thought I gave you the day off."

"Yes, Captain. However, I thought, given the company to be received today, that the appearance of another sub-captain would not be deemed inappropriate." Edward nodded, seeming to accept this answer before turning his gaze to Mara.

"The guard is ready, Captain. They await your command."

"Thank you," he replied, but did not meet her violet eyes.

A short time later, the prince arrived with several of his guardsmen and royal advisors. "Ah," the prince said as he approached. "The long-lost captain makes his appearance at last, and with my future bride by his side."

Mara felt herself visibly stiffen.

"Tell me, Princess, was it for the ability to carry a sword you surrendered your crown? Or was it instead for license to stand between two such as these?" He motioned to the men who stood beside her.

Mara did not answer, but instead allowed Edward to take the lead. "The queen awaits you in the study, Your Highness. If you would follow us this way."

He turned, leading the prince through a set of doors to their right and into the queen's private study. It was a room lined with rows of books and old rolls of parchment. A fire blazed against the far wall where multiple chairs had been placed for the honored guests.

The queen stood a few paces in front of them, dressed in a full-length gown of black velvet with a scooped neckline and silver trim. A matching silver crown graced her brow and her long dark hair lay straight down her back. Sometimes it still amazed Mara how young and beautiful her aunt appeared, and how strikingly similar to Mara's own reflection.

Mara took her place beside the door as the prince stepped forward to bow before the queen. "Greetings, Your Majesty. May the blessings of the Muir Court be upon you."

"The same to you of the Lorcan," the queen replied before motioning to the chairs behind her. "Shall we sit and speak together?"

The prince nodded his consent before moving to take the offered seat. The two royals exchanged polite pleasantries until the conversation eventually shifted to matters of state. Edward, who stood on the opposite side of the room only a few paces from the queen, was as still as Mara had ever seen him. There was a tension to his frame, a tightness in the way his hand clutched the hilt of his silver Arius blade.

He caught her gaze and she suddenly found herself unable to look away. When was the last time he had looked at her like that? Was it before Liza had died? Or perhaps before that, before Liza had even been born? Liza had changed him—had changed them all, really. Made them softer, gentler. Now, that softness was but an ancient memory.

She forced her eyes back to a forward glance to the far wall which she maintained throughout the remainder of the meeting. Their talks were a quiet affair, at the end of which the guards were dismissed with simple instructions to return the next morning. And so it went continued until the last night when a banquet was held for the nobles and Mara cautiously added Brendan and Jacob to the roster of the Royal Guard. The royals drank and made merry until well into the night when suddenly, Erik stepped forward. "May I have the honor of a dance, Lady Mara?"

Startled, she raised her gaze to Phillip, who shrugged as though to say, *your choice*. Then she turned back to the Captain of the Muir Court. "I am flattered, my lord. But hardly dressed for the..."

"You look ravishing, my lady. Please, grant me this honor."

She nodded and allowed Erik to lead her onto the dance floor. A soft tune filled the room from the royal musicians as the two captains bowed and began to glide across the floor. As they transitioned into a more intimate portion of the dance, the captain said, "I am glad to see that you took my words to heart."

"They were well received," she replied quietly.

The two separated momentarily in the twisting of the dance and then turned again, one towards the other. "He is not what you think," Erik whispered as he twirled her in his arms. "He is a monster."

"What?" They came to a complete standstill as the music came to an end.

"Call on me tonight," he whispered as he gave a bow and left the floor.

Mara stood momentarily confounded before finally managing to find her way out of the crowd to resume her previous stance against the stone wall. She re-positioned her sword at her side and then looked up to find Edward's dark gaze upon her. She ignored him, waiting out the end of the festivities before turning to her chambers. She replayed the dance for some time before finally emerging from her room. She walked down a series of long hallways and eventually knocked on Brendan's door, awakening the young lord from his slumber. "Brendan," she said. "Do you remember that night, when I declared the right of substitution?"

"Yes, my lady."

"Good. I want you to keep that in mind when I tell you that I need a favor of absolute secrecy." He nodded without speaking, so Mara continued. "I need you to go to the rooms being occupied by the Muir Court and I need you to bring Captain Erik here to your chambers. I need you to tell no one—not even Phillip."

Brendan nodded and quickly left to carry out her bidding. A few minutes later, Brendan re-entered the chambers with the Muir Court captain following closely behind him. Upon his arrival, she turned to Brendan.

"Whatever you may hear, I charge you to absolute secrecy. Should you by any chance have been seen or be questioned as to the details of this meeting, you are to say that you, being a young knight, were honored by the chance to converse with such an esteemed captain. Tell them he told you of fighting in the Golden Age of the Roman Empire and for the glory of Ancient

Greece." Brendan gave a bow and moved towards the far wall without being asked. Then Mara turned her attention to the Muir captain. "My lord?"

Erik studied her for several moments before speaking. "Honor," he stated, "is such a tricky thing. Makes it difficult to know what can and cannot be spoken, before it exists no more."

"I find it hard to believe, my lord, that one such as yourself could lose your honor so easily. You are a hero among a sea of legends."

He offered a sad smile. "My lady, if you knew but a fraction of the things I have done to gain such a reputation, a 'hero' is the last thing you would see."

"And what would I see?"

"A killer," he replied. "Perhaps one of the greatest to ever live, but a killer, nonetheless." He took a step forward. "And one day, my lady, you shall be as well."

Mara stared at him for several long moments. "You would like to speak with me, my lord?"

"Only to tell you that the one you seek is within your grasp. And if you search long enough, are determined enough, you will find him. But beware—vengeance comes at a high cost and you may not like what you have become once it is achieved."

Mara's breath caught in her throat. "You know who killed her."

"That, I cannot say."

"Then why did you ask to speak with me?"

"To tell you to beware. You may have rejected your title, but the same royal blood which condemned the princess to her fate even now flows through your veins."

"Who killed our princess?" she asked again.

"I can say no more." Erik reached forward and traced his hand along the side of her face, brushing through the long strands of her dark hair. "I dread the day I see you across the field of battle. Yet, I know that the day will come." He continued to stare into her violet eyes and then, to her further surprise, he leaned down and kissed her. "When that day comes, my lady, consider this kindness I have shown. Kill me quickly and I shall consider the debt repaid."

CHAPTER XLVII

1200 AD

TWO DAYS LATER, AFTER THE members of the Muir Court had been seen safely back to the edge of their own kingdom, Mara was summoned to the door of the queen's chambers. When she arrived, it was to find other members of the guard, including Brendan and Phillip, had also been summoned. "I think she called all who worked on the royal detail while the Muir Court was in residence." Mara nodded and then proceeded to follow the crowd into the rooms beyond.

The queen stood near the center of the room dressed in a silver, full-length gown with long, flowing sleeves. "Your Majesty." Mara bowed, but the queen did not glance her way. Mara swept the room. Garreth, Edward and Jacob stood several feet to her left while Phillip and Brendan were on her right. Along the back wall stood several more members of the guard, but their faces were cast in shadow. She took a step towards Phillip, creating a half-circle around the queen, who had turned to address her captain.

"Is this all?" the queen inquired.

"Yes, my lady."

"Good." She nodded. "I would like to congratulate you all on a job well done. The royals of the Muir Court arrived and left safely. All appears to have gone smoothly. This speaks to the discipline and loyalty of the members of this guard."

Mara had to prevent herself from audibly sighing in relief. But relief had come too quickly.

"Or are you?" the queen suddenly asked the captain.

"My lady?"

"Are you, all of you, my most loyal of knights?" Her gaze traveled the room, but it was Brendan who her gaze finally settled upon.

"Yes, my queen," he answered tentatively.

"Then tell me, young knight. Where were you the night of the final banquet?"

"On guard in the dining halls, Your Majesty."

"And tell me, Brendan. What happened after the banquet?"

"My...after?"

"Yes," the queen answered. "What did you do after the banquet?"

"I..."

"What were you, barely more than a child, doing in a private meeting with the Captain of the Muir Guard?"

Brendan drew a breath and delivered the rehearsed answer. "Captain Erik offered to tell me a few stories of his victories in Rome and Ancient Greece." Brendan forced a nervous smile. "Did you know he actually fought beside Caesar? I had been dying to hear the tales."

The queen considered him for a moment. "In the middle of the night? You honestly expect me to believe this story?"

"There was no time during the day, Your Majesty. As the captains were in meetings every day of the trip. I was most honored by his agreement to come and speak with me."

The queen stepped closer to where Brendan stood until she was a few paces away. "Perhaps you are telling the truth." She paused. "Then again, perhaps you are not."

"I assure you, I am."

Mara's eyes closed tightly at the tone in the queen's voice—one she knew all too well.

"Hmm," the queen mused. "I suppose this is nothing a few rounds with the lash will not sort out."

Mara drew a breath to speak, when Edward called, "My queen, I have never known the boy to lie. You have my word to vouch for his honor."

"Your word?" the queen stated as she turned those dark eyes upon the captain.

"Yes." Edward took a step forward, his hand upon the hilt of the silver blade by his side. "If the boy says he is telling the truth, there is no reason to disbelieve him."

"So quick to come to his defense, Captain. Perhaps it is you who needs to be questioned." She closed the distance between them. "Hand me your blade."

Mara's heart began to race as Edward handed his sword hilt-first to his queen. She took the blade in her hand. "Such a magnificent weapon. To think with a single stroke, you would forever bear its mark." She shook her head and then tossed the blade aside. It struck the floor with a loud clatter. "Perhaps something a little less lethal." She pulled a smaller, thin blade from her side.

"My queen," Mara interjected, walking quickly across the floor. "The boy is not lying. He wanted to hear Erik's stories. I arranged the meeting myself. I can personally promise it was nothing untoward. There is no need for this."

"Hmm," the queen answered without removing herself from the man standing in front of her. "Then it seems only the captain is in need of a lesson."

"Please, Your Majesty." Mara paused a single pace from where the queen stood. "They did nothing wrong."

The queen did not reply, but instead raised the blade and sliced through the dark fabric of Edward's shirt, revealing the smooth lines of his pale chest.

Mara's breathing began to quicken. Her heart pounded even harder in her chest. "My queen," she tried again, "please don't." Phillip moved forward but froze as Mara took her last step, placing herself physically between the queen and her captain. "I arranged the meeting. Punish me, if you must. But Edward had nothing to do with it."

"Mara." Edward tried to move her, but she brushed him away.

"Be careful," the queen said. "You give away your weakness far too easily."

"That may be," she replied. "But it does not change the facts. Please." Mara slid to her knees and gazed up, meeting the queen's gaze with her violet eyes. "Aunt Clarissa, please."

The queen stared down for several moment and her voice grew cold. "That is not going to work, my child. Not this time." The queen moved her thin blade in a forward motion toward Edward's left side. It flew forward but instead of flesh, met the cold steel of Mara's silver blade.

CHAPTER XLVIII

Present Day

"WAIT," NOLAN EXCLAIMED FROM HIS seat beside Mara. "You raised your blade...to the queen?"

Mara shifted in her seat uncomfortably and exchanged a glance with Garreth, who cleared his throat. "Yes," he answered for her. "Mara raised her blade to the queen."

1200 AD

GARRETH COULD RECALL THE SCENE as though it had happened only moments before. The sound of colliding metal echoing through the dark room. The silence which followed. The men against the far wall surging forward, only to hesitate as the sub-captains pulled their own swords to meet them. All eyes slowly turning to where Mara sat frozen upon the stone floor, her blade crossed with that of the queen's.

It was the queen who broke the silence. "I could have you killed for this."

Mara met her aunt's gaze directly. Her heart pounded against her chest, yet her grip upon her sword remained steady. It was the queen who pulled back first, lowering her sword to her side. "Clear the room," she commanded. "I wish to speak with my niece alone."

The crowd thinned quickly, most relieved to escape the storm to come. Yet Garreth, Phillip and Edward remained. "I said, alone," the queen repeated.

"Your Majesty," Edward said from his place behind Mara. "If I could just—"

"Do as she commands," Mara cut him off. "She is right. This is between family. Isn't it, Aunt Clarissa?"

"Yes. Garreth, you stay. The rest of you leave, or face my wrath."

"Mara." Edward's voice betrayed them both.

"Go," she said, knowing that if she turned into his dark eyes she would lose all of her hard-won resolve. Phillip stepped forward and gently began to lead Edward from the room when he suddenly knelt down and grabbed both her arms. "Mara..."

"Too late," she replied refusing to look into his eyes. "I cannot do this with you here." He stared at her for a moment. Then he stood and left the room without another word.

When only Garreth remained, the queen turned her dark eyes upon her niece. "You earned a death sentence today, Mara. Were you aware of this, when you pulled a blade upon your sovereign queen?" Mara met the queen's gaze directly, attempting desperately to slow the frantic beating of her heart. "Do you understand me, niece? For what you have done, I have the right to take your life."

"Then take it, and let us be done with it."

"Still in love with him," the queen said quietly. "Who would have guessed that after all these years—after all the pain he has put you through—that you would still love him enough to put your life between his flesh and my blade." She shook her head. "How painful it must be to love someone that much, knowing he has nothing to offer in return. How...tragic." She paused. "What a horrifyingly incredible thing, to love as you do. So...like your mother."

The queen knelt down until she was eye level with Mara. "Tell me, niece, if I ordered Edward's life to be taken in your place, would you choose, as did your mother, to follow him to the funeral pyre?"

The words crashed down upon the younger woman, pulling memories from the darkest recesses of her mind. Her mother crumpling in Garreth's arms as she learned of her husband's death. The complete abandonment as her mother was incoherently carried to the bedroom, leaving Edward, to inform the young princess that her father was never coming home. Mara's breath caught in her throat, memories devouring her making it difficult to think, to speak, to breathe. The queen leaned closer and gently caressed the side of Mara's face with a tenderness she had never known from her aunt. "Tell me, Mellissa," she called Mara by her mother's name, "what is it like to love that much? To give your entire being into the hands of another and to have them offer the same? What is it like, Mellissa?"

Mara parted her lips to answer, then began to trembled as a thick, green vine appeared along the back wall of the room. "Unbearable," tumbled from her lips as purple roses began to bloom along the single vine. "Like having your heart ripped from your chest, every time he looks into your eyes."

"You could have come to me, Mellissa." Her aunt continued to gently run her hand through the long strands of Mara's dark hair and more vines cascaded over the wall, more roses spilled forth as they had once done for Mara's mother. "Why did you not come to me? I would have helped you."

Tears burned the surface of Mara's eyes at the tenderness in her aunt's voice and the knowledge that the words were not meant for her. "I would have helped you."

"No. You could not help her." Mara drew a stuttered breath. "She stopped living the day he died."

Her mother had lay in bed for weeks, refusing to move, to eat, to live. People watched her, healers were called and they forced food down her throat against her will. They bathed and dressed her each morning, but she gave no response of her own. Mara sat at the foot of her bed each night, begging her mother to please wake up, but for months it was to no avail. It was Edward and Garreth who watched over her. They who had held her as her father's body had burned upon the funeral pyre. They who helped her to understand the truth of what had happened. Who had helped her through her father's death. Months later, her mother began to function again, but she was never the same. Sadness surrounded her and the depth of her pain was enough to steal the courage of even the bravest of souls. Then one day she lay down and, as Mara held her hand, had chosen to let go of the breath that sustained her, joining her lost love in eternal sleep.

"She died with him. And if you kill Edward...so will I." A tear spilled from the corner of her eye. Her aunt moved a hand to stop its trail down her pale cheek. "Please," she begged on a trembling breath. "Do not kill the man I love. Take my life if you must, but I cannot, I could not...watch you hurt him again." Her words fell to complete sobs. "Please, Aunt Clarissa. I beg you. Don't hurt him. Please don't hurt him."

The queen shushed her as she pulled Mara close, taking the younger woman into her arms and resumed running her fingers through her long dark hair.

"I'm sorry. I'm sorry. *ignosce mihi.* Please, forgive me."

"You poor, motherless child. Do not fear. I will not harm him, this man you love."

Mara's entire body began to shake. She rested her head against her aunt's breast and began to sob in her arms. Clarissa soothed her for what seemed a long time until her sobs subsided and her trembling began to cease.

When the queen finally drew back, she caressed Mara's face, wiping the last of the tears from her cheeks. "There," she said. "No more tears."

Mara drew a deep breath and nodded. Then, the queen added. "After all, you will need all your strength for what is to come."

CHAPTER XLIX

1200 AD

MARA'S HEART SANK AS THE roses along the wall withered and died upon the vine.

"Do not fear, niece. Your royal blood will save your life. But it will not save you from the punishment you have earned by daring to raise your blade to your queen." Clarissa stood from the floor and took several steps towards Garreth. "One hundred lashes," she informed him. "Twenty-five for each of the men she saved, and fifty for daring to raise her sword to me. And a half hour under the knife; let's see what designs we can make on that flawless skin."

"One hundred." Garreth could not hide his shock. "Surely, my lady—"

"One hundred. Care to make it more?" Garreth lowered his gaze to the ground as the queen continued. "She should consider herself fortunate that I do not give her to the men when you are finished." She gazed back to where Mara still knelt upon the floor. "If her children would not have a claim to my throne, I would." With that, the queen turned and left the room.

By the time Garreth reached her, she was physically shaking. "Breathe, Mara. Please, you have to breathe." Most days the centuries between their births seemed non-existent, but as Garreth gathered her into his arms, those years had never seemed more present. "My girl," he said softly. "My brave, brave girl." He held her tightly against his chest, clutching her close. "Oh Gods, Mara. Thank you." His own voice rose unsteadily. "Thank you for doing what I could not." He laid a gentle kiss upon her brow.

"She's mad," Mara whispered against his chest. "Completely mad."

"I know," he said, trying to soothe her.

"You can't tell Edward. Please, you can't tell him. He can't know how bad this is going to be. Please." She shook her head. "He can't know."

"Okay," Garreth replied. "We will tell him it was very little. That she forgave you because of your royal blood."

Mara gave a shaking nod. "My mother..." she said suddenly. "I begged my mother not to. I tried to..."

"I know," he assured her. "I know you did. There was nothing anyone could have done to save your mother. You know this. Not you—not even the queen."

Mara nodded as Garreth placed her upon the ground. "You have to walk out on your own, Mara. If Edward is waiting, you are going to have to be convincing; otherwise he will see right through you." She nodded again and Garreth opened the tall doors of the queen's chambers. Much to Mara's relief, it was Phillip, not Edward, who awaited them.

"I sent Edward to his chambers," were the first words to escape his lips. "He was a mess. I told him you needed him to be strong and to wait for you there. And I did not want the queen to see him standing here and decide to change her mind about letting him leave."

As the relief washed over her, Mara collapsed and would have tumbled to the ground if Garreth had not been there to catch her.

"My lady," Phillip stepped forward. "Is she injured?"

Garreth again gathered Mara into his arms and glanced at Phillip. "Not yet."

"I see," came the response, the tips of his fingers tightening against his palms. "I am going with you." Garreth did not argue but instead began to move down the hall to stairwell, all the while cradling Mara in his strong arms. Phillip moved ahead of them and proceeded to open doors and clear each hallway before they entered it, minimizing the risk of anyone seeing Mara in such a condition. When they finally reached the cursed chambers, Garreth walked Mara slowly to the stone table in the center of the room.

"How bad?" Phillip inquired. "You would not look this worried if it wasn't bad." He motioned to where Mara lay silently in Garreth's arms. "I've never seen her afraid. Angry, hurt, exhausted, yes—but never afraid."

"It's not physical," Garreth replied. "The queen called her by her mother's name and it...emotionally it..."

Phillip gave a nod. "I remember when her mother died."

"Yes," Garreth answered, his mind traveling back to that day all too easily. The tiny girl delivered to his door, clinging to Edward's hand. When Edward tried to leave her that night, the orphaned princess had begun to cry, begging and pleading for him not to go. He had finally moved with her to the bed, placing her head upon his chest and held her through the night as Garreth looked on helplessly.

Mellissa had died three days before she was found, with Mara kneeling at the edge of the bed holding her dead mother's hand. *Three days,* Edward had said over and over.

Even at that tender age, Mara held a special bond with Edward that seemed unbreakable. By the time she was seventeen, Edward could deny her nothing, including his heart and entrance to the Queen's Royal Guard. The queen had asked Mara how she could place herself between a blade and the man she loved, after all the pain they had endured. Garreth wondered, *how could she not?*

"Shall I get the captain?" Phillip asked.

Garreth felt himself fighting back his own tears as he said, "No." He raised his eyes to the other man's. "She asked us not to. I don't think she could live with herself if she forced him to watch this; not after what happened to him when Liza died." Yet even as he spoke, he found himself silently praying: *By the Gods, let me be right.*

"Shall we secure her?"

"No." He drew a deep breath and turned his attention back to the girl in his arms. "Mara," he said as gently as he could. "I need you to look at me." When she did not respond, Garreth ran a finger down her cheek. "I am going to put you on the table, Mara. I need you to tell me that you understand." She did not respond. "If you cannot look at me now, I will have no choice but to get Edward."

"Edward," she repeated his name. "Edward."

Phillip shook his head and began to walk towards the doors. "I will get the captain."

"No, wait. Mara," he said, adding a touch of force to his words. "Sub-Captain Mara." Her eyes moved to his at the use of her title. "Captain," he said again. "I am going to move you to the table."

She did not speak, but instead offered a shaky nod, terror running through her violet eyes. He moved her from his arms onto the table as gently as possible, then proceeded to pull a knife from his side. He cut carefully through the silk which covered her back. "It won't offer protection and we do not want to cause her more pain later by trying to pry the torn pieces of fabric from her skin." Phillip nodded and then Garreth moved to the floor and positioned himself near the front of the table she lay upon. "Give me your hands, Mara." Her arms shook as she reached forward. Garreth grasped her trembling fingers and slid his hand inside her own. "Mara, if you want Edward, tell me now. If you, at any point, decide you want him here, say the world and I will bring him to your side. Do you understand?"

Yes, she screamed silently. *Yes, I want him.* But she forced herself to swallow her pleas. Watching this would only harm him further, and that she could not do. "No," she informed her cousin. "No matter what happens, don't let him see this."

Garreth gave a painful nod and positioned his hands further into Mara's grasp. "Hold on to me. Break my hand if you have to."

She gave a trembling nod and Garreth said, "We love you," as the first lash crashed down upon the center of her exposed flesh.

"How many?" Phillip asked.

Garreth looked up with haunted eyes. "Until she stops screaming."

The whip crashed down in a steady rhythm, never quite hitting the same place twice. On the fifteenth, Mara let out an ear-shattering scream and by the thirtieth, she was begging for them to stop. "Garreth," Phillip was exhausted, "how many?"

"One hundred."

"What?"

"One hundred."

"By the Gods." He shook his head. "I...I can't. It's too many. I'm going to get the captain."

"Dam nit, Phillip! How can we ask her to be strong if we are not ourselves?" He looked down at the girl writhing on the table. Her skin was split open alone the sides of her spine. Exposed muscles showed through layers of stripped flesh. Blood gushed, cascading over the sides of the stone slab to splash into a pool which streamed wildly in all directions. Garreth closed his eyes tightly to draw an unsteady breath, but gagged at the overwhelming smell of blood. Phillip again brought the whip down upon her. A few strokes more and she became delirious.

She screamed Edward's name, begging for him to stop the pain. She called for mercy, to the Gods above, and finally, for her mother. She thrashed upon the table, breaking several of Garreth's fingers as she struggled to escape her torment and eventually, fell to an almost death-like stillness, too injured to move.

As she lay, her eyes fell to the far side of the room where a stream of her blood was quickly working its way across the stone floor. There was a crack in the wall where a stray vine had erupted from the garden above. Upon its branch lay a series of white roses. Lacking the strength to move her head, Mara watched as the crimson stream moved forward to paint the white petals of the rose. Yet as Mara's blood touched the first, delicate petal, the roses on the vine turned not the crimson of Mara's blood, but the black of a starless night. "Black Rose," she whispered in a voice all but destroyed from her screams.

"Stop!" Garreth instructed the other man, who instantly complied. Garreth leaned forward and placed his ear closer to Mara's cracked lips. "What did you say?"

"Black Rose."

Garreth raised his eyes to Phillip's. "Did she just?"

"Yes."

"No one has taken the Vow of the Black Rose in centuries."

"No court has had a murdered princess either," came Garreth's response. "She was Liza's captain. The vow is hers to take."

"And if she takes the Order of the Black Rose..."

"It places her beyond the power of the courts—including the queen."

"Along with all those who choose to serve her," Phillip finished for him.

"Yes." The two men exchanged a bewildered glance. "If she takes the Vow of the Black Rose, she won't only save Edward, she will save us all."

"It is a mad quest. If our entire force cannot find Liza's killers, then how can she be expected to...?"

"Does it matter?" Garreth replied. "As long as it gets her away from this?" Both men turned their gaze to the unrecognizable form of the girl lying between them. "Mara Sethian," Garreth said in a reserved tone, "the Captain of the Black Rose."

CHAPTER L

1200 AD

GARRETH AND PHILLIP HELD OFF Edward's demands to see Mara for the next three days. They lied, informing him that she had received only a minor punishment and the queen, despite her initial anger, had softened at the reminder that Mara was, in fact, her niece. They said that she was recovering from these minor injuries and begged his patience before she saw him again. However, on the third day, he could stand it no more and told Phillip coldly that if she would not come to him, then he would go to her.

Every muscle screamed as the flesh of Mara's back ripped even further apart with every motion. Yet when she reached Edward's door, she pushed Garreth away, refusing assistance as she stepped forward to slowly meet her captain. "Not a word," she hissed to Garreth in a strained voice. "Not one single word."

She walked forward, her back far too straight, her steps careful and slow. When she reached the center of the room, she knelt down, lowering herself gingerly to the stone floor.

"Mara." He spoke her name softly and her eyes closed at the sound. She had to resist the urge to fall apart. "Mara," he said again.

"Edward." She spoke his name and offered a silent prayer for strength. "I'm leaving, Edward."

A long pause followed the statement before he finally asked, "What do you mean, leaving? Where is she sending you? Is it because of what you did for me?"

"She is not sending me anywhere," Mara replied.

"I don't understand. Where are you going? For how long? I need you here."

"No," Mara shook her head. "You needed me, for a time. But today, you placed yourself between the queen and your men. You do not need me, not anymore."

"Yes, I do! If you had not been there, the queen would have...she..."

"Edward," Mara cut through his words. "Don't you see? You did not act further, because I did not let you; and it was not my place to intercede."

"You swore an oath to serve the queen. What makes you think you can...I don't understand."

Mara fought to control a swirl of emotions. "When I joined this guard, I swore a vow of obedience to the captain of this guard. I swore another to Liza when you named me her captain. I never once, nor was I ever asked, to swear an oath of loyalty to the queen." She inhaled deeply, "Now, I have sworn another."

"And what vow would that be?"

"I have taken the Order of the Black Rose." Mara's right arm began to shake from the effort required to remain kneeling. "I will take vengeance upon those who killed her."

"The Black Rose?" Edward asked in a tone of disbelief. "No one has taken that oath since...it must have been the beginning of the Roman Empire."

"Nevertheless, I have taken the oath and will, from this day forward, be sworn to avenge the death of our princess. And Edward, I want you to come with me." She paused for several heartbeats to allow him to process her words before she added, "Come away from here. I know the men would follow you—as would I. It is only fitting that she be avenged by your hand."

Edward shook his head, pushing himself to a seated position on the bed. "Mara," he finally replied. "The queen—"

"Cannot prevent you from leaving." The trembling throughout Mara's body became steadily worse. "She cannot stop you, not if you take the Vow of the Black Rose." Edward's dark eyes seemed to stare straight to her soul. "Please, come with me, Edward. I..." She fought to keep the desperation from her voice. "Please, I cannot watch her hurt you anymore. Please." The word escaped as a sob. "Don't make me. I just...can't do it anymore." She lost her battle as a stream of tears escaped the corner of her eye. "Please."

"Mara, I am the Captain of the Queen's Guard. I can't."

Mara gazed into the jet black eyes of the man she had loved all her life, and broached the forbidden subject. "The queen," she paused between each word, "who killed her daughter."

Edward was unable to hide the shock from showing on his face. "What? You do not know that. How could you say such a thing? How could you even begin to believe it? They could kill you for saying such a thing!"

"Then how did she die?" Mara's tears ceased as her voice grew in intensity. "She was killed by an enchanted blade. The only sword unaccounted for was hers. Don't you see?" She tilted her head slightly as her voice began to hollow. "It does not matter whose hand made the stroke. Liza died by the queen's own blade."

"You don't know that!" Edward's voice was as firm as Mara had ever heard. "There could be another. You will not make accusations against the queen of this court and you will not repeat your words to anyone. Do you understand me, Mara? Not to anyone!"

Mara stared into his eyes and spoke the unforgivable words. "You cannot issue me orders, Edward. You are not my captain anymore." The words cut deep. "But I will make you this promise, for the love that Liza bore you." She gave a hard swallow. "I will not raise my blade to the queen as long as you stand before her. You, who Liza loved above all others."

Deadly silence stood between them when Edward finally asked, "And what is to stop me then, from killing you now, for this threat you have made against my queen?"

"Nothing," Mara replied. "But I ask you to think well upon your choice, Captain. If you wish my life, take it now, for tomorrow I ride to Lethia Castle with a hundred men sworn to trade their lives for mine."

Mara's left hand touched the ground beneath her, physically lacking the strength to remain in her kneeling position. Edward leaned forward and grabbed her arm. He jerked her forward, causing her to slide across the floor, her chest crashing against the side of the bed. His hand rose to Mara's chin, raising her face to meet his eyes as his fingers pressed against the hollow of her throat. Mara leaned forward, increasing the pressure of Edward's fingers against her delicate skin. "If you wish my life, my lord, you have but to ask."

In response, Edward leaned forward and pressed his lips to hers. Time seemed to seep into a small eternity as their kiss lingered and deepened. Then as Edward drew back to draw breath, the moment was broken.

Mara closed her eyes tightly, but was unable to keep fresh tears from spilling down her face. She drew several ragged breaths and finally returned her gaze to the man before her. She reached her arm forward until her fingertips touched the left side of his face. She offered this single caress. "Goodbye, Edward."

Goodbye, my love.

CHAPTER LI

1200 AD

IT WAS THE NEXT MORNING when Edward realized the truth. His chambers being one of few which held a window for morning light, he awoke to find the path to his bed smeared with blood, saturating the spot where Mara had knelt before him.

Edward rose quickly and flew to Garreth's chambers where he proceeded to bang upon the door. "Come in!"

Edward opened the door so hard it slammed against the wall behind him. "Minor punishment!" he all but screamed. "What, by all the Gods, happened to her? How dare you lie to me! How dare you!"

"It was her secret to keep. And I'm shocked you didn't see. She could barely stand when she entered your chambers last night. Did you notice how she had to reach down to support herself? There is no way she held a kneeling position without doing so."

"What happened?"

"What do you think? She pulled a blade on the queen!" Garreth shook his head and spoke through gritted teeth. "What. Do. You. Think?"

Edward's gaze dropped to the floor. "I didn't want... Why didn't she call for me?"

"She did," Garreth answered with tears searing the corner of his eyes. "She screamed for you as we cut into her... As we... She had made me promise that no matter what she said, I would not tell you. And I know it was wrong, I know I should have, we..." He grabbed a goblet from his bedside and threw it hard against the wall. "Damn you! She made me swear. She begged no matter what. But yes, yes, she called for you. Screamed for you!" Garreth paused to breathe and then forced himself to continue. "The queen called her by her mother's name, screwed her up so much emotionally that I'm not even sure she knew what we were about to do until it had already begun. She...I...I couldn't." He buried his face in his hands. "I knew she needed you, but Gods...what would you have done? I wanted to kill the queen myself. If you had been there; if you had seen, Edward I..." He suddenly looked up and met his captain's eyes. "I don't know what you would have done. Do you?"

Edward's voice was as controlled as it had been angry moments before. "It was that bad, wasn't it?"

Garreth simply nodded. "I've seen worse, but...only once."

"By the Gods, I am such a fool." Edward turned towards the door. "I have to find her. I have to tell her that...I have to tell her..."

"It's too late. The next time you see her, it will be at the head of the Black Rose Guard."

"And you?"

"Will join her. I am sorry, Edward. You are my captain and my brother, but...I can't watch the queen do this anymore. Just...no more."

CHAPTER LII

Present Day

"A FEW DAYS LATER OUR men gathered in the rose garden outside these walls. Like those of the Ciar Court, every single rose had turned black. As they have been ever since...until now." Mara's voice faded in the quiet room where she sat between Garreth and Nolan.

"My lady." Jonathan, who had slipped into the room part way through the story, approached from the left side of the room. "I thought you should know..."

"What is it?"

"The roses, they are not just red. They are violet as well."

Her eyes moved to Garreth's. "At the Ciar Court?"

"They were violet as well."

She turned back to Jonathan. "When did you see this?"

"Right before the fight. Brendan and I were standing near the garden and they literally transformed before our eyes. One moment they were red and then random petals began to bleed purple."

Just as they turned black all those years ago, Mara thought.

"Red, purple, black. What does it mean?" Nolan asked.

Mara turned to Garreth, allowing him to answer the question.

"The myth of the roses," he began, "is that the roses are connected to the royal family. They transform to different colors depending on which member of the royal family is near them. Once, they turned red for Mara. But..."

"The night I took the Vow of the Black Rose," Mara said, "every rose in the courts turned black."

"The men took it as a sign," Garreth stated. "That the Gods had blessed Mara's quest for vengeance. Men flocked to take their vows from the youngest to the most experienced of knights. She rode out with well over a hundred men. The number grew to well over three hundred before the year was over." He looked at Jonathan. "When did you say the roses changed?"

"Just before the fight began. We were trying to figure out what was going on with the roses, which is why we were not in the castle at the time of the attack."

Mara turned back to Garreth. "What were you doing before you saw the roses at the Ciar Court?"

Garreth gazed at her for several moments attempting to recall what had sent him to the garden. "I had just finished escorting Lady Sandra to see Edward."

Her head turned slowly from Garreth to where Regald stood in the far corner of the room. "And when you escorted her to the ancient grounds, what happened?"

"The roses turned purple and red."

"Wait," Nolan interrupted. "What is violet?"

The captains exchanged multiple glances. "Royalty," Mara answered.

"Well," Regald said, "she is engaged to the prince."

"But not of royal blood," Garreth stated. "The roses only respond to those of the royal bloodline. They never change for those who merely marry into the line. Or at least, they never have before." His expression became focused on Regald. "Could she be carrying the prince's child?"

"It's possible, though not likely. I mean, they could be...intimate. But I do not think they are. They have a massive wedding planned and Mathew has always been protective of ensuring the legitimacy of his bloodline. A trait I believe he has passed down to his son."

"Lady Sandra," Mara interjected. "Who is she?"

"See, that is the thing. No one is really sure. She was found with only a few scattered memories. I was the one who found her." He drew a deep breath. "She was in bad shape, like she had been in a major accident of some kind. She was eventually taken in by one of the noble families as a lady-in-waiting and eventually found herself working in the queen's household. She met the prince a few years ago. The marriage was arranged and I was officially placed on her guard detail."

"Mathew put you, his captain, on another's detail?"

"I thought it was strange at first too, but I had been watching over her ever since I found her, so I was happy to take the assignment."

"There is another possibility." Edward suddenly joined the conversation, drawing all eyes to where he stood along the back wall. "I would like to speak with Mara first to discuss it."

She did not question this, but instead glanced around the room before her eyes settled on Jonathan. "It is getting late. We should all get some sleep and reconvene tomorrow." She drew a breath as she addressed Jonathan directly. "Keep no fewer than four men on the outer doors at all times and call the men back to the castle."

"Who, my lady?"

"All of them. I want every single member of the Black Rose called back. They have forty-eight hours. Mathew's challenge cannot go unanswered."

"Yes, Captain. It shall be done."

Chapter LIII

Mara turned to face Edward from the privacy of her personal chambers. Edward stood a few feet away from her, dressed in a clean, black shirt that had been borrowed from Brendan's wardrobe. "The outfit looks good on you," she said, "but then again, I always knew it would." She took a few steps closer, standing about half-way between the door and the bed. "You said you wished to speak with me, Captain?"

"Don't do that, Mara."

She paused. "You're right. I am sorry, Edward. What is it you wish to speak with me about?"

It was his turn to pause. "I am really not sure how to begin. I don't want to hurt you."

"That doesn't sound like a very good start."

Edward sighed and then drew a deep breath. "I spoke with Lady Sandra on the way over here. We talked about her past, what little she could remember of it. She had a few, scattered memories about her mother. She claimed that her mother told her stories as a child."

"Stories? What stories?"

"Stories about me," he answered. "And they are of such vivid clarity, filled with details that no one should know...let alone someone so young."

"What do you mean?"

"She knows things, Mara. Things she should not. About that night..."

"The night you were tortured? How could she know?"

"It got me thinking," Edward stated slowly. "Her loss of memory could be from an accident, as she says..."

"Or?"

"From an enchantment."

"An enchantment? That seems a bit of a stretch."

Edward stepped forward and gently took her hand. "Come here." He led her over to the bed where she took a seat at his bequest. "Mara." He spoke her name gently, taking a knee before her. "I need to ask you something."

"Yes?"

"But first, you must hear me."

She shifted on the bed uncomfortably. "What is it?"

He gazed up directly into her eyes. "I love you, Mara. Nothing you say will change that. I have left you alone for six hundred years." He pursed his lips as he attempted to draw breath. "I will never leave you again."

"Edward, you're scaring me."

"And it is the last thing I ever want to do."

"Ask your question."

"She spoke of her mother—a woman of moonlit skin, dark hair and violet eyes." Mara's head titled slowly to the left, her eyes narrowing as she stared at him. "I need to know, my lady. If there is any way that this girl is your daughter? She...she looks like you."

Mara's eyes narrowed still further, transforming her gaze from violet to silver. "What?"

"She looks like you," he said again. "Dark hair, pale skin and her mother had your eyes; the rarest of any within the royal bloodlines."

Mara stood from the bed, jerking her hands from his. "How dare you? How could you ask me such a thing?" She stepped several paces forward, drawing a series of long breaths before turning back to face him, anger shining through her. "Do you really think I would have kept a child from you? Do you find me that heartless?"

"No," he said firmly, rising from his kneeling position. "Not heartless, Mara. Protective to a fault. If you hid a child to protect her from the queen—"

"From you, Edward? You honestly believe that I could have bore your child and hidden its very existence from you?"

"Mara, I'm sorry. With the roses and the appearance...I had to ask."

Her head lowered slightly, her expression tightening with a pained expression. "No, you don't think I would keep *your* child from you. You thought I would keep another's."

"Mara, your daughter would be of royal blood. It would have explained why all of these things are happening." He shook his head. "I'm sorry. I had to ask."

Anger continued to flow through her. "How could you? How could you think I would?" She pressed the back of her hand against her forehead, then jerked her arm back to her side. "I love you. I have always loved you. You and no other. Not in twelve hundred years! How could you not know?" Edward stepped closer and grabbed her arm. He forced her against his chest. "How could you?" she asked again, but the anger was quickly leaving her voice.

His tone matched her pain. "I am sorry, Mara. I am so sorry." He pulled her closer.

"I love you," she sobbed. "I have always loved you. I have always..."

"Forgive me. Please, Mara. *ignosce mihi, mea rosa, mi amor.*" He moved his left hand to the back of her head, completely enfolding her into his embrace.

"I've loved you all my life. I swear, I..."

"I know," he soothed her. "Gods, I know." He lifted her in his arms, carrying her towards the bed. He sat down on its edge, continuing to hold her, slipping his arms around her back to keep her body against his chest. "Mara, my Mara. *mea rosa immortalis.*" He dipped his head and kissed her with all that he was worth. When he was forced to pull back to draw breath, he kept his eyes upon hers. "I would give anything to undo the pain that I have caused you. Anything. But I can't. All I can say is that I love you. *te amo, rosa, mea rosa immortalis.* I love you. I will never leave you again."

She searched his dark eyes and found nothing but the conviction of the strong, powerful man who had stolen her heart and never let it go. "Edward," was all she could manage before he leaned down and offered another searing kiss.

CHAPTER LIV

THE FIRST RAYS OF THE morning sun had come and gone long before Mara finally awoke wrapped in the circle of Edward's arms. Her cheek was resting on his chest, her arm across his torso. His hand lay gently upon her bare back, holding her close as she slept. She had unpleasant dreams, struggling against a ghost that could not be seen, only felt, and he had woken at her movements. He pulled her from the nightmare. "Don't leave me."

"I won't," he promised.

She had closed her eyes at his words, enfolded in the safety of his arms. When her breathing had finally settled to the steady rhythm of sleep, he lay awake watching as dawn rose. "*ignosce mihi, mea rosa, mi amor.* I am so sorry."

When she had arrived in the Arum Court, he thought he was surely hallucinating. Her soft, strong voice sliding through the room. *I must be dying*, he had thought. *She has come to me at last.* Yet she had been real. The exact image of the vision he had attempted so desperately to banish from his mind over those hundreds of years of solitude and loneliness.

His hand moved slowly down her side, pushing her hair back as his eyes roamed her pale skin, his fingers trailing over her body as though attempting to memorize every inch of her.

Her shoulders were slender, but strong from years of carrying the heavy blades he had taught her to use as a child. Her long arms and slender wrists, so smooth to the touch. Then his finger reached her side and over the long, jagged scar, the only flaw to her otherwise pristine skin.

Edward had not seen Mara since the destruction of the Muir Court. He had been sent in search of a child, the last prince of the fallen court. Instead he had found Mara, kneeling at the edge of the sea. The water was a deep, beautiful blue with sunlight dancing off the edge of the waves as they crashed upon the white sand.

1400 AD

MARA'S SILVER SWORD LAY ON the ground beside her, blood staining the dark metal, seeping into the ground below. "My lady," Edward's deep voice fought through the strong breeze to reach her. "Have you seen a boy? They say he might have run this way."

Mara did not acknowledge his words. She remained perfectly still, watching the sun slowly lower itself into the rising tides of the sea.

"Mara, have you seen a child?" His inquiry was again met with silence. "Mara?"

She drew a breath and slowly answered his question, her gaze remaining upon the blue waves. "There is no child, Edward." The water shimmered in the falling sunlight.

"What...I don't understand."

"It is not complicated, my lord."

"Are you saying that you have not seen the child?"

"There is no child, Edward," Mara stated again. "Not anymore."

Silence fell over them as Edward began to digest her meaning. "Are you saying that you..."

"The line of the Muir Court has ended." Her voice sounded hollow. She finally turned to face him, meeting his gaze directly. "Liza's death has been avenged."

"But..."

"That," she spoke firmly, "is all you ever need know."

She stood from her kneeling position, raising her blade from the blood-soaked earth—a splash of crimson on a sea of white sand. She took several steps forward, walking carefully until she reached the edge of the ocean's waves. She paused, staring into the brilliance of the falling sun, then stepped into the edge of the water, the blue waves stroking the edge of her long dark skirt.

She knelt down, lowering her sword into their gentle grasp. For a moment, the blue waves turned to red as the water cleansed the blood of its court from the edge of Mara's blade. Then the water cleared, the last blood of the Muir Court carried away by the powerful ocean tide.

Mara stared into the clear water for what seemed a long time before slowly turning and walking back to where Edward stood, watching silently. When she reached him, she looked up and stared into his dark eyes. "It's done, Edward. My vow is, at long last, fulfilled."

Edward studied her for several moment moments before finally replying in an almost haunted voice. "You killed the child."

"I killed the Crown Prince of the Muir Court and avenged the death of our princess."

"He was a child."

"So was I," Mara replied. "And yet look what my vengeance has bought them, this court of the sea who killed our sweet, sweet Liza."

"But he was a—"

"Prince. A young prince who would become a man. A man who would remember this day until the rest of the world had long forgotten it. Don't you see?" She drew a sharp breath. "He would remember this day and then, many years from now, he would seek his vengeance upon those who destroyed everything and everyone he ever held dear. And he would come for us, Edward. For you, for me, or worse...someone else."

"Mara." It was Edward's turn to sound hollow. "You have gone too far. This..." He shook his head. "This is against everything we are. Against our codes. The codes I taught you!"

"You taught me to fulfill my vows, Edward!" Anger began to spill into her previously calm voice. "The first rule of being a knight. Protect the realm and always, always keep your vows. I swore to destroy this court. I have done my job. Perhaps it is time that you start doing yours!"

The wind became stronger, causing sand to rise and swirl between the two captains. "What are you implying?"

"You haven't done your job since the night she died! You are useless, a shell of the man I knew. The man I followed. That I pledged my life to. The man I..." She had to fight down the words. "The man she loved." Tears burned the surface of Mara's eyes, but she refused to let them fall. "I did my job. Her death has been avenged. I only pray it allows you to find some measure of peace."

"You did not do this for me!" Edward shouted. "This, all of this," he motioned behind him to where thick, black smoke rose from the remnants of the castle from unseen flames, "you did this for yourself! As though it could make things better. As though you could bring her back from the dead with your vengeance."

"Is that so?" The threat of tears subsided as anger rose. "I am not the one who vowed to love one woman, and then gave his heart to another at the first possible opportunity! The one woman," Mara's left hand clenched tightly at her side, "the only woman, in the entire kingdom that he could not have. You lost your head, Captain, and we have all paid the price. Our entire court has paid the price for your forbidden love. And now the Muir Court has paid as well. All because of you! You are responsible for every life lost since that night, Captain."

"Mara!" Edward interjected, his voice crisp in its own anger. "You cannot begin to imagine... You cannot."

"Yes, I did it for you! All this, every life I have taken, every vow broken, every horror, all for you. How dare you! You want to blame someone, then blame yourself. You did this. You did this to your men, to my men, to the dead men of the Muir Court. All of them dead—because of you!"

Mara raised her sword a single moment before Edward's came crashing down upon it. The sound of their colliding metal sailed down the beach with the rush of the fierce wind. The two stood frozen, their swords pressed together by the weight of their bodies. Too startled to move, she stared into the dark eyes of the man she loved.

The look on Edward's face was as surprised as hers. "Mara." He took a step back, his sword sliding along the edge of hers until the blades finally separated.

"These are Arius blades, Edward. You...we..." She drew shallow breaths then her anger transformed to an uncontrollable rage. Her hand tightened on the hilt of her sword.

"Mara."

"You could have killed me! We could have killed each other! You, my captain, my friend, my..." The word love refused to leave her lips.

"I didn't mean—"

Mara raised her silver blade. Edward stepped forward just in time to block her movement, the sound of metal again twisting its way across an ocean of white sand. "Mara, don't!"

"Why not?" she screamed, again bringing her sword down upon his. "You want a fight? Here I am!" Their blades began to dance, the two captains circling each other in a tight, dangerous spiral.

She swung her sword in an upward arc, but Edward took a step to his left, sidestepping the motion altogether. She had some difficulty regaining her stance, as her feet sank into the sand. She turned just in time to block Edward's own motion, his blade sweeping towards her left side. The two swords again sang through the air. Edward again swung his blade down. Mara bent her knees, placing both hands tightly upon the hilt of her blade, twisting it sideways. The ancient swords collided with enough force to throw both off balance, turning in opposite directions to keep from completely falling into the sand.

They recovered quickly, turning back to face each other, clutching their blades. Mara brought her sword up in a series of long strokes, moving towards Edward's left side with tremendous speed. He turned, blocking her first two swings with ease. However, the third bit lightly into his left arm, causing him to hiss in pain. He took several steps back, and she paused to draw a deep breath from the cool breeze before moving to follow him.

She moved forward and Edward's blade raced toward her right side. She moved her sword up and blocked, but the force knocked her sidewise. He turned his sword towards her, lower this time.

She threw herself to the left, holding onto her sword as tightly as she could. She struggled with the sand as she rose to a crouching position, holding her blade carefully in front of her. Edward advanced, but she swung her blade low, forcing him to step back to prevent her sword from slicing across his legs.

She used that moment to regain a standing position. She stepped forward, and Edward again brought his blade down upon her. She parried, sending a cloud of sand into the air as she did so. Her sword again struck his, and then she turned in a full, tight circle, bringing her blade down to his left. He blocked her sword mere inches from his skin. She pulled back, readjusting her grip.

He swung left. She attempted to side-step the movement when the sand suddenly gave way under her left foot. She slid deeper into the unstable ground and attempted to twist away. She was too slow.

Edward's silver sword entered her right side, stabbing through her ribcage. She cried out as the sword forced its way both in and out of her chest. Spots appeared in her vision, so severe was the pain. Yet she drew a wheezing breath and swung her blade towards Edward's right. She knew that in a few moments, she would be unable to continue; this would be her only chance.

She swung her sword to Edward's right side, smashing the two blades against each other. She lunged toward his left arm. He parried. She brought it up again, then jerked her arm down at the last moment and drove the sword toward his legs.

He jumped back. Mara followed him. She brought her blade down. He blocked the attack , but she allowed no respite, and brought her blade down upon his with all her strength. Edward's sword slipped from his hand and Mara's blade was suddenly at his throat. Pain and anger raged as she stared down into his dark eyes for several long moments before Edward suddenly decided to speak.

"Admit it," he said, the emotions in his voice matching her own. "You blame me for Liza's death!"

At these words, Mara took several steps back, sinking to her knees in the sand. She dropped her blade and moved her hands to her injured side attempting not to grimace as she did so. She shook her head and spoke through labored breaths.

"No, Edward. I was responsible for Liza. I was her captain and she died on my watch. I am responsi—" She fought down a surge of emotions before turning to the eyes of the man who still, even now, she loved more than life itself. "I was responsible, Edward."

Her words settled over the land as the sun continued to dip lower into the sea. Blood seeped from her side, turning sticky against her hands. Edward's anger vanished at her words. "It was not your fault, Mara."

"Yes," she murmured, tears falling from her eyes. "It was. But today, I have done my duty. I have avenged her death."

She attempted to draw a deep breath, but the pain in her side was too much and she ended up in a fit of coughing before she was able to continue.

"I don't blame you, Edward. That failure lies with me. But today, I have washed my sins with the blood of those who killed her."

She rose slowly to her feet, forcing her blade back into the leather sheath at her side. Then she walked slowly through the sand to where Edward still knelt. She leaned down slowly and wrapped her fingers around Edward's deadly blade. "I will take this," she stated. "It bears the blood of roses."

"Mara." She stared down at him. "I...I almost...I am so sorry."

More blood spilled from her side, hidden in her dark clothes. "I love you," she said. "You are my soul."

"Don't leave me."

She took a sharp intake of air, tears streaming down her flushed cheeks. "I am sorry, *mi amor.* But I have to go now. I have to go."

He had remained kneeling as she walked slowly down the beach with the last rays of the setting sun. Almost completely from view, Edward saw her fall. However, before he could so much as rise from the sand, Garreth appeared and gathered her in his arms with Mathew beside him, carrying the Arius blades.

It had been the last time Edward had laid his eyes upon her.

CHAPTER LV

Present Day

IT HAD BEEN DAYS LATER before Edward learned that Mara had watched Phillip die that night. They said she had walked towards the sea as though she were one of the dead. How much pain she must have endured, kneeling by the edge of the sea, realizing that the man who had protected and counseled her all her life would never again stand by her side.

Edward drew a deep breath, his mind trailing back from the recesses of memory to the room where he now lay. Mara still slept securely against him, her head upon his chest while his hand slowly soothed the bare skin of her back. "My lady."

She woke to the sounds of his voice, scared that it existed only in the realm of her dreams. His hand trailed down her back, sliding along her long dark hair. She opened her eyes slowly. "Edward." He offered a smile. She lay still, listening to the beat of his heart and the gentle rise and fall of his chest. "You're here."

"Yes," he said solemnly. "Mara. Gods, Mara, I am so..."

She lifted her head to stare down at him. He reached his hand to the back of her neck and drew her forward for a kiss, her breasts touching his chest. When she finally pulled back, it was to again collapse upon the bed beside him. They spent the day lying there, enjoying the simplicity of being together after all the centuries apart.

"I always knew that you would be the last thing I ever saw," she said. "I just never thought you would be real."

"It doesn't matter anymore. I am here. That is all that matters."

"I don't want to move. I don't want to breathe. I don't want to wake."

"This is not a dream, Mara. I promise you it is not." Edward pulled her closer, moving her head against his shoulder. They held each other, celebrating the simple act of touch which they had denied themselves for far too long.

They did not rise until the next day when they entered the whirlpool tub that had been installed a few years before. Though easily big enough to accommodate multiple people, this was the first time it had played host to more than the room's single occupant. When they finally emerged from the steaming water, they dressed quickly. Mara pulled her familiar outfit from her closet while Edward dressed in clothes that he borrowed from Brendan's. She watched as Edward donned the uniform of the Black Rose.

He offered her his arm as they walked down the wide hallways toward the top of the spiral staircase. Moments before emerging behind the stone wall, Mara removed his arm from hers. Turning the last corner, she walked to the rail and gazed down upon the grand entrance.

A loud clamor rose from the vaulted room, but the sound began to vanish at the sight of the Black Rose captain standing with Edward only a few paces behind her. Two hundred men stood below, gathered in various clusters around the room.

When was the last time that the entirety of the Rose had been called together? Mara was uncertain. Then she realized that, among the sea of black, there also stood several men of garbed in the silver of the Ciar Court as well.

Mara motioned to Edward who took a few steps forward to stand beside her at the railing which lined the path between the two spiral staircases. As the last of the chatter began to fade, Mara drew a breath to address those gathered. "My lords," she stated, attempting to project her voice through the vast hall. "Two days ago, members of the Arum Court invaded these sacred halls. They attacked your fellow members of the Black Rose, including myself, and threatened us with torture unto death." She paused, allowing her words to settle over the room. "They also threatened and tortured our fellow knight, Captain Edward of the Ciar Royal Guard. With this attack, the Arum Court has violated the peace that has been maintained between the courts—the peace that we of the Black Rose are sworn to protect."

A murmur rose and fell among those gathered. "They have also taken by force a young woman, who walked as a guest inside these walls. Another insult to the Black Rose and all it stands for. And last..." It was here that she found herself fighting to steady her voice. Edward wanted nothing more than to offer comfort, but feared making her appear weak in the full view of her guard. "Members of Arum Guard have killed Brendan, your sub-captain and my second-in-command. He died bravely, a death of honor and valor. A death that makes me proud to have called him my fellow guardsman and captain."

She forced herself to draw another breath. "These threats and attacks upon our sacred grounds will not go unanswered. And the death of our captain must be avenged."

Here she paused, unsure how to continue, when a voice called from the crowd, "May the Black Rose protect you in life!"

Mara stared down and nodded. "And avenge you in death."

Mara then walked down the long stairwell with Edward mirroring her steps from the opposite side. The crowd parted before them as they stepped forward. "Follow us."

Mara and Edward led the crowd along an old dirt path and into the ancient rose garden. They approached to find that the violet associated with Sandra's appearance had vanished and the roses were now a mixture of deep crimsons and the familiar black. Gasps were heard from among the crowd at the splash of color that had entered the garden, some pausing in their steps as though they could not believe it to be true.

Brendan's body had been arranged upon a funeral pyre, dressed in a clean uniform. His arms were folded upon his chest, his hands clasped around the hilt of his silver blade. His expression seemed peaceful, a harsh contrast to the agony of his final moments.

Mara moved closer to the pyre while the men spread around in a circle that extended to the garden walls. She walked to the body and placed a single black rose upon his chest and watched it turn crimson before her eyes. She turned and gazed out over the faces of those sworn to serve her when Garreth suddenly appeared by her side holding a torch. "My lady."

Mara lowered her head, and forced herself to breathe before giving a single nod. Garreth turned and lit the pyre. Covered in specially selected oils, the flames quickly cascaded over the wood upon which he lay to ignite the shell that was all that remained of the young man Mara had once laid down her blood and flesh to protect from harm. She turned, heat and smoke from the flames burning her eyes. Behind her, yet another yelled, "May the Black Rose protect you in life and avenge you in death!" The cry was repeated by another voice and then another until it became a deafening chant with the twisting flames. The chant did not die until the last of the flames were mere embers blown by the powerful mountain winds.

"*Rosa Nigra te in vita tueatur teque in morte ulciscatur.*" She spoke the ancient words. *May the Black Rose protect you in life and avenge you in death.*

"Goodbye, my friend. May you walk with her upon the sacred ocean waves and know peace forevermore."

The story will continue in...

HEART OF THE ROSE

Now Available

Read on for a preview...

Heart of the Rose

A Preview

900 AD

MARA ENTERED THE ROOM WITHOUT knocking to find Edward lying on the expansive bed, draped in layers of dark pelts. Bared to the waist, his shoulder-length black hair unkempt, he turned toward her. "Mara?" he asked, as he struggled to disentangle himself from the furs.

She did not speak, but walked to the bed, falling to her knees in her floor-length gown. "Take me with you." The words escaped her lips before she could stop them. "I know we decided I would stay away, but...please, Edward. I cannot bear it. Please take me with you."

He moved to the edge of the bed and stared down at the young woman kneeling before him. "Mara." She looked intensely at the stone floor, her body trembling. He moved his hand and traced a finger down her cheek before raising her gaze to his dark eyes. He leaned down, the pain in her expression making his heart ache.

"Mara," he again spoke her name, before his lips claimed hers in a deep, passionate kiss. She closed her eyes at his touch and fought back a flurry of emotions.

Edward pulled back and pressed his palm against her cheek. "*me paenitet, mi amor*," he whispered. "I am so sorry."

She drew several sharp breaths and opened her violet eyes. "I know. It's only...it's..."

"Come here." He pulled her from her knees and guided her to a seated position on the bed's edge.

"I know we decided I should stay away," she said. "That it would be easier for both for both of us. But I couldn't. I can't."

"I know, Mara. It's all right." Edward wrapped his arms around her, gently kissing her forehead.

"I didn't mean to. I was trying to be strong." Shame strangled her flurry of words. "I don't want to make this any harder. I couldn't stay away. It's your last night. I couldn't stand it."

"Mara," he cut her off, raising his hand to brush a long strand of dark hair from her eyes. "I want you here. I wanted you here so badly."

"Let me stay."

"Yes, *mea rosa*." He soothed her. "I don't want to be alone tonight." He moved to the center of the bed and lay down, his pale skin standing in contrast to the dark furs beneath him. Mara moved into his offered embrace, laying her head against his chest as his arms engulfed her. He ran his fingers down her back, holding her closely. "My love, you are the strongest, most beautiful woman I know. I wish to the gods that I did not have to leave you this way." She buried her face against his chest, listening to the steady rhythm of his heart. "*me paenitet, mi amor. ignosce mihi, mea rosa, mi amor. ignosce mihi. mea rosa immortalis*." He continued to murmur softly until her breathing settled into a steady rhythm.

"You'll come back," she whispered.

"*promitto, Mara*. I promise. *me paenitet, mi amor*." He continued to hold his love securely until exhaustion overcame her. A pain resided inside him that he feared would never heal, and with each breath she drew, his terror deepened. His mind wandered back to that night, many years ago, when he found her kneeling over her mother's grave.

Father left her alone and the isolation was unbearable, Mara had spoken of her mother's suicide. *My mother knew she would never love again. She was alone. Everyone leaves.*

I won't, he had promised. *You will never be alone.*

Yet, here he was preparing to break the only promise she'd ever asked of him. The gravity, and guilt, threatened to overwhelm him. It took all of his strength not to give in and take her with him. To throw all duty, all honor, all sanity to the wind and steal her away from the guard, the courts, and the threats of an increasingly dangerous queen. "Forgive me," he whispered again to the woman in his arms. He held her until the first rays of sunlight seeped into the room, then woke her with a heavy heart.

"My lady," he said, as she opened her violet eyes to reveal their silver center. "I need you to listen to me now, *mi amor*." She blinked several times, clearing her vision. "Mara, I need you to swear to me, to promise me, that no matter what happens or how hard this becomes, you will be strong for me. I will come back. I swear I will. But I need to know, without a shadow of a doubt, that you will make it through my absence."

He ran his fingers through her long, dark tresses, stirring the scent of the rosewater she used to rinse her hair. *Everyone leaves*, her words haunted him. *They always leave.*

"It breaks my heart to abandon you this way, my lady. Promise me, swear to me, that you will be strong."

"*promitto*, Edward. And when you come back, I will be waiting."

He drew her into a tight embrace, clutching her close for what seemed a long time, then finally forced himself to draw back and rise from the bed. He dressed quickly and gathered the few things he was taking with him into a small bag: a change of clothes, a warm blanket to fight off the cold night air, and a few miscellaneous items. He removed his silver Arius blade, encased in a black sheath lined with diamonds, from its place upon the wall. He tied the rare, deadly sword few were entrusted to carry around his waist with a belt, the golden hilt a stark contrast to his dark attire, and pulled a long woolen cloak around his shoulders, securing it with a pin. Finally, he turned back toward Mara, who had risen to stand beside the bed.

He tried to speak, but his voice betrayed him. "Mara, I..."

She walked toward him and grasped his hands in her own. "You have to go."

"Yes."

His heart ached as he watched the young woman fight heroically against tears, refusing to make his departure any harder. Instead, she leaned down and kissed his hand. "May the gods protect you, my lord, and see your swift return." He touched the side of her face. She closed her eyes tightly to prevent tears from falling, but was unable to control the tremor which slid up her spine. "I love you, Edward."

He leaned forward and kissed her, molding his lips to hers. "Forgive me."

"Gladly," she answered, as he pulled her close and buried his face into her tousled, dark hair. "I love you," she said again, "but you must go now, Captain. You must go."

He pulled back and stared down into her violet eyes one last time as though trying to memorize their depths, then forced himself to turn toward the door. "I will come back," he promised forcefully. "I will come for you, Mara. *tibi semper adveniam, mi amor.* I will always come for you."

The door closed with a loud clap of stone, leaving Mara standing alone in the dimly lit room. Frozen in place for a long time, she found the strength to walk back toward the bed. Numb, she crawled between his still-warm fur blankets and clutched her sides as she curled into a fetal position, knowing her world would never be the same.

Thanks & Acknowledgements

I would like to offer a special thanks to a few people who both assisted and supported me throughout the creation of this novel.

I would like to thank Scott of the Vancouver Taekwondo Academy for his assistance in my research; both through an extensive interview and allowing me to observe several of his classes. Second, to the instructors and students at East West Martial Arts of West Vancouver for also allowing me to observe their courses and for making themselves available to answer questions.

I would also like to thank my long time writing mentors, Kate and Mike, for instilling within me a passion for writing and reminding me of that passion when it was needed most. Also, to my writing partner, Jonny, for all the hours spent discussing the finer points of writing in that little coffee shop. Also a thanks to the Watling Street Writers group of St. Albans, who helped shape the direction of the beginning of this novel, offering both support and critique along the way.

A big thank you to Sarah C. for assisting me with some promotional graphics which turned out nothing short of amazing and for a ton of advice on this journey towards publication.

Also to my promotional team, and especially Kim and Karen, who have walked me through the media and promotional process from the beginning of this story.

To my family for their never-ending love and support. This never would have been completed without them.

To my content editor, Melissa, who helped me work through some of the most difficult scenes and finally, to my amazing editor and cover designer, Skyla, who takes the jumbled pictures in my head and consistently turns them into the beautiful covers you see upon the books. Your work is nothing short of marvelous!

About the Author

K.L. Bone has a Masters degree in Modern Literary Cultures. An American, currently living in Ireland working toward her PhD with a focus in vampire and children's literature. She wrote her first short story at the age of fifteen and grew up with an equally great love of both classical literature and speculative fiction. Bone has spent the last few years as a bit of a world traveler, living in California, London, and most recently, Dublin. When not immersed in words, of her own creation or studies, you'll find Kristin traveling to mythical sites and Game of Thrones filming locations.

Follow her at: www.klbone.com
On Twitter: @kl_bone
Or on Facebook: https://www.facebook.com/klboneauthor

Made in the USA
Middletown, DE
15 April 2016